The Mistress of Alderley

The Mistress of Alderley

ROBERT BARNARD

First published in Great Britain in 2002 by
Allison & Busby Limited
Bon Marche Centre
241-251 Ferndale Road
Brixton, London SW9 8BJ
http://www.allisonandbusby.com

ISBN 0 7490 0554 8

Printed and bound in Ebbw Vale,
by Creative Print & Design

Chapter One

Rural Idyll

When Caroline came in from the garden, she was pleased to find that Mrs Hogbin had gone upstairs to do the bathrooms. Caroline had had cleaning ladies in the past whom she'd regarded as friends, whom she'd been more pleased to sit down with over a cup of tea and a scone than any of the theatrical people she called her friends. Mrs Hogbin wasn't one of them.

She came through to the spacious hallway and poked her head round the door of what had once been a box-room.

"Tea, Alex? Coffee, Coke, milk?"

"No thanks," her son said, hardly looking up from the screen that mesmerised him. "Mum: I need a whole lot of new software."

"Then you're going to have to need for quite a while."

"Oh Mum! I've got to have it! I bet Marius buys all the latest stuff for Guy."

That was a line Caroline always felt she had to nip in the bud. Guy was not the spoilt child of a rich man: he was not given lavish pocket-money, or bought everything his young mind could covet.

"Maybe, and maybe not. Anyway Guy is nearly twenty, he's Marius's son, and he's about to start a computer degree course at St. Andrew's University."

"So what? He's been computer mad for years, and has stuff I could only dream about. You have to start young to be really on top of them. I bet if I asked –"

"Don't even *think* of asking Marius. Just think of all the calls he has on his money. My God – doesn't he do enough for us all?"

She shut the door on his already-opening mouth. At least he'd looked up from that bloody screen. Unfortunately before she could get to the sitting room she was caught by Mrs Hogbin, descending the stairs with a bucket.

"I'll be finished in half an hour, Mrs Fawley. If I could have your company, just to the bus stop –"

"Of course, Thora. You never used to be so nervous, though –"

"It's all those feedopiles. It doesn't feel like nobody's safe in their beds any longer."

As she waddled through to the kitchen it occurred to Caroline that Thora not only did not know how to pronounce paedophile, she had no idea what they were. So much for the educational mission of the popular press. The word had become for Mrs Hogbin a synonym for what in Caroline's childhood used to be called a "sex maniac".

Luckily when the half hour was up and Mrs Hogbin was pulling on her wholly unnecessary coat, Alexander said he needed to go down to the village shop for his chocolate supply. In fact he was going for cigarettes, but so far he had successfully kept this habit from his mother, and even from his sister Stella. He was a naturally secretive boy, who collected and collated information obsessively, but never willingly shared it.

Caroline went into the sitting room, then crossed to the large window that looked out on to the garden. The roses at the far end were looking better in their second flowering than they had in their first. There had been an interesting blend in the two big rosebeds when she and Marius had taken the house over, but she had introduced one or two more unusual types that had enhanced the effect. People commented, and inspected the new varieties closely, and that pleased Caroline.

The lawn had been splendid all year, but that had not been due to her. The mowing had mostly been done by Alexander, and Mr Wilks from the village had come to spray the lawn feed and keep down the moss and dandelions. The whole garden had looked a picture and when she had been asked, in an emergency, if the village fête could be switched to Alderley she had quite happily agreed. Everyone was complimentary, there had been no tensions or disapproving glances, and the vicar had been sweet as always – extra-sweet, in fact.

So unlike the Rector of Conningham, that Sunday when they'd gone to communion there. She had coped well, with her stage training, but Marius had been fuming, and obviously so. Clearly there were Yorkshire villages still in the dark ages, as well as others, like Marsham, that had moved with the times.

Wandering round the house, which she rather liked having to herself for the odd half hour, Caroline felt suffused with happiness. She felt none of the pains of *missing* which she had rather feared: acting was behind her, a thing of the past. She felt no nostalgia for the applause, laughter or edge-of-seat involvement of a live audience, no retrospective affection for the recognition that appearances on television bring, no regrets for backstage backbiting, patently false compliments on her acting or appearance – the whole fake superstructure of the acting profession (*trade*, she corrected herself) had disappeared from her life, and her life was the better for it.

Marius had done this for her. The transformation had been worked by him. And on Friday he would be down for another gorgeous, snatched, relished weekend.

From her bedroom window Caroline saw Alexander and Mrs Hogbin going through the front gate. She'll be pumping him, she thought. Well, let her. She was ashamed of nothing about her present life. Anyway, she'd back Alexander against Mrs Hogbin any day.

* * *

Alexander, in fact, in his secretive way, was rather enjoying himself. Knowledge was power, and though he had no desire to be a dictator, or even a prime minister, this was the sort of power he enjoyed, hoarding it, telling it over, like a miser his money.

"So Mr Fleetwood will be coming down this weekend, will he?" Mrs Hogbin asked.

"He generally does," said Alexander, using one of his strategies for avoiding a straight yes or no.

"And have Mr Fleetwood and your mother any plans?"

"If they have they wouldn't involve me. I'm a big boy now. I do my own thing."

"Sit over that bleeding word progressor every hour God sends," said Mrs Hogbin, who was always free with her opinions.

9

"That's not true," said Alexander. "I spend a lot of time meditating on life's great mysteries. Such as why you never see orange cars."

Mrs Hogbin shot him a glance, then gave it up.

"But I meant – like – *larger plans.*"

"Oh, I suppose everyone has plans and dreams, don't they?"

"Not when you get to my age you don't. But your mother's still a young woman, and Mr Fleetwood's not much older I wouldn't think. Plenty of people that age get married ..."

"I expect you're right. I haven't studied the statistics."

"Stastistics?" spat out Mrs Hogbin, exasperated. "I'm not talking about stastistics. I'm talking about being in love. And it's plain as the nose on my face that them two are in love. Even you must see that."

Alexander put on his pretentious-actor voice.

"'What is love? 'Tis not hereafter:
Present mirth hath present laughter.'"

"Now you've lost me."

"It's a quote from *Twelfth Night.* My mother played Viola in *Twelfth Night,* but she was a bit too old for it by the time she was asked to do it. Come to that, she's been in *Present Laughter* as well."

Mrs Hogbin frowned in bewilderment.

"You're getting off the point, Mr Alexander. And the point is, if they love each other, they should be married. It would make people round here a lot happier if they were."

"Well, I never realised the purpose of marriage was to make other people happy. This *has* been an interesting conversation, Mrs Hogbin. Here's your bus stop. Byee!"

* * *

It was an hour or so later, when Alexander was home and doing something-or-other at the far end of the garden – which pleased Caroline, as getting him out of doors and away from that damned computer – that she heard a car draw up on the circular front drive, and then a ring at the doorbell. The car had a distinctive knock at slow speeds, and she knew who the visitor was.

"Jack!" she said, as she opened the door. "This is a pleasant surprise. Come in."

"You're *sure* I haven't come at an inconvenient time?" Jack said with his accustomed diffidence.

"I don't really have inconvenient times any more," Caroline said, then added: "except at weekends, of course."

Sir John Mortyn-Crosse ("Bart." it insisted on his card, to distinguish him as a baronet from the myriad creation of knights and Life Peers over the last twenty years or so) was as estimable a man as Caroline had ever known: courteous, considerate, infinitely charitable within his straitened means. It was unfortunate that her children ignored all these qualities and focused on the workings of the poor man's insides, which were indeed like the plumbing of an old and neglected house, resulting in loud bubbling or heaving noises and periodical loud reports with consequent pervading smells. "Fart Fart the Bart" her eldest daughter would sing if she heard his car approach, and since Olivia was a dramatic soprano Caroline was always afraid that Jack would hear her as he got out of the car.

As he sat down in the armchair that was "his", his stomach obligingly produced a noise like the maelstrom preparing for action. As always, Jack ignored it.

"I've come to ask a favour – " he began.

"Ask away."

" – and you've got to say 'no' if it's the least bit inconvenient."

"I'm not sure I'll promise that, but go on."

"I was wondering – Meta and I were wondering – if the arrangement for the fête this year could become a permanent one." He hurried ahead, out of some kind of embarrassment that Caroline thought excessive. "You see, it's been a delight having it at the Dower House all these years – one small relic of the past, of former glories – but in the end it *is* a bit of a chore, and though everyone is very nice, and takes care, and comes and helps with the clearing up afterwards, Meta *does* hate the damage to the garden. She's not getting any younger, you know, and we have no help, and the fact is the grounds here at Alderley are much bigger, and with people being

11

able to use both the back garden and the front without traipsing through the house –"

"Jack – *Jack*! It's all right. I thought when we had the fête here it was ideal, and I enjoyed enormously having it, and all the people, and the things for the children. So I'd love it to come here, and I can see that you and Meta must feel you've done your bit, having had it all those years."

Jack looked at her impishly.

"I have to admit that, having said it was a delight having it for so long, I should have added that this year the delight was *not* having it."

Actually Caroline was rather surprised that Meta was letting the fête be transferred to Alderley, because she was a bit of a dragon, albeit a comic one, and was very hot on her position in the village. She frequently suggested by a succession of piggy stares that she disapproved of Caroline and Marius's unwed state. Still, with only two houses in the village capable of playing host to the fête, she didn't have a great deal of choice if she wanted to be rid of the burden.

Relieved to have that bit of business out of the way, Jack Mortyn-Crosse relaxed in the chair and settled in for a good session of village gossip, breaking wind at regular intervals. The vicar's wife wanted to get a job, or at least wanted the income that a job might produce, Mr Patel at the village shop-cum-post-office was threatening to sell up or close, one of the (few) children in the village had been raiding the little patch of apple trees that was all that was left of Marsham Manor's orchard. The manor itself, where Jack's family had lived, if not for centuries, at least for a hundred and fifteen years, had been sold twenty years before, and its demolition had led to a large estate of instant homes on the site of house and grounds. Jack and his sister lived in the Dower House, in a relationship which veered between the just-tolerant and the downright hostile. Jack's long-ago wife, who had died in childbirth with the longed for baby, was barely a memory in the village, though mention of her always brought a look of pain to Jack's pleasant face.

"And Marius will be down for the weekend?"

"Of course."

"Any plans?"

"Not yet, but no doubt something nice will emerge. Olivia's rehearsing with Opera North, so she may be able to get away for a bit. Not that she'd expect us to do anything special for her. She's happy shutting herself away and singing scales."

"Wonderful voice. I've heard her singing Schubert."

Caroline bent forward to fill his cup, hiding her reddening face.

"It's a bit too big a voice for lieder these days. Or perhaps it's personality. She seems to overpower the songs. Verdi's more the mark."

"And yet she's still young. It must be God given ... So you and Marius will be able to get away to something-or-other?"

"Oh yes – meal, play, or whatever. There's *Dangerous Corner* on at the Leeds Playhouse, and there was something or other on at the Palace, Manchester that Marius said he fancied seeing. Manchester's just an hour or so away these days."

"Couldn't be too far, if I had my way. Don't you ever –?"

Jack had an infinite number of ways of asking whether Caroline didn't miss the stage. The burden of his concern seemed to be that she was forsaking her Art – one of many common man touches in Jack's thinking. Caroline, as always, laughed.

"No, I don't long to be treading the boards still. I have no regrets about quitting the stage – neither performing, nor all the back-stage and off-stage stuff."

"I expect you will, though."

"Jack! It's as if you *want* me to be frustrated and unfulfilled."

"Seems such a waste," Jack muttered. "Anyway, it's as well to have plenty of strings to your bow."

"I've got quite enough strings to my bow, thank you very much. My life is so *restful* now, Jack: so serene, so rich. I see more of my children than I ever have, and I love that. Even Olivia I see plenty of, though she has been out on her own for years now."

"I suppose you were building your career when she was young."

"That's right. And so was Rick, my first husband – the archetypal Thespian nasty. Olivia's life was all nannies and baby-sitters, poor love. It's no wonder that ... Anyway, the main thing is, there's a base for all three of the children when they need it. And they all get on so well with Marius – and with his brood, the few times they've met."

"Everyone would love it if –"

"I know, Jack, I know. But I've been there, done that. Rick, my first, I can hardly bear to think about, let alone talk to. Evelyn, my second, the creature from the swamp, I had to bully my younger two to have the most minimal contact with before he took himself off to an embassy in Central America. I've given up reminding them when his birthday is: I just buy cards for them and guide their hands when they sign. Marriage is a disaster zone I don't intend to stray into again a third time. In any case, as you well know, Marius is still technically married."

"But he could –"

"I don't want him to, and there wouldn't be any point. End of conversation, please Jack."

Which fairly effectively put an end to the visit as well. Jack murmured something about "thought I ought to bring it up", like a vicar apologising for mentioning God every time he paid a visit, and then he went out to his car. As he got into his ageing Honda Civic Shuttle he emitted a loud report that sent a passing squirrel scuttling up a tree. Alexander, coming round from the back with – if his mother had only had a stronger sense of smell – a fair whiff of nicotine about him, looked after the departing car.

"Fart Fart the Bart was looking a bit hang-dog," he remarked.

"He brought up the business of marriage again."

"Why can't they let you alone to do what you want?"

"Amen to that."

"You've slaved away on stages and in studios long enough."

"You know," she said, looking around her, "I think it's this place, Alderley, that makes people do it. If Marius had set me up in a suburban semi they wouldn't think it half so important that he should make an honest woman of me."

"There wouldn't be any point in setting you up in a suburban semi: we had one already."

"True. Anyway, I think the appeal of Alderley is aesthetic to Marius."

"Don't talk to me about aesthetics, Mum. You know that's my blind spot. I suppose you just mean he likes a good lay in pleasant surroundings."

And Alexander drifted back indoors to continue his trawl through the fatuities and ego-trips on the Internet.

Caroline rather enjoyed his last remark. It was characteristic of Alexander – his instinct to earth everything, to deflate pretensions and pomposities, to prick bubbles. Not something she would have wanted in a lover, but something she found quite useful in a son. She was just turning to follow Alexander back into the house when she saw someone approaching from the direction of the village up the narrow country road outside the gate. So few walked it – it only led by the most roundabout route to the next village – that she stayed outside, wondering if it was a friend of one of her children.

It was a boy, a young man – she soon saw that. She saw too that he had a smallish rucksack on his back. The shorts and open shirt bespoke the hiker. The *walk* – there was something in the walk that reminded her ... of who? Not one of her husbands, thank God. When he got to the gate without seeing her he stopped and got out a map.

As he stood there peering at it, Caroline got a good view of his face. Of course! What his walk and face reminded her of was Marius.

As she watched him from the shadow of the tree she was convinced he had not seen her, though his face was in her direction. After a minute or two with his finger tracing a route on the map the young man folded it carefully, then continued on his way along the road.

Chapter Two

The Wandering Boy

On thinking it over, Caroline became convinced that she would see the boy again.

If she had passed in the street a young man who conspicuously resembled Marius she would have been intrigued, but she would quite soon have put it out of her mind: there was not an infinite number of facial types or personal features. And if it was not mere coincidence, then the boy could very well be a relative – a nephew, or some kind of cousin. Caroline knew next to nothing about Marius's family, apart from his children, and she cared not a whit about anyone more distant. She had "done" families in the course of her two marriages, and had discovered nobody she particularly liked, apart from the mother of her first husband, who was quite as bemused by the awfulness of the product of her womb as anyone less intimately related to him could have been. Caroline now felt she had Marius, cared about his children Guy and Helena, and was interested in his wife, but that was it.

But the fact was that she had *not* seen the boy casually in the street: he had come to the gate of Alderley, brought there apparently by a map, and this must mean that he had at least an intention of making himself known, and had decided against doing it at that time. At some stage, surely, he would come back, tell her who he was, and would probably turn out to be the result of one of Marius's earlier indiscretions. In fact, she felt she would be rather disappointed if he did not – if his appearance in the road outside Alderley turned out to be merely the result of a curiosity that was satisfied by a sight of the house in which Marius had installed his mistress. That would be a let-down, because she felt she wanted to talk to the boy, and since Marius had made no secret of several youthful and not-so-youthful entanglements she saw no reason for embarrassment on either side. Without any conscious decision having been made on her part, Caroline stayed within the house and garden for the next day or two. That was no penance. Alderley was the first place in her life where she was entirely happy.

She had seen the boy on Tuesday. It was Thursday when he rang on the doorbell. Caroline was working round the side of the house, waiting for a promised visit from the Rector and Sir John, and the windows of Alderley were open to the summer sun. She went round to the front, vaguely wiping her earthy hands, and recognised her visitor at once.

"Oh hello," she said. "I wondered whether you'd come back."

"Back?"

"I saw you when you went past the house before. I was puzzled at first, by your resemblance to somebody."

The boy smiled a slow smile. He did not take her up on her words, but went at the matter obliquely, rather reminding Caroline of Alexander.

"I hope you don't think it's cheek, visiting you like this."

"Not at all. I'm delighted. Do come in and have a cup of tea or coffee. I'm Caroline Fawley, by the way."

"I know. I'm Pete Bagshaw."

They shook hands awkwardly, then laughed, and Caroline led the way inside. She regretted that Alexander and Stella were both out, and she hoped she could persuade Pete to stay to dinner, or stay the night even. The children could help with that, and she hoped she could delay him until they were back. She put him in the lounge, found that he would prefer coffee, and asked if there was anything else that he wanted.

"A bath. I'd die for a bath."

"Bath or coffee first?"

"I should say bath, but I'm parched."

"Right. There's a paper there if you're interested in the news."

When Caroline came back with a coffee pot and two large cups and saucers she saw he was somewhat confusedly finding his way through the various sections of *The Times*. She poured a cup, then said:

"Anything particular you're looking for?"

"Sport."

"Oh, it sometimes has a section to itself, sometimes it's with Business. I'm afraid it's not something I even glance at." She handed him his cup, and he helped himself to two heaped teapoons of sugar. Out of tune with his time, she thought. When he tasted the coffee he had to suppress a grimace of surprise or distaste. Caroline kicked herself for a failure of sympathy. He was a Nescafé boy, and probably a tabloid one. She didn't often put her foot in it when it came to that sort of judgment. She thought perhaps it had come about because she had thought of him as Marius's son. It came to her that she had made the mistake because she was nervous. Silly reaction, she told herself: she had known many gauche but harmless young men, usually friends of her children. She had nothing to fear from the likes of Pete Bagshaw.

"Try some cream," she said. "It will take away the bitterness. I was a bit lavish with the coffee grounds."

The cream did seem to make the brew more palatable.

"It's a grand house," Pete said.

"Isn't it? I just loved it the moment I saw it."

"And lovely gardens too."

"They are – small thanks to me. The Rector and a neighbour should be here soon to talk about next year's fête. It's being moved to here, which is a great honour. You can disappear to the bathroom if you prefer. It's top of the stairs, then second to your right. I expect Alexander and Stella will be back by late afternoon. I'd like you to meet them."

Unspoken so far was why she would like him to meet them. The boy remained silent, giving her no opening.

"I suppose you're on some kind of walking tour, aren't you?"

"That's right."

"Where do you live?"

"Armley, near Leeds."

"Oh, I know Leeds quite well. It's good for shopping, and I've played there in my time."

"It's just a small house. My mum works in a supermarket."

"Is she married?"

Pete shook his head, unembarrassed like all young people.

"No. And no one around at the moment. I did have a sort of step-dad for a time, but it didn't work out. Doesn't bother me. We're all right as we are."

"I'm sure you are. Still – " But she was just beginning to get to the heart of the matter when the doorbell rang. Pete said "I'll have that bath, if you don't mind," grabbed something from his backpack in flight, then went up the stairs two at a time.

The visiting party consisted not just of Sir John Mortyn-Crosse and the Rector, but the Rector's wife as well. Caroline was on swap-trivialities terms with Mrs Watters, and wondered whether she was being inspected for hitherto-unknown depravities or given some kind of social absolution for sin. On the surface however she was notably, almost ostentatiously, friendly. Mr Watters explained that, with the prospect of the much larger grounds of Alderley, he thought his wife could contribute a great deal to the discussion of how they could best be used. As they went around cordiality and acceptance reigned, and Mrs Watters tentatively decided on the positioning of the various major stalls, and even began suggesting they could branch out into children's games and races.

"But where are the children to come from?" asked Caroline.

"Oh, the fête is for all of my husband's parishes," said Mrs Watters. "There are three villages in all. We'll hope for quite a lot of young people."

"I must make sure Marius keeps the day free," said Caroline.

"We shall be honoured if he can be with us," said the Rector. "But you of course will be the big attraction."

"Oh, I'm sure no one remembers –"

"But they *do* remember, Mrs Fawley. Especially faces. They may not remember the various things you were in on television, or what they were *about*, but they remember *you*. That was notable this year, and will be even more so when word gets around more. A business-man is all very well, and I'm sure everyone is impressed by Mr Fleetwood's standing in the world of commerce, but in the end, for getting people through the turnstile so to speak, a businessman can't compete with an actress."

"I'll tell Marius that," said Caroline. At that moment Jack let

19

fly with a loud one, and they all moved over to admire the chrysanthemums.

Caroline was wondering how she would introduce Pete when she asked them all in for tea, but luckily the Rector had an appointment with a pair of new parents to discuss the christening of their baby son – "though it will probably be the little chap's only time in church if he is anything like his mum and dad" – so Caroline was able to wave them all goodbye in the Rector's old car and go back into Alderley on her own.

Pete wasn't in the sitting room, and after poking her head around various doors Caroline found him in the scullery, bending over the washing machine.

"I hope you don't mind – I'm washing a few things."

"Of course not. I'm impressed you can work it."

Pete obviously thought that smacked of soft soap.

"Piece o' cake. It's difficult on a walking tour unless you go to one of the bigger towns with a laundrette, and you're not supposed to do that."

"Not supposed to? –"

"Duke of Edinburgh's Award. I've done several things for that. August is a good time to do them."

"Oh –" said Caroline, inevitably vague, because she had very little idea of what the Duke of Edinburgh's Award consisted of, or was given for. She was saved from exposing her ignorance by the sound of the front door.

"Hi, Mum. Oh –" Alexander and Stella, coming in from a shopping trip to Doncaster, stopped short at the sight of the visitor.

"Alex, Stella, this is Peter Bagshaw –"

"Pete."

"Alex and Stella are the children of my second marriage, and we're all called Fawley, which was my stage and maiden name. Pete is on a walking tour for the Duke of Edinburgh's Award. He's just giving his dirty clothes a wash, and I hope he's going to have a meal with us."

It all sounded unlikely, bordering on the absurd. She wondered if her children saw the resemblance. It was less obvious when he was

20

standing still – it had been his walk as much as anything that had told her who he was. Alexander broke the brief silence by nodding, then turning to his mother.

"They had this new scanner in at Compuware in Doncaster. I paid for it out of the cheque you gave me for my birthday."

"What have you got?" asked Pete. He didn't need to explain what he was interested in. Alex thumbed in the direction of the little box-room, and they went off together, to be immersed in computerbabble for the two hours until dinner. Caroline sighed.

"He's not bad looking," commented Stella. "Mum, there was this skirt in Principles, it was fabulous, and I couldn't resist it."

So for the women it was clothes until the time for cooking arrived. Clothes were a subject which interested Caroline less and less as far as herself was concerned, but she simulated an interest in them for Stella's sake. Stella tried on the skirt – a short, slit number that was very sexy, and she left it on for Pete's benefit, Caroline suspected. Stella had not her elder sister's frank and hungry interest in men, but she was definitely developing an eye for them. Caroline was rather glad than otherwise, in spite of her earlier misjudgements. Misjudgements were all a vital part of the lifelong sexual game, she thought, and fourteen was about the age to start playing it.

The boys did not emerge from the box-room until she shouted that dinner was ready. By then they gave the appearance of being bosom friends without knowing anything whatever about each other except their taste in computer software. They continued their conversation over the soup (which Pete seemed uncertain how to deal with), and their talk could well have been in Hungarian for all Caroline could understand of it. She wished they would get on to something she could follow, so she could make for herself an opening. Stella did understand, but she got increasingly impatient.

"What do you do, then?" she asked Pete, putting down her spoon.

"Degree in Computer Science," he said, disappointingly. "At Leeds Metropolitan University."

"Leeds is a good place to go, isn't it?" Stella persevered. "For clubs and underground parties and things. I can't imagine Oxford or Cambridge is any good for having a wild time in."

"Quite apart from the fact that you will never have the remotest chance of getting into Oxford or Cambridge," Caroline pointed out.

"Oh, I know I'm not ac*adem*ic," said Stella, as if that was the last consideration when deciding to go to university. "And I don't suppose *you* are either," she said, turning back to Peter – "computer science and that."

"Means to an end," muttered Pete.

"'Course it is. Means to the end of having a good time."

"Getting a good job, in my case."

"Oh that. I suppose so. I'm too young to think about getting jobs, aren't I, Mum?"

Caroline made a moue.

"I'd have said so when I was your age. But people seem to think about it from nursery school these days." She was coming back from the kitchen with a tray of plates containing lamb chops and boiled potatoes (she had forsworn new potatoes when they lost all their taste).

"I've had to think about earning a good living," said Pete, but not aggressively. "My mum is stuck in a rotten little job, and we've always lived on the breadline. I want to get something that brings in a lot, so she can chuck her job in and put her feet up."

"Young people always think that," said Caroline. "Then they meet a girl and get married, and Mum suddenly is at the bottom of their list of priorities."

Pete shook his head, then, having watched the others, began tackling his lamb chops. Caroline guessed he was used to microwaved shepherd's pies and takeaway pizzas. The chops were tender, and he coped very well.

"What are you doing on this walking trip?" pursued Stella.

Pete seemed a touch embarrassed.

"It's part of the Duke of Edinburgh's Awards Scheme."

"I heard Mum say that. Isn't that some kind of Outward Bound thing, with everyone doing gung-ho kind of exploits?"

22

"Don't be rude, Stella, and don't screw up your face as if you knew what you were talking about," said her mother.

"Well, I mean – OK, I don't know much about it, but it's for kids, isn't it? People at university don't do that sort of thing."

"I started it years ago," said Pete, unembarrassed. "It'll look good on my C.V. Employers like that kind of thing."

"You have got this job thing bad."

"Stella!"

"Oh, all right, Mum. I'll keep quiet. Demure, downcast looks, listen to the men's talk with suitably humble expression. Like you do when Marius gets on to his business and state-of-the-economy talk."

"I do *not*, Stella. I just switch off."

She had looked at Pete to see how he reacted to this talk of Marius, but his face was a complete blank.

"You get an automatic look of sweet but baffled interest on you face," said Stella. "You learnt a lot when you were an actress. Mainly about pleasing men."

"If I wanted to do that I was very bad at it. Both my husbands walked out on me."

"Only to get in first, because they knew you were planning to walk out on *them*. That's what you've always told us. Mind you, I wouldn't blame any woman for walking out on number one. Our dad we hardly know, but number one was the pits." She turned to Pete. "Did your mum walk out on your father?"

This time Pete did look embarrassed, and almost didn't answer.

"Before my time," he mumbled. "Before I began to take notice, anyway."

"But your mother must have told you."

Pete looked at his watch ostentatiously – pure amateur acting in the early stages of rehearsal.

"I must go," he said.

"Oh, but I've got gooseberry pie," said Caroline. "And I hoped you could stay the night."

"We're not allowed to sleep in private homes. It's out in the open or in a hostel. I have to get to the hostel in Doncaster by ten if I'm to get a bed."

Caroline tried to avoid seeing the expression on Stella's face, which was openly sceptical.

"Well, I wouldn't want to cause you to break the rules," she said, following him into the hall. His newly-washed shirt and underclothes were lying on top of his backpack, and he now began unzipping it and packing them away. "I'm sorry about Stella. She's a curious child – inquisitive, I mean. She always likes to know everything about anybody she meets. She doesn't mean to be rude."

Pete swung the pack round to sit squarely on his shoulders.

"That's all right. I don't have to answer."

"No, of course not. You handled it well. I won't compound my daughter's rudeness, but it would be nice if you could pay us a visit one weekend when Marius is here."

The boy turned at the front door and looked at her.

"Better not, don't you think?" he said, then lifted the latch and was gone. Caroline stood for a moment, absorbing what he had said, then went back to the dining room.

"Well, I'm not the only one who's adept at scaring men away," she said.

"Oh Mum, I didn't *scare* him. He just didn't want to talk about Marius," said Stella.

"Marius? Why should he talk about Marius?" asked Alexander. The women looked at each other.

"You really didn't notice?" asked Stella.

"Notice? Notice what? We were looking at the screen most of the time."

"I bet. Well, for your information, Pete was the spitting image of Marius."

"Not the spitting image,'" amended Caroline. "But like."

Alexander shrugged.

"Didn't notice. So what? He's probably some relation."

"Could be," admitted Stella. "Much more interesting if he's a long-lost son."

"Why on earth should you think that? Marius was hardly mentioned."

"Well actually," said Caroline hesitantly, "while we were in the

24

hall I suggested he might come back again when Marius was here, and he said 'Better not, don't you think?'"

"Oooh!" said Stella, now thoroughly interested. "Well, well: that more or less proves it, doesn't it? I wonder what Marius will say when we tell him."

"Stella," said Caroline, at her most impressive. "Stop smirking. You will say *nothing* to Marius about this, nothing about the boy's visit at all. Do I make myself clear? Anything said about it will come from me, and I'm not sure it wouldn't be best for me to keep shtoom as well. You two will keep well out of it. Understood?"

"OK, Mum," said Stella.

Alexander shrugged.

"I'm not interested." That, Caroline suspected, was not true. She was confirmed in this opinion by her son's next words. "I can't think why he bothered to come at all. He did nothing beyond *see* you – see us. And how did he know about you, and where you lived?"

"Yes,'" said Caroline. "That was one of the things I'd like to have asked him."

Chapter Three

Sweet and Sour

The next day was Friday, and Marius arrived at Alderley earlier than usual. Luckily Alex and Stella had already gone out – Marius had waved to them at the bus stop, in fact. He arrived at his usual top speed, and held her in a long, long embrace in the hall. He did not immediately start undressing her and leading her upstairs, and Caroline was very glad that he didn't. At their age it would have been ridiculous, and long years of playing comedy had honed her sense of *that* danger. In fact she immediately put dinner on, got him his favourite dry Amontillado, and they ate over candlelight (just on the right side of the ridiculous, that, in Caroline's view) the veal escalopes and sorbets she had prepared, with the New Zealand chardonnay which was Marius's preferred wine for other than special occasions. Then they went up to bed, and to the long, loving, tender sex that made Caroline so happy.

"Dress, or not to dress?" Marius asked later.

"Dressing gown will do, surely. My children aren't nursery school kids. Alexander was going to the cinema anyway, and won't be back till eleven or so. Stella hadn't decided. By the way, Stella is becoming decidedly interested in boys." Then would have been the time to tell him about Pete, but she muffed the chance: she lamely added: "I wouldn't want it any other way," and Marius started talking about his wife Sheila.

"If only she enjoyed it as you enjoy it," he said.

"I'm not at all sure I'd be happy about that," said Caroline. "In fact, I *much* prefer it the the way it is."

The two children arrived back just as Caroline and Marius reached the landing on their way back to bed. Caroline called out "Goodnight", and the children called "Goodnight" back, and then went on with their argument about the film, which apparently they'd both been to see. They came up to bed twenty minutes later, and Marius's hand paused as he waited for their doors to shut, and then began again its wonderfully exciting attentions.

26

It was close to midnight, and the pair of them were still awake, though drowsy, when they heard a car draw up outside. Caroline slipped out of bed.

"It'll be Olivia," said Marius softly.

"I like to *know*," said Caroline. She drew the curtains aside a fraction.

Down below, getting out of a middle-market car, was her daughter. She came round to the driver's door, but it was opening. Caroline got a look at a large young man, but couldn't see his face as he enveloped her daughter in a passionate hug, bending her over the car to kiss her. She let the curtain drop, feeling she was intruding, but seconds later she heard the front door opening, then the car driving away.

"Olivia, driven home by her latest," she said, then amended it: "or one of the current ones." Olivia was not usually monogamous, even in her short-term relationships.

Caroline got back into bed, laid her head on Marius's shoulder, and was soon fast asleep.

Morning began with mugs of tea from the Teasmaid. Caroline always said that was the best cup of tea of the day, because any preparation for it had been done so long ago that it was genuinely like maid service. That Saturday morning their enjoyment was accompanied by Olivia's singing exercises from somewhere in the distance.

"I'd say that was a gorgeous sound," said Marius, "if you didn't know me to be an absolute cloth-ears where music is concerned, whose opinion is of no use or interest whatsoever."

"Well, your cloth-ears happen for once to be right: she has a wonderful voice."

"She gets her looks from you – pale shadow though they are. Where does the voice come from?"

Caroline grimaced. It was an instinct she had, when her first husband was mentioned.

"Rick Radshaw was gunning for parts in musicals about the time we were married. Still does them whenever he can get them. The dizzy summit of his career was Freddy Eynsford-Hill in the first touring production of *My Fair Lady*. We had 'On the Street Where You Live' non-stop around the flat for months."

"I think I've heard that one," said Marius. Caroline looked at him with amused affection. How wonderfully unselfconscious he was!

"Anyway, one thing I can assure you: *La Forza del Destino* stands up to oft-repeated hearings a great deal better than Lerner and Loewe do."

"When's the first night?"

"Today three weeks. You'll be down that weekend, won't you?"

"How many weekends do I miss, darling? I keep them free with the ferocity of a cat keeping a mouse to herself. I suppose you'll insist on buying me a ticket?"

"It was bought long ago. First nights are always at a premium, and one on a Saturday is a bit unusual."

"So long as Olivia won't be hurt if I don't sit through the whole thing."

"She'll *expect* you to duck out after about half an hour, as you have for everything of hers you've been to. And then maybe come back for curtain calls."

"That's the nice thing about opera: they tell you in the foyer when it's due to end. People assume I've been involved in some frightfully high-powered business dealings during the intervening hours."

"Whereas in fact you've been propping up a bar."

"Sometimes. I've been known to go and see a film if the damned opera is long enough."

Later, at breakfast, Olivia paid them a visit, popping her head round the door to see that Marius was still eating, not yet smoking. She sat down with them, took a piece of toast from the rack, spread it with the strawberry jam that Marius preferred at breakfast time, then poured herself a strong cup of tea.

"Your voice sounded lovely," commented Caroline.

"Mmmm," said Olivia complacently. "It's going to grow, get richer, acquire the sort of *weight* the role needs, the solidity, till this time Saturday three weeks – Bingo!" Then she seemed to think she was pushing her luck. "If all goes well," she added.

Caroline looked at her daughter with motherly pride. Her looks, as Marius had implied, were not the equal of hers: in themselves they would not have got her parts on the dramatic stage, though they were a cause for comment in the world of opera. Caroline regarded her daughter's gift of a voice – rich, powerful, capable of bringing tears to the eyes, shivers down the spine – as more than compensation for her rather ordinary good looks. And she envied, without always approving of, her voracious hunger for life, experience, fame. Time enough, in ten years' time, to slow down and accept the more everyday as her lot. If, of course, the life of an international star turned out to be beyond her grasp.

"By 'if all goes well' I suppose you mean if your love-life goes well," she commented.

"What else? It affects the voice. *Of course* it affects the voice."

Caroline thought this was probably superstition, or a convenient fable, but she didn't say so.

"And who was the man who brought you home last night?"

Olivia shrugged.

"*Not* the love of my life, anyway. He's the Alvaro in *Forza*. Sort-of-Irish, sort-of-American. Studied and trained in America. Nice enough voice."

Caroline sighed.

"You're not going to do the Ingrid Bergman thing of always having an affair with your current leading man, are you? That always seemed a bit calculating to me."

"I am *not* having an affair with Colm ... Not by any usual definition of the word."

Caroline wondered vaguely who she was having an affair with (baritone? bass? conductor? director?) but decided she wouldn't bother to ask since the name would mean little or nothing to her. Having gobbled her toast and jam and gulped down her tea Olivia took herself off, and soon she was to be heard floating phrases from Leonora's big arias, and eventually singing one of the arias complete. Her half-sister had enough skill at the piano to provide a skeleton accompaniment, though she had to be bribed with money – nothing else did – to give up her time.

Later, walking arm in arm with Marius in the late summer sun, Caroline asked:

"How is Sheila?"

Marius never let his face betray any sign of distaste or irritation when the subject of his wife came up. Today it only showed perfect blankness.

"As ever. Perfectly friendly but a bit remote. I think she misses the children now they're not around the house so much. It's left a hole. She actually came with me to a film premiere on Wednesday."

"Oh? Not the sort of thing you go to often, is it?"

"Fleetwood Enterprises have sunk a bit of money into it. Not a lot of money, because for every British film that makes a packet there's forty or fifty that are lucky if they're let out on video. *Putting the Boot In* looks as if it's going to be in the former category, I'm glad to say."

"Most of what you invest in does."

"Ten per cent daring, ninety per cent caution – that's my motto."

"Did Sheila enjoy it?"

"Not at all. Much too violent. It was one of those films designed to show that the Britain leads the world in gangsterism, though I shouldn't think we hold a candle to America or Italy or Russia. I think we'll have to find one of those upper-class comedies with wet British actors to put our money into next."

"I suppose Sheila would like that better."

"*Much* better." He shot a shy look in her direction. "You've been in plenty of upper-class comedies yourself."

"True enough. I wasn't being sarcastic."

"Sheila's a perfectly nice woman, you know. And intelligent too."

"You've always made that plain."

"I was moderately faithful to her, till she made it clear that *that* side of the marriage was over as far as she was concerned."

Caroline laughed, then squeezed his arm.

"I love your idea of being moderately faithful. Put a sock in it, Marius. Have I ever pressured you to get a divorce?"

"Never."

"I've done with marriage myself, though not with *that* side of it, as you call it."

30

"Decidedly not."

"I don't want the sort of commitment that gets written down on a sheet of paper. But I *am* totally committed."

"Me too, darling. I just don't want to hurt Sheila."

"And nor do I ... What do you think she will do, when the children are really gone, and her husband is semi-detached? How will she fill in her life?"

"Who knows?" Marius shrugged. "Good causes? Jam-making? A young boyfriend?"

"That doesn't seem likely, if she's gone off sex."

"If. Perhaps she's just gone off it with me. She wouldn't tell me if so. She's not in the hurting business. Anyway, it's her affair. I would never talk to her about my relationship with you, though she certainly knows about it, and I wouldn't want her to talk about any relationship she gets into. There's a lot to be said for tact and keeping quiet about things. Reticence doesn't get much of a press these days, but it's been very useful over the centuries. Think what an awful mess the Restoration rakes made of their lives by being totally open and flagrant."

"Charles II seems to have managed pretty well," said Caroline, who had once played the part of the Duchess of Cleveland in *In Good King Charles's Golden Days*.

"Kings have advantages over lesser mortals. No, I prefer the example of the Victorian lechers who managed to keep their lives in separate compartments."

"Well, we certainly do that, and you won't find me complaining."

For some reason the topic of Sheila Fleetwood was in the air that weekend. Most of the times they were together she barely got a mention. In the car that evening, on the way to *Dangerous Corner* at the West Yorkshire Playhouse in Leeds, Caroline said:

"I really wasn't being sarcastic about Sheila preferring an upper-class comedy to gangsterism and thuggery. I'd certainly prefer it myself. The truth is that these days neither category is very satisfying as far as I'm concerned: I'd never go to either type of film a second time."

"You're a bit of a culture snob, aren't you Caroline?"

"I don't know about that," she said, almost miffed. "I've spent much of my acting career in fairly ordinary pieces. It was a real lift to get *Streetcar* early on – Stella, not Blanche of course – and then Candida, and Rebecca West in Glasgow. But they were high spots. I spent much of my career in drawing-room comedies and whodunnits."

"Sheila's a real culture-vulture, to tell you the truth. It upset her a lot when Guy decided to do that computer stuff at university. Beneath contempt, she thought."

Now would have been another good chance to mention Pete Bagshaw. But the moment passed. Caroline let it pass, again.

"She sounds like a woman after my own heart," she said. "Though as far as computers are concerned I'm not *against* them. I don't despise them, I'm just ignorant, and I want to keep my ignorance."

"Sheila feels everything is becoming automated and dumbed down. She shudders when she opens the arts pages of *The Times*. She's of a generation that can hardly think of films – or 'Film' as they call it – as an art form at all."

"Nonsense, she's of my generation. And I do think that's going a bit far."

"Well, pop music, then. She sits on cultural bodies and she's on all the cultural grapevines. She knows when anything significant is coming at the theatre long before it actually opens. She'd bound to have heard that Olivia is going to be a sensation in *Forza*. She'd probably come if it wasn't –"

"Yes, if it wasn't." Caroline pondered for a moment. "*Are* the grapevines saying Olivia is going to be a sensation? It's news to me."

"Oh yes. People have commented, wished her well through me. That's people who know about you and me, of course."

"Well, that's wonderful news if it's true. I've always had a feeling in my bones about Olivia's voice, but of course I'm only an amateur as far as opera is concerned."

The topic of Marius's wife did not come up again, but interval time at the West Yorkshire Playhouse did lead to more discussion of Olivia's approaching appearance as Leonora. There were various people from the acting trade in the audience – people appearing in or otherwise involved with plays in the West Yorkshire area. The ones who knew Caroline, and even one or two who didn't, came up, asked what she was doing ("Being a kept woman," she said to one of those "and very pleasant it is too") and several had heard on the local arts network that rehearsals were going sensationally well for Olivia.

"They say it's a wonderfully rich voice," said an elderly actor who had seen every operatic sensation since Callas's Covent Garden Norma, "and with the bloom still on. Lucky old us."

"We hear a lot of it, but we still think it's pretty magnificent," said Caroline. "If there's going to be a lot of advance hype, I hope it doesn't arouse too high expectations though."

"It's not hype, darling. It's informed report passed by word of mouth between people in the know."

Going back into the auditorium Caroline got a warm glow of anticipation. She was soon going to be known as the mother of Olivia Fawley. She felt not the slightest twinge of jealousy, no sense of anti-climax. Her career had never aimed at the highest peaks, and her life, now her career was over, was both happier and – oddly – more fulfilled. Part of that fulfilment was the excellent relationship she had with her children.

That thought brought in its train other thoughts about parents and children. But with Marius's comforting presence beside her, she put those thoughts away from her. She *would* think about Marius and Pete, she would think through the implications of what Pete had let slip, but she would do so when Marius was not there to influence her conclusions. And she would not be so silly as to take the off-hand and ambiguous remarks of a post-adolescent young man as gospel truth. Marius deserved better than that from her.

It was as they were leaving the theatre with a sense of two hours pleasantly spent that Caroline saw Lauren Spender and Lauren saw her. Lauren was the current partner of Rick Radshaw, her first husband.

"Darling! How come I didn't spot you at interval?"

"I didn't spot you either, Lauren. Perhaps we weren't looking."

"Darling, what are you doing at the moment?"

"Being a kept woman. You know how it is, Lauren."

"Oh, catty! Actually I'm opening in *Loot* next week. So I won't be able to come to *Forza*. But Rick will be there, to support his talented offspring. We're in a cottage in the Dales. Heaven! Bye, darling."

"Don't darling me, you bitch," muttered Caroline as she got into the car.

"Do I gather that is the dreadful Rick's wife, partner or appendage?" asked Marius as they drove off.

"Partner."

"Why the bitchiness?"

"I've always loathed her. Everything is false about her except her spleen."

"Sounds like she and Rick are well-matched."

"Ideally. But what does that say about me, who married him and let him father my first child."

"That you were hardly more than a child yourself at the time."

"I've known toddlers that had more sense and better judgment. And now I'll have to be nice, *specially* nice, to him at the first night – as if he has had anything to do with Olivia's success."

"Well, he is the parent with the singing voice you said this morning."

"Oh, I give him that. But that's exactly like saying a parent has given its child brown eyes or fair hair or flat feet. Not something you can accept credit or blame for."

"Certainly not something you're going to give him any credit for," commented Marius. Caroline laughed.

"You bring out the best in me. I can hardly forgive you for that. Let's forget about Rick."

And for the rest of the trip back to Alderley they laughed, were catty about the night's supporting actors, and forgot all about Sheila, and Rick, and Pete. Marius, of course, probably never thought about Pete.

Chapter Four

Newcomers

"I've discovered how that Pete Whatsisname found out about you and where we live," announced Alexander at breakfast on Tuesday.

"Oh? How?"

"The rector's daughter is at Leeds Metropolitan University."

"Oh really? I thought she was at the older one."

"Oh, they leave it vague," said Alexander, with his habitual pleasure in finding out things. "They say 'Gina will be going back to Leeds next week' – that sort of thing. I don't think she makes any secret of it herself, but she's hardly been around all summer."

"I can't see why anyone should make a secret of it," said Caroline.

"Don't you? It doesn't have the prestige of Leeds University. Just a harmless little bit of snobbery on the vicar's part. Added to which, these new universities that used to be polytechnics are where people go who want to do wacky things like Sports Studies or the Social History of Sanitary Engineering."

"I bow to your superior knowledge," said Caroline. "I suppose it's possible. But have you any evidence that they know each other?"

"No. But it's obvious."

"Hmmm. Well a course in logic might be a good idea for you, whatever you do as your main subject."

"It may not stick out a mile, Mum," said Stella, "but you've got to admit it's fairly likely."

After breakfast, washing-up and a rather perfunctory tidying of things away, Caroline walked to the village shop, half a mile away.

She was not surprised to see Jack walking in the opposite direction from the Dower House. They quite often did meet up in the shop, because Jack had come to know her habits – though he was sensible enough not to contrive it too often so that it was obvious that their meetings were no longer accidental.

They greeted each other, walked the remaining short distance, then bought far more than they wanted as a way of placating Mr

Patel (who had no intention of closing down, but put out the rumours periodically for commercial reasons). Then they repaired together to the White Hart for coffee and biscuits.

"Has the rector's wife been in touch?" Jack asked.

"Just a phone call. Said she wanted to talk to me about these new events and attractions she's planning. I felt like saying 'There's months to go!'"

"Oh things have to be prepared, to mature slowly. But it's good they're involving you."

"Say it how you mean it, Jack: it's good that I'm being accepted, that's what you're thinking."

Jack let fly, and as usual took no notice of sound or smell.

"Well, something like that."

"It's rather touching your caring so much – more than I do."

"I see shifting the fête as a sort of symbol. And you'll be much better as the host than I or Meta ever were."

Caroline smiled a worldly-wise smile.

"I suppose it comes from playing Lady of the Manor roles in highly forgettable drawing-room comedies. Not that Alderley is a manor, quite. Still, it's a lovely old house and the largest one *I've* ever lived in!"

"You should have seen the real manor," said Jack with a sigh. "People don't realize how much I miss it. You could get away from people there. Still, no point in regrets. If you can't keep it up, and no one has a use for it, then it has to go. Yes, Alderley's a nice house."

"I always feel it should have alder trees in the garden. Maybe it once did."

Jack shot her a glance.

"Oh no. It was always called Hallam's Croft until the nineteen-hundreds, after the man who had built it forty or more years before. His children didn't want it, and it was bought by another man who'd made his fortune in cotton, and he named it after his three children."

"His children?"

"Yes. Alice, Derek and Leyton, the last named after a maternal uncle the family had expectations from. He put the names together. Nothing to do with trees."

"Oh."

Caroline felt distinctly deflated, as if her beloved house had been devalued. It was like people calling their semis Philmar or Valjon. She shook herself for being silly, but she felt the house deserved better.

"What happened to the three children?" she asked.

"Derek – it was rather an uncommon name then – was killed in the Battle of the Somme. Leyton was killed three weeks before Armistice Day, and he'd never got the legacy from his maternal uncle that everyone hoped for. If he had, Alice would have been quite well off. As it was she and her husband struggled with the house for years and years, but finally had to sell it in the 'fifties. It had various owners – the last one was Alfred Beck, who was your predecessor. It was too big for him after his wife died. He rattled around in it. He's much happier in his bungalow in Hornsea. He made his money in Whitby, out of fishing, and he always missed the sea."

Jack seemed about to say something more, then decided against it.

"Marius was lucky to find Alderley anyway," said Caroline to fill in the silence. "Or rather, *I* was lucky he found it."

"On the contrary, we are lucky you came to live among us," said Jack, with his usual gallantry.

"I wonder if the situation would be acceptable in any village around the country," mused Caroline, "or is Marsham exceptionally tolerant? It would be quite unacceptable in parts of Scotland, I would guess. And Wales too, don't you think? But in most parts attitudes have changed enormously. Think – not so very long ago I would have been discreetly housed in a flat in Maida Vale."

"I don't really know London," said Jack. "Is Maida Vale so dreadful?"

"Not at all. But if I'm to be the acknowledged mistress of someone, I do very much prefer being it at Alderley, rather than shut away in a 'thirties flat in a 'thirties suburb of London."

Jack looked at her.

"Marriage is better, you know. Particularly for a woman."

"Marriage is *worse* for this woman! I should know, if anyone knows. I've learned by experience."

They smiled and went on to talk about village matters.

Marius usually phoned Caroline mid-week. When she heard the ring early on Wednesday evening she knew it was him, and settled comfortably in an armchair before picking it up.

"What have you been doing?" he asked, after the preliminaries.

"Coffee with Jack, gardening, listening to Mrs Hogbin on the evils of drugs, though she doesn't know her cannabis from her crack, reading silly magazines, settling a quarrel between Stella and Alexander. All very much as usual."

"Are you getting bored?"

"*Bored*? You must be joking. I feel I'm acting a part in an idyll. I get intense pleasure just thinking what to give you for dinner on Friday."

"Don't."

"*Don't*? You mean you won't be down for the weekend?"

"I love the sound of the disappointment in your voice. You sound absolutely crushed. I'll be down – in fact probably earlier than usual. We'll go out to eat."

"But we usually do something like that on Saturday."

"Not this weekend. I've something to tell you."

"Well tell me now."

"It's not the sort of thing that should be told on the phone."

"Anything can be told on the phone, Marius. Come on! You've not got the idea you're being bugged, have you?"

"No, of course I haven't."

"Then tell me."

"No. Book a table for Friday, at some place where we can be pretty sure of getting a bit of privacy – Sheffield, Leeds, Doncaster, York – anywhere."

"That rules out several of our favourite places. *La Grillade* has several little poky areas though. But tell me *now*. Is it nice news?"

"Not particularly."

"Then why on earth go out to a nice meal to break it to me?"

"It's really, when I think about it, not nice or nasty. But it's unexpected and – well – interesting. So book that table."

And he rang off. Caroline, feeling dissatisfied and gripped by curiosity, got up, poured herself a drink, and began pacing the living room.

Her first thought was to wonder whether Pete Bagshaw had made contact with his father. That might qualify as a happening that was neither nice nor nasty. There was an ambiguity about the boy that nagged in Caroline's mind. She had been adept enough at *suggesting* a character's ambiguity on stage (Stella Kowalski and Rebecca West sprang to mind), but she now found she didn't feel easy in real life with a person whose characteristics seemed shifting, two-sided, ungraspable. The boy had both seemed to like her yet resent her. Or had that latter emotion been supplied by herself, by her guilt? Here she was at Alderley, and there he was, growing up in Armley with a wage-slave mother, obsessed with rising out of his environment, getting a well-paid job.

But the question of Pete Bagshaw raised very pressingly the question: *if* he was Marius's by-blow, why had his father done so little for him over the first twenty years of his life? It would surely be natural for Pete to feel some resentment.

And yet, *assuming* he was Marius's child, it could be seen from the father's point of view too. Twenty-odd years ago, as far as she could guess, the chain of supermarkets in the South and West of the country were no more than a link of two or three, though the ambition for something much greater was certainly there. If Marius had a child by someone of his own background and class, he could be expected to pay maintenance appropriate to his then financial position. Why should his meteoric rise in fortunes lead to a massive increase in the sum to be paid "Mrs" Bagshaw for maintenance? Would that even be kind to the mother and boy, granted that a sudden access of funds which they would be unused to handling could have disastrous consequences. A sudden thought struck Caroline: Pete was only a year or two older than Guy. Perhaps conceived at about the time of Marius's marriage to Sheila. It was a disconcerting idea.

Caroline had just got to this point in her thoughts when a car drew up in the gathering darkness outside. Going to the window she thought she recognised the shape from the one seen from her bedroom window the Saturday before. She put down her sherry glass. Of course mothers should wait until their children *decided* to introduce their boy – or girlfriends, but ... If she waited for Olivia to do that, she would never meet the long and varied list of men she was interested in or involved with.

She went into the hall and opened the front door. Both front doors of the car were open now, and getting out of the driver's seat was a large young man with an Irish chin and a definite presence. There was no particular distinction to his face, but he seemed pleasant, thoughtful, and very taken with Olivia. Caroline liked men to be wholehearted, committed, but with Olivia that was likely to prove disheartening. Poor chap, she thought, for the umpteenth time about one of her daughter's boyfriends.

"Mrs Fawley?" the young man said, swerving from Olivia's door and coming over, hand outstretched. Caroline made a face.

"Call me Caroline."

"I'm Colm Fitzgerald."

"I thought you might be. Everyone's very excited about *Forza* I hear. Are you coming to rehearse here?"

"No, I'm just bringing Olivia home. She wanted a bit of peace and quiet and luxury. We've finished rehearsing for the day, and we're not needed again till late tomorrow."

"Thanks for the lift, love," said Olivia coolly, bending her head back and accepting, rather than reciprocating, a kiss. Caroline had been intending to ask the young man in, but Olivia said "See you tomorrow," and started towards the front door.

Colm Fitzgerald, obediently but reluctantly, got back into his car. As she turned to wave, Olivia said:

"You didn't have to do that 'Call me Caroline' bit. I told you: he's not a boyfriend."

"I see. Just a chauffeur," said Caroline, with a touch of tartness.

As she watched the young man drive off she noted the drooping set of his shoulders, and wondered whether he had overheard Olivia's words.

"So to what do we owe this honour?" she asked.

"It's like Colm said: I just got fed to the back teeth with the racketty and bitchy world of opera. The rehearsal period is worst, of course. I just felt I had to get away from it all, *them* all, and be myself for a few hours in a peaceful atmosphere, with nobody shouting or emoting or calling attention to themselves."

"I see."

Being some kind of refuge was one degree better than being the laundress for a week's wash, which she had been when Olivia was at music college, but she was not altogether happy with the new role. It felt like conniving at the brutality with which her daughter treated her boyfriends.

"Well, I thought he seemed a nice young man," she said, "and I hope next time you will invite him in."

"He just wants to be the baggage I carry round with me if I become a star," said Olivia contemptuously. "He should get real."

Olivia spent the next day in vocal exercises, a long rest, and some swanning round the garden. Colm arrived to fetch her back promptly at three, and Olivia kissed her mother at the front door.

"Thanks, Mum."

"You *use* that young man, Olivia."

"Use, that ye be not used," said her daughter. "He would if he could."

But he didn't look at all like the type who would. All in all Caroline did not regard it as a very satisfactory visit, and Alexander and Stella both made comments which included the words "prima donna".

Marius coming on Friday, early in the afternoon as he had promised, made everything right. He embraced her, and sat happily drinking coffee and eating some nibbly cakes she had made specially for him, deprived of the chance to cook him a special welcoming dinner. Then they went upstairs to bed and stayed there till it was time to drive to Leeds, braving some sardonic remarks from the children as they left. Caroline was so preoccupied with what Marius was about to reveal that she even forgot to ask her usual question, what Alex and Stella would do about an evening meal. Marius drove with his usual brisk flair and efficiency, and they were in Wellington Street by seven o'clock, and had had an apéritif, chosen their meal, and been seated in their little alcove by half past.

"I told them when I booked that we would like to be as alone as possible," Caroline said.

"They probably took you for a teenager," said Marius.

"They know me, know my voice," said Caroline. "I think they'll try and keep the other tables vacant if they can. *Now –*"

"Wait. Here comes our food."

She looked at him – at the lock of brown hair that occasionally fell over the warm brown eyes, at the high forehead and full cheeks, the red, almost feminine lips. The tiny surge of irritation she had felt vanished. She looked down at her plate and took up her knife and fork. And it was after five minutes of satisfying eating that Caroline again said: "*Now.*"

Marius shifted in his chair.

"This is going to come as a bit of a surprise to you. I know it did to me."

Caroline said nothing, just kept looking at him.

"Sheila is pregnant."

42

Chapter Five

Reactions

There were all sorts of questions Caroline wanted to ask but felt it would be unwise to. In the end the question she did ask came out sounding slightly absurd.

"How *old* is Sheila?"

"Forty-three. Five years younger than me."

And seven years younger than me, Caroline thought. Marius had left his wife for an older woman. Somehow she felt that must have hurt more than if he had left her for a bimbo. Even if he hadn't, strictly speaking, left her: he had merely supplemented her.

"Go on, ask the question you want to ask," said Marius.

"No. You know I tr –"

"Go on – ask it."

The understanding between them was too total for Caroline to hold back any longer, though she was still reluctant.

"Are you the father?"

"No."

"Do you know who is?"

"No." Marius's face screwed up into an expression of puzzlement. "As you know, Sheila and I are just friends, though perfectly good ones, and with a long history behind our friendship. It's because it works so well, our friendship, that we've never opted for divorce. Why change something that, by and large, works well."

"So you've discussed it?" Caroline asked.

"Oh yes."

"I thought it might be the children."

"That was the other thing. I'm afraid I'm rather traditional. I believe children need stability. I can come the heavy father if necessary. You can't do that coming from a position of weakness."

"So you've stayed together, but both gone your own way?"

"Sheila has a lot of – let's say pals, something more casual. She

43

goes around with them to charity do's, arts events. I thought she'd gone off sex, though I did suggest it might be that she'd just gone off sex with me."

"Difficult to imagine. And you think it's one of these culture-vulture friends, or one of her charity junkies, who's the father of this baby-to-be?"

Marius shrugged.

"Maybe. I just don't know. If I was a betting man –"

"Yes?"

"I'd bet on one of her arty friends, maybe one a lot younger than her."

"I see ..."

"One that she wouldn't think of having a long-term relationship with."

"But I take it she told you about the pregnancy. Didn't you ask about the father?"

"Of course. She just said it wasn't important."

Caroline's eyebrows shot up.

"Well, that really is downgrading the male role. Is she some kind of extreme feminist?"

"You know she's not."

"So what she meant by it, I presume," said Caroline slowly, "is that this doesn't change anything."

"I assume so. When I'd had time to think through what she might have meant, that's what I thought it must be."

"That you go on as you have been doing, and the child when it comes is treated as yours."

"Yes."

"That's a decision only the two of you together can make."

"Of course."

"And are you willing to go along with it?"

Marius chewed for a few moments, thoughtfully.

"I don't know ... Why don't you eat up?"

Caroline looked down at her lamb chops as if she didn't know how they had got there, and then up at Marius who had continued attacking his swordfish. How could things suddenly be so ordinary again? She put her knife into the bright pink flesh and conveyed a piece to her mouth.

"To get back to your question," Marius said, "it occurred to me that if I went along with this, I'd only be doing what some man has probably done with an offspring of mine. That thought seems to give it a bit of perspective."

"You have a lot of such offspring?"

"One or two. On the other side, Sheila is asking me to wink at the sort of activity that she has had to wink at from time to time with me."

"Rather more than that, surely. She's never had to be pretend-mother."

"True. The really crucial question, I think, is what sort of a father I'd be likely to be to the child. If I know myself I feel I'd be pretty unlikely to give it the sort of love and attention that I give my own children. Sad – bad perhaps – but true."

"Honest, anyway."

"It's a situation that calls for honesty. On your side too. I need to know whether you're really being straight with me when you say you're not interested in getting married."

Caroline didn't need to consider.

"Of course. I shall never be married again. I'm quite happy for the situation to continue as it is."

Marius scraped the last fragments of fish and sauce from his plate and then laid down his fork.

"There is a possible halfway-house situation."

Caroline frowned.

"I'm not sure I like the sound of that. I've never been one for messy compromises."

"I don't know that this one is messy. I more or less move in with you, and keep the marriage up merely as a façade. I couldn't run the businesses from the wilds of South Yorkshire, so it would mean your moving to London."

"Oh God – Maida Vale."

"I think we could manage Islington."

"I've lived in Islington before it became fashionable. I've *done*

Islington. Oh dear, I had hoped to have seen the last of London. I do so enjoy being at Alderley."

"Being the mistress of Alderley. I know you do. I *see* you enjoying the role. And it suits you down to the ground. The house was made for you, and you for it."

"And then again, perhaps living with you would be too much like being in a marriage. Perhaps it's not marriage as such that doesn't work for me. Perhaps it's living with someone all the time."

"Sounds like heaven to me, but if it's not that for you ..."

"Oh darling, you're making me sound ungrateful and half-hearted. I'm not. But I have to be clear-eyed about myself, and about us."

"That's exactly what I want both of us to be. Now – have another glass of wine, think things through, and then tell me how the situation appears to you after proper reflection. And then perhaps we can think about what we should do."

Caroline had had periods between the men in her life, and was used to eating quietly by herself and using the time to think things through. So she went back to her lamb, finished the plate almost greedily, then wiped her mouth while she considered what next.

"We take it as read, I suppose," she said finally, "that Sheila is not only not considering marriage to this child's father, but is not considering entering into a relationship of any sort with him. Beyond casual and no-strings-attached sex."

"Yes, I think we can take that as read."

"That being the case, she will certainly need someone around at the time of the birth. OK, it's not her first, but the others are nearly grown-up, and at her age there could be problems."

"So you think I should stay with her until the birth?"

"Yes. Unless she has someone else lined up to be with her and play that role – mother, sister, whatever."

"She hasn't. Hasn't got either, for a start, and no best friend who fits the bill. There's Helena, of course – they are great mates, Sheila and her – more mates than mother and daughter. But she is only fifteen. She just doesn't measure up to the responsibility, I'm afraid. It would be unfair to put it on her."

"Then it comes down to you, doesn't it?"

"I suppose so. There's not really a problem in my staying on until the birth. The question is what to do after the birth. Me there in the house with a small kid I have no particular feeling for, and a wife who is that only in name."

"You care for Sheila. That counts a lot. And we would still have our weekends." The waiter was hovering, and she turned to him with an instant decision to get rid of him. "I'll have the lemon sorbet."

"And I'll have the apricot flan," said Marius. "So what you're saying is: keep the arrangement as it now is, because it suits us, and see how things develop – circumstances, relationships – after the birth. Is that it?"

"Yes, I think it is."

"Maybe it's the least worst solution."

"Oh dear – you do keep putting me off. I hate least worst solutions. They often result in fact in the worst of both worlds. But in this case ... To put it shortly, I feel so happy that I don't want this new situation to stop me being happy in this wonderful way."

"It won't, my darling. It won't."

He was looking at her with such love, but also with such a little boy air, that suddenly what she had been waiting to say to him for two weeks came out without premeditation.

"We had a hitchhiker drop by the other week, and do you know he had the look of a young you."

It was not at all how Caroline had intended bringing it up, if she brought it up at all. She had decided to discuss it seriously, look at ramifications such as the family's poverty, the boy's future. But it had just come out as a Funny Thing Happened to Me on the Way to the Forum type of remark – as if she were narrating an incidental oddity.

"Oh? What was he called?"

"Pete Bagshaw."

"Not one of my offspring. Where was he from?"

"Here in Leeds. Armley."

"I was based in Manchester in my early years. Could be some

kind of throwback ... Or, come to think of it, it could be one of my brother Phil's youthful sins."

"I didn't know you had a brother."

"I don't. He died in a motorcycle accident when he was twenty-two. But he was living in Leeds then – back, oh, twenty-two or -three years ago. How old was this boy?"

Caroline puzzled her brain.

"I don't think he said. But early twenties anyway. He's at university, doing computer science."

"Good God. It seems to run in the blood. Guy and him, and probably Alexander in a few years' time."

"Alexander's not your blood."

"But he begins to feel like it. I hope these young chaps don't get disappointed: what seems like a smart career move now could mean they're sent out into an industry over-populated already with computer experts."

"Tell that to Alex, and try to persuade him to take something else."

"People should never be persuaded in matters of education or career. In the end they have to make their own mistakes, otherwise they blame you for life."

"So what sort of man was your brother Phil?"

Marius's eyes went distant. He seemed hardly able to remember.

"A real tearaway. The motorbike was sort of symbolic. He was a rebel, he slept around as if there was no tomorrow, had a succession of jobs and often no job at all, and was into petty crime. Maybe he would have come through that phase, maybe not. To tell you the truth I didn't know him well enough to say. He was six years younger than me, and when he grew up and started going off the rails I kept my distance. I was launching myself into the big world of commerce on my own account. One thing I could do without was a black sheep in my family."

"Well, maybe this boy Pete was his, maybe he is some kind of throwback, with both of you having a common ancestor –"

"Or maybe it was just coincidence. I assure you I never kept a mistress in glamorous Armley, or had a son by anyone in Leeds."

And there they left it. Though the conversation was so different from the way she had planned it, Caroline in the event felt perfectly happy with it. In fact, it had cleared the air, and left her for the rest of the weekend with a feeling of blissful contentment. Pete Bagshaw as the son of Marius's scapegrace brother was a satisfactory explanation, though she did wonder whether he had somehow got it wrong and took Marius to be his father. That was the only way she could explain his final remark to her. That could be embarrassing or dangerous. As to the other matter, the solution they had come to began to seem to her to come close to the ideal: if, after the birth, Marius should find living with Sheila and the baby intolerable, he could get a flat in London, and she would visit him from time to time – something she would enjoy, and which she could not do so long as he remained with his wife. It could turn out to be a situation even better than the present one, she decided.

Stella touched on that question on the Saturday, while Marius was away discussing business matters in Middlesbrough, where he was thinking of opening a supermarket, precursor to a possible expansion in the North. Stella always came out with what she was thinking, apparently artlessly, though in fact she had found by trial and error that it was the best way to get her mother to talk.

"So did you and Marius talk through what was bothering you over dinner?"

"Nothing was bothering me," said Caroline, temporising. "It was Marius who had the problem. Yes, thank you: we talked it through, and came to a decision."

"And what was the problem?"

Caroline sighed.

"You are the most persistent ... Oh well, I suppose you'll find out. Sheila Fleetwood is pregnant."

Stella whistled.

"My God! They're a bit ancient for that, aren't they?"

"She's forty-three. And there's no question of 'they'. It's not Marius's. He thinks it's by some younger casual boyfriend."

"So why isn't she getting rid of it?"

Caroline couldn't think why she hadn't asked Marius the same question.

"I suppose because she doesn't want to or doesn't believe in it."

"Seems the most sensible solution if your marriage is falling apart and your husband is screwing a gorgeous actress he's set up in a bijou stately home two hundred miles away."

"You put things so sweetly, Stella. Perhaps she thinks a baby will give her an interest, fill a gap in her life."

"A man would do it better, and be much less trouble."

"*Some men*," said Caroline, with deadly emphasis. "A lot of the men I've had to do with wouldn't. Maybe she doesn't know anybody suitable. You can't just buy a man over the counter at Harrods."

"I bet you could if Mr al-Fayed had the bright idea of stocking them. Anyway, what was the decision you both came to?"

"To let things go on pretty much as they are, for the moment anyway."

"Probably sensible," said Stella, with all the worldly wisdom of fourteen. "You're happy as you are, and if Marius is unhappy he's certainly not showing it. You'd probably notice if he was getting itchy."

"Itchy? You do use the most awful words, Stella."

Stella opened her mouth, but at that moment Marius's car was heard on the gravelled drive, and the weekend resumed its normal course.

Olivia came as usual on Sunday. This time Caroline spotted Colm Fitzgerald's car as it came through the gates, and she went out to meet him and invite him in. Olivia, she could tell, was not pleased. Colm had tea and cakes, met Marius, and was given a tour of the house and gardens. It was Caroline who gave him the tour, followed a few feet behind by Stella, who seemed taken by the large yet somehow forlorn tenor. When they got back into the house Olivia was practising: great arching phrases, unaccompanied, proceeded from what they now called the Music Room. Colm asked to use the lavatory, and two minutes later, coming back into the hall, Caroline caught Stella watching him from the security of the study while he himself, motionless halfway down the stairs, was watching Olivia –

singing great swathes of glorious melody to cloth-eared Marius through the open door of the Music Room.

"She's in wonderful voice," said Caroline, to make him realize she was there.

"She leaves me for dead," he said, and he seemed to be summing up their personal rather than their vocal relationship. He reluctantly tore himself away from the sound, and went towards the front door.

"I'll drive Olivia to the station tomorrow morning," said Caroline. Colm seemed about to protest, but then he just nodded miserably and went out to his car.

As the first night of *Forza* approached Olivia was getting jumpy. Two minutes after Colm drove away she broke in mid-phrase and announced: "It's not right yet." Two hours later she was practising again. Stella accompanied her. She was doing rather well out of these sessions, but she looked as if she would rather be doing something else. The next morning when Caroline drove Olivia to Doncaster station she was still in taciturn mood. Caroline understood. She had been through it all in a milder way at high-points in her stage career. She had the impression that opera singers did what actors did, but in an aggravated form.

"Another idyllic weekend over," said Stella to Alexander as they walked towards the bus stop on their way to school that same morning. "And Marius on his way back to his other woman."

"His mysteriously pregnant wife," said Alexander, who had been whispered to on the subject. "If I was Mum I'd be suspicious."

"Maybe. But Mum has this instinct for not rocking the apple-cart."

"Boat," said Alexander. "If I was the latest in a long line of girl-friends and mistresses, which seems to be the case, my suspicion antennae would be perpetually on the quiver."

"So would mine. But Mum's used to all this in theatrical circles. Let's face it, Marius acts no worse than most of Mum's friends."

"Or our beloved elder sister, come to that."

"The man eater. The human boa constrictor. She was on tenter-hooks yesterday, wasn't she? I think she's thrown over that tenor. Pity – I thought he was dishy. I might ask her: 'Got a spare tenor, Lady?'"

"Very funny," said Alexander, unsmiling. "Knowing her she'll have someone else already."

"Maybe we should have said we'd go to *Forza*. Try and spot which of the cast is her current."

"Could be the director, or designer, or lighting man."

"Can't see her stooping to the lighting man. Still, you're right. It wouldn't be worth sitting through three or four hours of opera on the off-chance. But she's really a cat on heat, isn't she?"

"Except that she's on heat the whole time ... She had a letter on Thursday morning."

Stella looked at him, puzzled.

"Why shouldn't she?"

"She was supposed to have come on Wednesday night on an impulse, to get away from things operatic."

Stella considered this.

"She used to get letters when she was here for three weeks last summer. Possibly someone's still got this address for her."

"Maybe. She snatched it when I took it in to her while she was practising, and didn't look at it while I was there .... Marius said Ghastly Guy might be coming with him in a fortnight's time."

"Guy's not so bad."

"He's only got one topic of conversation." Stella hardly bothered to suppress a smile.

"He may be mad about money but I prefer him to Helena. Bossy little thing she is. At least she won't be coming. At home tending her mother over those first few difficult weeks. Yuck!"

Alexander put on his most mature and thoughtful expression.

"They've probably both had difficult childhoods, what with Marius's affairs and all that."

"Just like us. We seem to be surrounded by multiple adulterers." They looked at each other. "Marvellous that we've grown up so normal and nice, isn't it?"

They roared with laughter, but as Alexander saw the bus approaching and put out his arm for it he said: "I just hope Mum knows what she's doing, that's all."

"When has she ever known *that*?" said Stella.

Chapter Six

Behind the Idyll

The next weekend was a rare one away from home for Caroline. It was the 25th anniversary of the first Fleetwood's supermarket, in Cardiff, and Marius was obliged to be there and speak at the celebratory dinner. He wanted Caroline with him, or at least near him, and though she probably disliked such occasions as much as Sheila (who had flatly refused to go) she agreed to accompany him, to sit discreetly at one of the lower tables, and to take nominal occupancy of an adjacent suite in the hotel.

"If it was any other sort of do we wouldn't have to be so hole-in-the-corner," said Marius. "But a Fleetwood company event with lots of flattering publicity calls for caution."

So Caroline undertook a horrendous journey with Virgin Trains that left her feeling dirty and angry, and the two children had the house to themselves. Caroline felt she knew them well enough to know they would not throw an orgy, suddenly start in on sex and drugs. With Olivia at the same age she would have been more apprehensive.

In fact, as Stella remarked to her brother, it was a hideously dull weekend. If Alexander had been old enough to drive his mother's car things might have been different, but he couldn't even think of having lessons until he was seventeen. Stella had to take the bus to Doncaster and go to an afternoon showing of a film (last time they had had a lift home arranged, but in spite of ringing round all their acquaintances Stella had not found one going in that weekend, and would have risked being stranded there overnight). For Alexander the best thing that offered in the way of entertainment was an afternoon walk to the village.

As it turned out, Marsham did offer better entertainment than he had expected. First he went to Mr Patel's shop, where he didn't buy more things than he needed or wanted because he was too hard-up and too canny, but he did buy two packets of cigarettes with which he intended to smoke himself silly over the weekend if he could do it without Stella guessing his new vice. One of Alexander's pleasures was doing things without people knowing.

As he left the shop with cheery farewells to its owner he bumped into Gina Watters, the vicar's daughter. Gina was the sort of girl Alexander thought he might fancy, if he went in for older women. Neat, rounded where it mattered, but quite sharp and funny.

"Hi, Gina. I thought you'd be back in Leeds."

Her face creased into a smile of anticipation.

"Tuesday. I can't wait. It seems like months since I went clubbing. Well – it is months. I've been working like a navvy to finance the good life once I get away from this dump. Here – wait a sec: I only want a box of tissues, then you can walk me home."

Alexander wondered where the idea of walking a girl home came from, and concluded it was from her antediluvian parents. When she came out clutching her box, he asked her:

"And is the Metropolitan University convenient for the club scene in Leeds?"

Gina stopped and looked at him.

"You're a little Sherlock, aren't you?"

"It's no big deal, is it? I thought it was your parents, not you, who made a secret of it."

"It is. And do you know – we've never talked about it, them and me. I noticed when I got my place that they always just said 'Leeds', and when I twigged what was going on I thought I ought to go along with it. It's a fairly harmless piece of snobbery, isn't it? And it's not as though Leeds University proper is one of the world's great universities."

"But it's a pretty good one, isn't it? Whereas the Metropolitan University ..."

"Now who's being a snob? It suits me. It has the sort of course I can manage without too much sweat."

"That's nice. Do you tell the people there about Mum having come to live in the village?"

She stopped again to look at him.

"What's all this about?"

"I'm just asking."

54

"Well, I *may* do. I mean, we haven't got much in this little arsehole of a place, have we? There's those from Manchester at Uni who boast about all the rock groups there, and how they've met this or that lead singer, slept with that one maybe ..."

"Do you believe them?"

"Some people will sleep with *any*one. Anyway, we haven't got much here, and you can't boast about a baronet in Leeds Metropolitan circles, so it has to be your mum."

"And Marius?"

"Well, yes. The 'mistress installed in state' story needs the rich lover as the other part of the equation. Why?"

"Do you know someone called Pete Bagshaw?"

Gina creased her brow.

"My best friend's on-off boyfriend is called Pete, and then something common. It could be Bagshaw. I barely know him."

"But you could have told your best friend –"

"About your mother? I've definitely told Trix. She's my flatmate. We talk about everything."

"And she could have told her boyfriend?"

"Yes. What *is* this?"

They were now outside the Rectory, and Alexander did not answer her, saying instead:

"Mum's getting the idea that she's being accepted in the village."

"Well, she is, in a way."

"What way's that?"

"Well, you know – " Gina was very hot on "you know"s, which she could have caught from the Prime Minister – "everyone's chuffed as hell at having an actress and a television star living here, and the fact of having a multi-millionaire businessman whose picture appears in the financial pages of the broadsheets goes down pretty well too, with the broadsheet type of person. Your mother *is* accepted, as the mistress of a supermarket tycoon."

"That's what I thought."

"Well, it's a bloody sight better than being *ost*racised for the same reason, isn't it?" Gina was getting quite red, and seemed to

Alexander much less attractive than he'd thought. "I mean, my parents call on her, and so does Sir Jack."

"You're sounding as old-fashioned as them."

"Yes, well, here in Marsham I'm my parent's child. I go along with their little snobberies and foibles. When I go to Leeds I do a climb-down act: there I don't tell them Gina is short for Georgina because it's a stuffy sort of name. I couldn't go to a concert, not a classical one, and not to a play unless there was some kind of scandal attached – gay scenes, nudity, explicit sex. I take E, and I sleep around a bit. You have to fit in with your background, don't you?"

That seemed to Alexander a pretty craven sort of attitude but he just said: "I suppose so ... So your parents don't *really* accept her and Marius."

Gina smiled in a way that was positively unpleasant.

"They swallow hard whenever they have to meet her. 'Bye, Alex!"

* * *

In bed that night in the best hotel in Cardiff, Caroline said to Marius:
"Happy?"

"Mmmm. I'm always happy when I've had you."

"I mean with the evening."

Marius's bare shoulder sketched a shrug.

"Duty done."

"Your speech went marvellously. Just what the occasion demanded."

Marius was used to flattery from his mistresses, and Caroline had sensed from the beginning that he expected it. It wasn't something she had given to any of her other lovers, or her husbands. But it added to his little-boy appeal for her, her sense of being somehow responsible for him. His speech in fact had been adequate but a little laboured, the jokes good but not particularly well told. Caroline felt that he could have done with a bit of coaching from her.

"How were things at table seventeen?" he asked.

"Oh fine. Everyone very pleased and interested. Lots of questions about television stars – Joanna Lumley, Jason Green, that sort of thing. Someone even remembered my episode of *Morse*."

"I don't think I've seen that."

"It was one of the very early ones, and a good meaty part ... One of the wives more or less asked me why I was there."

Marius snarled at the far wall.

"*Which* one?"

"Never you mind. I don't want anyone carpeted or sacked."

"They'd all been properly briefed, *and* told to brief their wives."

"I expect they had, but they forgot in the presence of someone they'd seen on the box. Anyway I just told the truth: how we'd met in a London restaurant and then again at a Booker prizegiving, omitting all the concentrated bedding in between. Then I changed the subject."

"Good ... " But it rankled that his word had not been law. "I bet it was that silly cow Ellie Thackley. Men who marry women as vapid as that should do the decent thing and divorce them."

"You're not the right man to lecture others on their duty to divorce."

"Sheila is not silly. Or vapid."

"I didn't say she was. I get quite another impression of Sheila, and quite a pleasant one."

"Good, because she is pleasant. I can say that because I married her, and I wouldn't want you to think I'd made a daft choice." Caroline was silent, so he added: "What are you thinking about?"

"Wondering if all your mistresses have been as understanding as I am about your wife."

"Some of them. Anyway it's the wife who's supposed to be understanding about the mistresses."

"Or not as the case may be."

"You're exceptional because you're not only understanding about my wife but also about my mistresses."

"Moderately," said Caroline, snuggling up to him. "I can contemplate the idea of a long string, provided it's in the past. I don't think I'd be at all happy with competition in the present."

"I don't know how you can even think about it. As far as I'm concerned two women are more than enough to handle."

But next morning, when they had driven out to Llandaff for

communion, and when Marius's voice was ringing out for "Glorious things of thee are spoken" as if to prove that, though he was cloth-eared he definitely wasn't tone-deaf, he stopped singing at the line "Fading is the worldling's pleasure" and muttered to Caroline in his rich, experienced-it-all voice:

"Oh no it isn't, Mr John Newton, whoever you are: worldlings' pleasures are doing very nicely, thank you very much. Not much sign of them fading today, thanks be to God!"

* * *

Alexander turned away from the Rectory and made tracks back through Marsham and towards home. His talk with Gina had made him thoughtful. He decided after a bit that it had taught him a lot about how his mother was regarded in the village. If the Rector and his wife were representative it made him like the village a lot less. But were they? He thought they might be a very special breed of person. In view of their advances to his mother about siting next year's fête at Alderley he could only conclude that they were a pair of holy hypocrites.

And really their daughter, in spite of her devotion to swinging Leeds, was hardly any better. She had practically said that Caroline should be grateful she wasn't ostracised. You could hardly get more Dark Ages than that, in Alexander's view. He had tolerated a lot of his mother's men-friends, and he was quite of her opinion that she shouldn't get married again. If not quite a one-woman disaster area, she was definitely accident-prone.

Coincidentally he had no sooner come to that conclusion than he heard the sound of some kind of crash behind him. Turning, he saw the impressive sight of Meta Mortyn-Crosse sprawled on the tarmac clutching a bottle aloft, her familiar bicycle a foot or so away, its pedals still turning. As he ran to help her she struggled to her feet and began dusting down her tweed skirt with her free hand.

"Bloody bike!" she swore. "You can't get a good upright ladies' bike any more."

Meta was built like a fork-lift truck, swung her shoulders when she walked, and generally gave the impression she must have joined her country's armed forces in the days when homosexuals went into the navy and lesbians into the army. In fact she had never done anything very much except live in Marsham Manor and later the Dower House. Local gossip suggested her sexual tastes were entirely mainstream, though she had had little chance of gratifying them as the men in her life had generally fled in the early days of the relationship. Now her face was very red, her cheeks and eyeballs popping out like footballs from her unlovely face. She mounted her bike, still clutching her bottle. Alexander made a note of the label, which was a very cheap kind of brandy.

"Are you sure you should be riding?" he asked.

"'Course I'm sure. Don't be so bloody rude."

"I wasn't being rude. You must have had a nasty shock in that fall. Anyway, it's difficult carrying anything with those low handlebars."

"That skinflint Pattel has run out of carriers." It was part of Meta's character to mispronounce in the English manner any foreign-sounding name. "I'd've been all right with a bag."

"Would you like me to carry the ... bottle up to the Dower House? It's not far." She stood astride her bike and brushed aside his offer which a shake of the head.

"Your mother's away for the weekend I hear."

"That's right."

"Off with Marius for a dirty – no. Can't really be a dirty weekend when they have one every week, can it?"

"I don't see why they can't have a dirty weekend anywhere they want to. Actually it's Cardiff."

"Not my idea of a place to have a sexy rendezvous, but what would I know? I've hardly left the village in the last twenty years." A grievance seemed to take hold of her not very clear brain, and she brandished her bottle in his face. "Reduced to buying cheap plonk because the coffers are so low. Next thing will be, Jack will want me to go out cleaning."

"I'm sure that won't happen." Nobody would employ you, Alexander thought.

"I wouldn't bank on it. What we need is a nice steep interest-rate rise, so that our money makes something for us, what there is of it."

"I expect there'd be inflation too, so it wouldn't help in the long run."

"Bloody economist too, are you?" She bent forward to look at him in the face, her bulging eyes fearsomely red. "If you're so bloody smart about money, you should give your mother some advice."

"I think she gets more advice than she can stomach."

"Jack, you mean? He has her interests at heart, at least. She gets advice given her because she needs it. Any woman who's a mistress not a wife does need it. Tell her to get something on paper, that's what Jack says."

"I'll tell her but –"

"Otherwise what will happen? Marius is a high-powered businessman. Life of tremendous stress, eh? So one day he drops down dead, and then where is she? Nowhere."

"I think Marius has –"

"No good thinking. Tell him she wants to see it, that's what your mother should do. Otherwise she'll have no money, no roof over her head, and a career that's dead in the water because she hasn't done any acting for yonks. She'd be a beggar. I don't give a damn, but Jack does. Tell her to get something definite in writing! Otherwise tea and sympathy is all she'll have, and not a great deal of the latter."

She hitched herself on to the saddle and rode off, turning at the next corner in the direction of the Dower House. Alexander walked on slowly, expecting to hear another crash, but Meta seemed to have negotiated the last part of her journey successfully. Over the rest of the mile-long walk home he pondered what Meta had said. He felt that, granted it had come from a drunken old harridan with a vicious streak to her, it had not been bad advice at all. Alexander did not hate Marius, but neither did he love him in the way Caroline had convinced herself both her children did. His mother was also sure she was something more than just one in a long line of mistresses that Marius had had. Doubtless words had been uttered that had convinced her that he had done, or would do, something that would give her special status a financial basis. OK then, let it be something not so lavish as to seriously damage his wife's or his children's position, but something generous and concrete. Something on paper. With witnesses. Even better, cash or title deeds in advance.

Stella, when he talked it over with her later that day, was in agreement, but she said the matter of talking to their mother about it would have to be his duty.

"You're the elder, and you're the one who's thought it through. Anyway Mum is convinced you are the really serious one in the family."

"I suppose it's just a matter of finding the right time," said Alexander dubiously.

After he had talked with her, or tried to, he was rather doubtful whether any time would have been right. When Caroline had settled back after her Cardiff trip he put Meta's points to her, and she clearly found the whole suggestion distasteful.

"Oh darling, how sordid!" she said, wrinkling up her face. "Like those awful film stars and tycoons who arrange the terms of their divorce before they even get married. You've got to trust each other if you love each other."

"Marius is a tycoon, so probably he wouldn't object. Meta says Jack is worried about this."

"Is *that* why he goes on and on about my acting, and how I should keep it up?"

"Probably. Remember you're not even Marius's partner, which would probably give you some rights. He's living with his wife. It surely wouldn't do any harm to be sure Marius has actually done for you in his will what he promised to do."

"Not just promised: he has made it quite clear, often, that he *has* done it. I wouldn't *think* of asking, Alex. He'd probably think I was planning to bump him off."

"He can't believe in your love for him if he imagined that."

Caroline sighed.

"*Joke*, darling. I'll put my mind to it some day, if it worries you. But you can't expect me to think of it with Olivia's first night in five days' time."

Or, probably, after it, Alexander felt sure.

Chapter Seven

First Night, Last Night

Guy Fleetwood came down with his father on the following Friday, the day before the first night of *Forza*. He was a good-looking boy, taller than Marius, with a nice manner. He would be a wow at St Andrew's, Caroline thought, where he was to study computer science. She had noticed on other times he'd been down that if Marius suggested he do something he jumped to and did it, and that if he disagreed with his father about anything he did so tentatively, almost apologetically. Caroline conjectured that his upbringing had been a great deal more traditional that her own brood's. Stella capitalised on this.

"Anyone feel like tennis?" she would say.

"Guy would like a game, wouldn't you Guy?" Marius would reply, as if his son was a ten-year-old. And Guy would tear himself away from Alexander's little computer room (where Guy could lord it rather, by virtue of his greater sophistication and the superior equipment he was used to at home) and go out and bash a ball around in the tennis court that Caroline had brought back from its very overgrown state when she had taken over Alderley. Caroline didn't know that he made very little attempt to be agreeable during the game.

Marius was to take Guy to York Station on Monday morning early for the train to Edinburgh, and then continue on back to his workaday life in London. Meanwhile there was the opera premiere to prepare for. Caroline knew better than to ring Olivia on Saturday to wish her well. The day of a first performance was one which one had to have entirely to oneself – either alone, or losing oneself in a crowd, for example of shoppers. Caroline wouldn't put it past Olivia to go and watch Leeds United that Saturday afternoon. Anyway, she phoned a florist's in Leeds and had roses delivered to her daughter's dressing room. Then she found that anything she settled down to didn't serve its purpose, and when she jettisoned it for something else that turned out to be equally useless at calming her nerves. "It's worse than if it were *my* first night," she said to Marius. She cooked a risotto followed by T-bone steaks for their early dinner. Marius and the children ate heartily, but she had to force anything down. After dinner she dressed, and Marius put on his swankiest suit, they kissed the children goodbye, said "Cross your fingers for Olivia" and drove off.

"Right," said Guy, as they stood at the sitting-room window watching the Mercedes go down the drive. "Where does your mother keep her car keys? We're going to hit the town."

* * *

"I don't suppose you're looking forward to this evening," said Caroline, as Marius's Mercedes glided past Wakefield.

"On the contrary, I'm looking forward to it immensely."

"Not much fun if you're cloth-eared, sitting through even half an hour or an hour of opera."

"I'm cloth-eared but I'm not tone-deaf. You know that. And I shall enjoy the curtain-calls immensely. I know my connection with the new star is tenuous, but I shall bask in your maternal pride, and get high on the cheers for your sake."

"Let's hope there *are* cheers. All sorts of things can go wrong – with the voice, the production, the *feel* of the whole event."

"The feel is going to be one of enormous expectation. That can't be bad. And I pay Olivia the compliment of saying that she knows her own voice, and how to take care of it. If she needed to cancel she'd cancel, but we know she isn't doing that."

Caroline had had a call from Colm just before dinner to say that Olivia was brimming with confidence and lively anticipation, though she didn't want to talk to anyone. Caroline had been awfully touched that he'd thought to ring.

"You'll have a lot of time to kill," she said. "What will you do?"

"Oh, maybe a film. Or there's something on in the Playhouse Courtyard Theatre that I could sample. I've never much cared for the pubs in the centre of Leeds, but things open up all the time there, or change managers. Don't worry about me. If there's nothing on I want to see I'll booze. I'll try anything except an Irish theme pub."

"It would have been better if we hadn't eaten early, then you could have had a good meal."

"Why should you sit through your daughter's triumph with a rumbling tummy? Anyway, you know me: if I feel like it I can eat a second dinner without any problem."

"I just hope we don't meet Rick."

"Well I hope we do. I'd like to cast my eye over Olivia's father. I could ask him for a rendition of 'On the Street Where You Live.'"

"Oh God! You're quite capable of doing that. And Rick is quite capable of obliging."

When they got to Leeds they drove to the concrete monstrosity of a car park in Woodhouse Lane, then walked down through the dank horror and sinister emptiness of the underpass, finally making it via Merrion Street to the Grand Theatre. They no sooner entered the semi-circular corridor around the stalls than they saw Rick. Caroline knew in her bones that he had been watching for them.

"Caroline! Darling! And is this your new rich bloke?"

"Marius, this is Rick."

Rick held out his hand, and Marius took his, his sparkling eyes aglow with curiosity.

"So glad to meet you at last," said Rick. "I've heard a lot about you. Funnily enough I've always got on well with Caroline's blokes, though she never returns the compliment with my chicks."

"Rick, you sound as if you got stuck in a groove round about 1964," said Caroline.

"Perhaps I did, darling. Not a bad era to get stuck in. But let's not spar. This isn't our night at all. It's that wonderful phenomenon we produced between us."

Caroline had to repress the urge to say "ugh".

"I hear you were in *My Fair Lady* when it first came over," said Marius.

"Well, not *quite* the first cast," said Rick, because Caroline knew the truth. "I suppose Caroline's told you how much she suffered from 'On the Street Where You Live', has she? She used to tell everyone at the time. Well, let me tell you, it's a *bloody* difficult song to get right. I've done quite a bit of Gilbert and Sullivan since, and it's shown me how very much the American musicals took from them, at least until Sondheim. For example, when I used to launch myself into the song in question which we won't name –"

Caroline drifted away. She knew that Rick, having proclaimed they were there for Olivia's sake, would from then on talk entirely and exclusively about himself. Anyway, Marius would be less likely to call for a reprise of that ghastly song if she wasn't there to get embarrassed. She stood in the crowd at the bar, was recognised by the barman, and got served at once. She got a gin and tonic for herself and a whisky and soda for Marius. She put it in his hand as she passed him and Rick, but pass she did.

"There's a whole treasury of forgotten English musicals, if we could only find a style to do them in," she could hear Rick saying. Caroline shuddered as she contemplated the thought of endless revivals of *Lilac Time* and *Bless the Bride* starring her one-time husband. She went and stood alone in a dark niche, to listen to the excited anticipation of the audience.

"Excuse me, but aren't you Caroline Fawley?" came a voice at her elbow. It was a pleasant, rather faded middle-aged woman. "I did so love you in *At the Kitchen Sink*. Nobody makes sitcoms like that these days."

Caroline purred. This was more like it.

"No, they don't," she said. "I sometimes wonder what has happened to the art of comedy."

* * *

Guy nosed the car around the streets of Leeds, looking for a parking place he wouldn't have to pay for. It was just seven o'clock, early enough for there still to be one or two left. Under Alexander's directions he kept well away from the Grand Theatre, where a capacity audience would have bagged all the places, and eventually found one behind the Law Courts.

"Now – what time do we have to meet up, so we're back before them?" he asked, turning to the two Fawleys. "When will this opera end?"

Alexander shrugged.

"It's quite long. But they put the time of ending up in the foyer at the Grand Theatre."

"Right. And they're going to a party afterwards. We'll be on the safe side and allow half an hour on to the time of finishing, and meet back here then. OK?"

They both nodded. Guy strode purposefully off, though he knew of Leeds only what he had learnt by driving round it. Alexander and Stella drifted off down to the Headrow, then she went in the direction of the cinema and he, with no particular purpose in mind, found himself going towards the station.

Oddly enough Guy, once he was out of sight, slackened his pace and began looking around him uncertainly. He was in a big town, new to him, and he needed to get his bearings. Needed, in fact, to read the indications that would tell him the most likely place to find what he wanted. He stopped in a doorway and began to observe the direction taken by most of the young people who passed.

* * *

The lights went down in the Grand promptly at seven-fifteen. The orchestra had been tuning up, and periodically phrases had emerged that Caroline recognised.

"I wondered if we should invite your Rick out to a meal after-wards," Marius whispered to her.

"It will be far too late after the party," she hissed back.

"Darling, eating late doesn't bother me."

"*No*. And he's not my Rick. He's any and everybody's Rick."

"I quite liked him. Though he's a bit of a bore."

"He could bore for England."

A large bearded man threaded his way through the orchestra, and (because directors abhor the vacuum of an overture) the moment the music started the curtain went up and a mute scene was played out with Olivia, as Leonora, preparing for bed. Caroline recognised that the set was a permanent one – a shape that dimly suggested a gun – which would be varied with odd props. As the music became more exciting Olivia sat on a bed, having her long hair, actually a wig, combed by her maid. Marius's fingers were tapping on his knee, but when Caroline looked down she saw that the taps bore no relation to the music that was being played.

The opera proper began with Leonora bidding goodnight to her father, then agonising in an aria over her decision to run off with her Indian-blooded lover: the aria was a second-sighted vision of herself as "Me pelegrina ed orfana" ("wandering alone and fatherless" in the translation), which was to become her fate in the course of the opera. Colm entered as the lover – a handsome figure, large if slightly strained of voice. They agonised together over the approaching elopement, as always in opera for a little too long: when they were interrupted by Leonora's father, Colm as Alvaro threw his pistol to the floor in surrender, it went off, and killed the father. The pair escaped into the night.

Olivia's voice had been large, securely-based, dramatic. Already the applause for the first scene was more than warm. Marius turned to Caroline.

"See you at curtain call, or the party afterwards," he whispered, then made his escape up the central aisle. It was seven-forty.

* * *

As the interval approached, Caroline wished she had someone beside her to share her growing excitement. Olivia had launched into "La vergine degli Angeli", and Caroline thought it was the most beautiful melody she had ever heard. Olivia sang it with the softness of strength: one sensed the solid base to the voice, knew there was immense power there as a potential, and yet relished the yearning and the striving towards peace that the soft singing suggested.

Caroline felt a surge of adrenalin. She had registered throughout the scene at the monastery that the audience was getting on to a high: their growing enthusiasm and excitement could not be mistaken by a theatre person, and it gripped her. Interval would come as soon as the aria, and Act II, ended, and she wondered whether there would be anything special in the way of first-half applause. An audience in the grip of an exhilaration such as this – and the emergence of a new star *involved* an audience, almost as if they were themselves responsible, and deserved credit for the discovery – needed some outlet, and some particular demonstration might be the result. Caroline felt in her bones that it must come.

And come it did. As the orchestra faded into silence the audience erupted into cheers – not end-of-opera cheers, but provisional cheers, a sort of down-payment towards the triumph they felt sure would come. The curtain went up again, with Leonora still at centre stage, with the Padre Guardiano some way behind her, and the chorus of monks a shadowy presence at the back. When Olivia had basked in the cheers for long enough she turned and drew the bass to share them with her. Then the curtain went down again, lights went up, and the audience began their invasion of the bars.

People who were in the know knew who Olivia was daughter of. As Caroline moved into the press of people in the centre aisle, people whom she knew and people whom she was sure she had never seen in her life began to shake her hand, pat her on the back, tell her how proud she must feel. Any sense of loneliness vanished. When the corridor around the stalls was gained a young man came up, asked her if she'd ordered an interval drink, and when she said she'd forgotten thrust his glass of wine into her hand and went back to join the scrum at the bar. "How kind!" she shouted after him.

Still the congratulations went on, and Caroline was struck by the sheer *pleasure* people felt at the emergence of a new voice. This was succeeded by a sense of the absurdity of their showering praise on her. She saw some of her little crowd nudge one another and nod their heads in the direction to her left. Looking that way Caroline saw Rick, hovering outside the group, which speedily evaporated to leave them alone. Very tactful, but just what she didn't want. Why, they probably thought Rick was her current bloke!

"Isn't it wonderful?" she said, to break the ice.

"Absolutely killing."

"But a bit absurd that we get praise for it."

"In point of fact I *wasn't* getting any praise for it, though if any-one –"

"All right," said Caroline loudly to his petulant face. "That's not in dispute. If Olivia has got her singing voice from anyone it's you." She nearly added that she had got her morals from the same source, but felt it wasn't the time or place. Caroline had a strong sense of the suitabilities of different sorts of occasion.

"Your Marius mooted the idea of a meal afterwards," said Rick, "but I'm not too sure."

"I wouldn't be able to eat a thing."

"I feel rather the same."

"Anyway, there's the party afterwards – there'll be the usual things there if either of us develops a hunger. I'd rather be up there, soaking up all the excitement and enthusiasm."

"Absolutely. We're theatre people, you and me, Caroline."

"Well, I *was*."

"Are. It's like if the Jesuits get you. Once you're a theatre person, that's what you are for life."

Looking away, to dissociate herself from Rich's yoking of herself and him as similar animals, Caroline saw through the doors to the street a young girl very like Stella walk past, look at the time of the opera's end, then walk quickly on. How absurd young people were today – dressing and even looking so alike! Caroline had shut from her mind the era of the mini-skirt. She turned back to Rick.

"So, no meal. We stay at the party and bask in the success of our offspring."

"That's the ticket. We probably won't be able to get near her. You know, that soft singing at the end, that was just like something I've always done as Frederick in *The Pirates of Penzance* –"

"Good God, surely Sullivan's wet-behind-the-ears heroes are a thing of the past for you, Rick."

"Bitch. Well, as Nanky-Poo then. You don't have to look seven-teen for him. In 'Wandering Minstrel' I try to refine the sound down to almost nothing, exactly like Olivia just now. Rather strange that, because she's never seen me do it. The *Manchester Evening News* said that I –"

Caroline switched off, then looked around rather desperately. She realised that she must have lost none of her ability to convey hidden emotions, because someone in the mass of people around her registered her desperation and came over to congratulate her and say that this was one of the most exciting opera evenings of his life. Caroline wondered whether she ought to introduce Rick, but decided he would only burble on about himself, so she kept the fan to herself for the rest of the interval. Where Rick went she neither knew nor cared.

* * *

Guy had sniffed early on that there was nothing doing at that hour in the clubs, and probably wouldn't be until well after the time fixed for their journey home. Ten-fifty he had to be back at the car. The young people seemed to go into pubs to get tanked up in advance, doubtless much more cheaply than in the myriad clubs that peppered the city centre. Many of the pubs and clubs seemed to cluster around the top end of Briggate and Vicar Lane, but with the Grand Theatre being within yards of them Guy was afraid of meeting his father there. Marius's inability to sit through an opera or ballet was a joke in his own family. Guy chose a pub in a little alley off the middle stretch of Briggate where there seemed to be a big and raucous crowd of young people.

Oddly enough, for all his apparent confidence, Guy did not feel altogether at home with this rowdy bunch. Truth to tell, his mother and father had always kept him on a fairly tight rein. He really knew almost nothing about the club scene in London, nothing at all about that in Leeds. But he intended to learn. And he intended to get what he had come for.

Stella walked on past the Grand Theatre, having registered that the opera ended at ten-twenty, then past the turn-off to the Headrow, then down Briggate proper. She was trying to look ordinary, as if things were normal, but she knew they were not. What she really wanted was somewhere quiet, somewhere where she could come to terms with what she had seen.

It had been so odd, so disturbing. She had been to a little restaurant off Merrion Street – had a plate of spaghetti and coffee, but they hadn't helped. Now she knew she had two hours still to waste. She looked up the little snickets that were like little mazes off the broad and traffic-free street. Many contained pubs, with noisy crowds of young people. One or two were just alleyways, dark and dank. She didn't fancy them. She lingered at the opening of one. There was a man with his back to her – a familiar back. She realized with a start it was Alexander. She wondered if he was peeing, but when his hand went up to his mouth she realized he was smoking. One of his little secrets. She was glad that for once she had found him out.

She lingered, though, because she would dearly have liked to confide in him what she had seen. But then she decided against it. He was not the only one who could nurse private secrets. She walked briskly on in search of a hamburger joint or pizza place. She preferred solitude among company to sordid back alleys.

* * *

It was ten o'clock, and the final scene of the opera was approaching. The tenor and the baritone were concluding the last of their big duets which were a feature of the second half of *La Forza del Destino*. Big healthy voices vowing eternal hatred – Caroline felt the appropriate surge of visceral excitement. Then in the darkness the permanent set shifted so that the shape vaguely suggestive of a gun split at the centre, where the trigger would be, to make a narrow gap: Leonora's penitential cave. And as the last scene began, with Olivia emerging through the gap to sing her prayer for peace, Caroline settled into her seat to enjoy the lead-up to her daughter's triumph. A big, heavy voice Olivia had said she was aiming at for this role, but one that could be gentle or agile when the score called for such qualities. Caroline decided she was well on the way to it, if not quite there. At the aria's end the conductor pressed on, ignoring the beginnings of applause so that Leonora's fighting brother and lover could bring the long saga of predestined disaster to its conclusion. The mortally-wounded brother stabbed his sister with his last burst of vengeful strength, and in the final trio the dying Leonora, her lover and the Padre Guardiano commended their souls to a God who Caroline thought hadn't come out of the preceding action with much credit.

Cheers. The audience had decided early on that this was to be a triumphant evening, and the bravos (with bravas and bravis from pedants) echoed round the theatre, and Caroline wished she could decently join in cheering her own daughter. She had a slight sense of anti-climax rather than climax in any case, and decided it was because Olivia had not had enough to do in the last scene, that things had been wound up too quickly after her long absence from the action. But the cheers went on, and the curtain went up and down and up again. The conductor acknowledged the source of the enthusiasm by pushing Olivia forward to take personal calls three times. Then, at last, the lights went up.

Walking again up the aisle, and enjoying a fresh burst of undeserved congratulations, Caroline wished Marius had slipped back in as he had said he would for the end of the opera and the acclaim. He loved that kind of excitement. But perhaps he had been watching from the back. When the wave of people got out into the corridor, Caroline slipped into the empty bar. No point in trying to get up to the Grand Circle where the party was until the Grand Circle patrons had made their way down the staircase and out into the street. She could see no Marius, either lurking in the corridor or the bar. She listened to the ecstatic comments of the departing audience with pleasure. One woman agreed with her.

"If only Verdi had given her a bit more to do in that last scene."

But there was no doubt it was a triumph. One didn't have to wait for the critics to know that. In fact only a dog in a manger could dissent.

When the swell of departing audience abated she emerged and made her way up to the bar in the Grand Circle. "Tell her we thought she was magnificent" a man she didn't know called to her. She smiled graciously and said that she would.

When she arrived at the Circle Bar she was taken under the wing of a member of the Opera North staff, who recognised her at once and fetched her a drink, as well as directing her to the trays with tempting eats on them.

"I couldn't eat a thing," said Caroline

"It is awfully exciting, isn't it?" said the woman. Caroline didn't tell her that what was preventing her regaining her appetite was not her daughter's triumph but worry about Marius.

"I'm Enid, by the way," said the woman. "Call me over if there's anything you need."

When she left a little group started gathering around her, but it parted as soon as Olivia made her entrance. She immediately spotted her mother and came darting over – getting me done first, said Caroline to herself, for she knew her daughter and knew theatrical priorities. The two of them folded each other in an embrace.

"Wonderful, darling," said Caroline.

"Room for improvement, especially the last scene," said Olivia, with a rueful grimace.

"I thought that was Verdi's fault."

"Not much point in asking for a rewrite at this moment in time. Where's Marius?"

"Hasn't arrived yet. He may have got caught up in something at the West Yorkshire Playhouse that ends late."

"Send him over when he comes, won't you? I don't want him to sneak away without talking to me."

"Marius isn't the sneaking away type. He'll want to be part of your triumph, even if he did only see the first scene."

Olivia nodded, then went to talk to the people who mattered – the company administrator, the conductor and director, a few words to the secretary and the chairman of the Friends. All eyes were on her, as if she were visiting royalty. Clutching her drink Caroline enjoyed her daughter's poise and purpose, but felt rather out of it, especially when Rick arrived with Lauren Spender, still dressed as the nurse from *Loot*. She had come in a taxi from Bradford where the play was being performed, and as she and Rick wafted past her on their way to pay their mead of tribute to Olivia, Lauren found the time to say:

"Been stood up, darling? Don't men treat us girls *rotten*!"

Caroline simply turned away. But she realised that she must have been looking rather out of things, rather bereft. Without Marius that was exactly how she felt. Still, that wasn't something that should happen at her daughter's triumph. She was just looking round for someone to talk to when there was a voice at her elbow.

"Are you worried about your partner? Is there anything I can do to help?"

It was Enid, the woman from the Opera North staff.

"Well, I *am* a bit worried," said Caroline. "Marius was so looking forward to the curtain calls and the party afterwards – he's not an opera person, I'm afraid. And it's not like him to promise to be somewhere and then miss it. He's a bit of a stickler that way. I wondered if he'd maybe got trapped at the Playhouse – maybe got a seat at something that goes on late."

"Both things on there end before ten – barring accidents, of course." Enid noticed that Caroline flinched at the word and said: "Would you like me to ring the police and the hospital, just to make sure?"

"Oh, I *would*. I know I'm being silly, but ... I mean, I'm not sure how I'm to get home if Marius *has* had an accident."

"Do you need to? I could find you a hotel."

"Oh, I really should. I've got children in their teens."

By now they were backstage, and the woman said quietly to one of the scene-shifters: "Could you stand by in case you're needed?" Then Caroline and she went up to her office, and Enid rang the police, where she had contacts, and the hospital, where she had to go through a bank of bureaucracy before she got an answer out of the Accident and Emergency Department. Neither had any news for her. There had been the odd fracas after the Leeds United home game, but they had all involved young people. No serious car accident. No news at all about a middle-aged supermarket owner.

"In any case I don't think Marius would have taken the car," said

Caroline. "Perhaps if I could just check that he hasn't arrived at the party, and then if that nice stage-hand *could* drive me home – Oh dear: I'm afraid I'll have to pay him by cheque."

"Oh, this is on us."

"No – I shall absolutely insist on paying," said Caroline briskly. "It's not as though you're rolling in money like Covent Garden."

So back Enid took her, and she stood at the door of the Circle Bar. Olivia was still surrounded by all the notables, though Colm had a lesser circle of admirers. Marius was in neither group, nor in any of the others. She shook her head, and the stage-hand who had followed them took her out of the theatre and down to the back, where a company car was waiting. As they began their drive to Alderley Caroline kept saying things like "I'm sure I'm being silly," then lapsing into silence. The last few miles Caroline had to direct the man, and when they got there she insisted on paying him, then rushed indoors to check the answer machine. There was nothing on it. From upstairs there was silence, so the children had probably been long in bed. Caroline wondered whether to pour herself a drink and wait for Marius, but she was washed over by tiredness and she took herself to bed.

She slept for an hour or two, then felt beside her to find only emptiness. The rest of the night consisted of alternately dozing uneasily and long spells of wakefulness. Sometimes she had something like a presentiment of future loneliness, at others only a resentment that Marius had spoilt one of the weekends she cherished so much.

Chapter Eight

The Morning After

The sun was up, and the city was starting to stir, but only mildly and tentatively, because Sunday still feels like a day of rest in the early hours, before the big chain stores open. Reg Liversedge was out with his Yorkie later than usual, and lingered longer at places of canine interest, because he wasn't going to work. He rented one of the flats over a shop in Briggate in Leeds. The shop sold mobile phones, but the establishment next door was a kebab takeaway, so the odours were sometimes pungent. Reg told himself he was part of the regeneration of the inner cities. He also told everyone who would listen that it was better than living with his wife, though if pressed he might have admitted that it was not better than living with *a* wife.

His dog Trueman was part of this guarded satisfaction with his present life. Reg took him for a walk every day around eight, before the city girded up its loins to start the day. He came home for his lunch break, gobbled the sandwich he had prepared at breakfast-time, then took him round the streets. After work he was almost always in, with an early-evening and later-evening stroll. Mostly, like ninety per cent of British people, he just watched the television. Trueman did too. The programme they both enjoyed most was *Pet Rescue*.

So today there was no work at Austin Reed's, no being friendly to customers he didn't give a damn about, no dealings with reps or company high-ups, all trying to guess next season's fashion trends. A lazy day. Reg turned up Briggate, crossed Merrion Street, and eventually made his way to the little oasis of green that surrounded the newly-built and unusual block of flats that were called CASPAR Apartments. Their distinction, their departure from the urban norm, was that they were round, were faced with wood, and looked from a distance like nothing so much as an Elizabethan theatre. Close to it might have seemed that they were very exclusive indeed, a little fortress for the moneyed, and way out of Reg's price league; in fact, however, CASPAR stood for Citycentre Apartments for Single People at Affordable Rents.

Trueman had no ambitions to live there, but he liked the greenery around it. The public was allowed on to the lawns, with their modest and low-care shrubs and bushes. Lingering now became the order of the day. Trueman could sniff to eternity before he decided which of the various growing things would be favoured with his urine. Sundays he could be pampered, and he took every advantage of this fact. Trueman was a dog of well-developed ego.

At the high point of the little patch of garden the Yorkie outdid himself in dilatoriness. Bored but obedient Reg turned away and looked down towards the centre of the city. He could see down Briggate, with the Grand Theatre to his left, the Odeon on the same side further down, then the main section of the street, with all the big chain stores – Debenhams, House of Fraser, Marks and Spencers – followed by Lower Briggate, which curved out of his sight.

Trueman had gone to the limits of his long lead, and was now tugging. Reg turned away from the city and followed the little dog. Something was drawing him, exciting him. Trueman pulled towards a flourishing shrub abutting a stretch of fencing. He scrambled into it, then turned around and barked. Reg peered into the dense and flowery vegetation. It looked like an arm. Appalled at the thought of a severed limb, Reg tried to edge through the row of bushes. The arm was not severed at all, but attached to a body – a smart, besuited middle-aged man. Reg dragged Trueman away, down the slope towards North Street, the dog protestingly barking that his little legs didn't *do* running. Then Reg came to what he was seeking and bundled Trueman and himself into a telephone booth to dial 999.

"It's a body, near those new flats past Upper Briggate – up from North Street, you know the ones, they're called CASPARS – it's a body hidden in the bushes around the flats. There's blood on his shirt. He's somebody, this chap. It's a very good suit – Armani or whatever – a *very* good suit indeed."

The constable taking the message thought it was an odd thing to put so much emphasis on, but then he knew nothing of the man who was ringing in. Clothes were Reg's business, so he was a man who noticed such things.

* * *

"Doncaster 3707 946."

"Is that Mrs Fawley?"

"That's right." Caroline's heart was thumping badly, and she had difficulty holding the telephone receiver without shaking.

"This is the West Yorkshire Police in Leeds, Mrs Fawley. I believe we had a telephone call last night from someone at the Grand Theatre on your behalf."

"Yes." Her voice was flat, while something in her brain blared BAD NEWS like a newspaper hoarding.

"This was an enquiry about a missing person, wasn't it? Your partner, I believe."

"Yes, Marius. Marius Fleetwood. Is there any –"

"There's nothing certain, Mrs Fawley. But I should tell you that a body has been found this morning."

"Oh God!" Caroline immediately began to sob.

"There's nothing definite, Mrs Fawley, like I say. Please don't jump to conclusions. But we wondered whether you could come to Leeds –"

"Yes!" She had to know. *Now* "Should I get a taxi?"

"No. We've lined up someone from the Doncaster force. He can be with you in fifteen minutes. Can you be ready by then?"

"I'll be ready."

She put the phone down, and saw that, standing on the stairs were her two younger children. They had been told of Marius's mysterious non-appearance at the party over breakfast. Caroline sank into the chair by the phone, her head in her hands, and did not notice Alexander and Stella look at each other with fear in their eyes, nor the legs of Guy as he listened from the landing above them.

* * *

The young uniformed constable who came for her from Doncaster had been out on another matter when he received the message to go to Alderley. He already knew Marsham, and was given instructions on how to find the way from there to the house itself. He bundled Caroline into the car with muttered expressions of sympathy and began the drive to Leeds at a goodly pace. Caroline sat, dazed and full of forebodings, for more than ten minutes.

"Was there anything on him – any papers or anything, with his name on them?" she asked at last.

"I'm afraid I don't know anything. I'm with the Doncaster force – we're just doing this as a favour .... The chap on my radio just said it was a bloke – a man – in a very good suit."

"Yes, Marius always knew how to dress," said Caroline.

It was another ten minutes, driving through suburbs and flat countryside of no interest, before she realized she had spoken of him as dead. She was already preparing herself for a sort of widowhood. She wondered how she ought to describe Marius. "My late partner," perhaps. Though a not-particularly-kind actress friend had once pointed out that "partner" was not strictly accurate since Marius had never left his wife, "My bloke," she said, would be better. "My late bloke", however, didn't sound at all right.

When they got to Leeds the young policeman drove her straight to Millgarth Police Headquarters and escorted her into the station. The constable on the desk knew at once who Caroline was, and spoke in a low voice into his phone. Soon she was being escorted into the station proper by a white detective of about her own age and a much younger black one who towered over her.

"My name is Oddie," said the senior one, "and this is Detective Sergeant Peace. This must be quite horrible for you. I don't know if you'd like a cup of tea or coffee, or if you'd prefer –"

"I'd prefer to see him now," said Caroline, interrupting him. Oddie nodded, signalled to Peace to wait, and then walked her to the mortuary. Caroline shivered when she got there, but went through the grisly ritual as if in a dream – or perhaps as if in a television cops drama. When the attendant drew down the sheet covering the body she just nodded and said:

"Yes, that's Marius."

"Marius Fleetwood?"

"Yes. The owner of the Fleetwood supermarket chain."

The sheet was pulled up again, and they walked back to Sergeant Peace in silence. When they got to him, and began to walk she knew not where, Caroline suddenly started talking as if she would never stop.

"I knew it would be him. It's not a shock. When someone you know and love does something entirely out of character, or *seems* to, then you get a presentiment of disaster, don't you? And Marius *never* went back on a promise or an arrangement. If he said he would be somewhere at a certain time, there he'd be. He said he'd be back for the curtain calls – that's for *Forza del Destino* at the Grand – and I knew he would be because he loved that sort of thing, and he'd be full of, well, *pride*, even though Olivia's not his child of course. And he'd be happy for me and her. So when he wasn't there, and wasn't standing at the back as I thought he might be, that told me there was something wrong, and when he wasn't at the party afterwards then I *knew* – almost knew, I mean I thought he might be in hospital, that was one of the things I feared, then I thought he might have been mugged and was just lying somewhere. Oh, I must tell Guy – all the children, of course, but Guy is his son, and he's at Alderley, and I suppose he'll have to ring his mother – oh dear, I suppose I could ring them from here, couldn't I?"

"Yes, of course you can. And then would you like to go home? We can leave detailed questions for the moment and concentrate on things this end, rather than on the background. There is a chance this is a sort of mugging or random attack."

"I would like to go home, very much. But first could I ... I'd like to see the place where he died. Or where he was found. So I could have some idea of his end, of his last hours – if he had that long."

"That will be all right. Sergeant Peace here can take you before he drives you home. You won't be able to be alone there, I'm afraid – at the scene of the crime, I mean: there will be policemen all over the place."

"I understand."

They had got to Oddie's office, and he opened the door and gestured towards the phone. Caroline stood still for a moment, seeming to steel herself, or perhaps deciding how she would break the news. Then she sat down at the desk and took up the phone and dialled.

"Stella? Darling, it's Mummy." A catch came into her voice, resisted unsuccessfully. "I'm afraid it's bad news. Yes, he's dead. Murder." She looked up at Oddie, who nodded. "Yes, it couldn't be worse. They're bringing me home, when I've just seen where he was ... *found*. Will you tell Guy, darling, and ask him to ring his mother ... Yes darling. I love *you* both. Be brave, be gentle with Guy, and I'll be home very soon."

Caroline let herself be taken by Sergeant Peace out to a car and seemed oblivious to her surroundings as he drove her up Eastgate, turning into Upper Briggate, then stopping in North Street. He led her up on to the grassed area, and her eyes immediately caught the knot of uniformed policemen and a little gang of people in white. She and Peace stopped at the ring of blue and white tape.

"Could we go closer?"

"Better not. It might complicate things. The body was found over there, behind that bush – Genesia I think it's called. The one with the yellow flowers."

"*Behind*? So he was probably not killed there?"

"Probably not. Hidden there so he wouldn't be found too soon."

"*How* did he die?"

"He was stabbed."

"Was the weapon still? –"

"No weapon has been found." Charlie Peace looked at one of the men in white, who nodded his head. Caroline frowned, then looked around her at the surrounding cityscape, as Reg Liversedge had done a few hours earlier.

"But I don't understand."

"What don't you understand?"

"I imagined Marius going to the town – to a pub, a restaurant, the Playhouse – something like that. But that's the Grand Theatre there, isn't it? If he was killed here he was coming *away* from anything he might have wanted to go to to to fill in time. There's nothing much here, is there?"

"Nothing much," agreed Charlie. "Those new flats. The odd seedy hotel. Otherwise just run-down businesses."

"That's what I thought, looking at it. I don't know Leeds well, but Marius did. He worked for the Morrisons supermarket chain in Manchester when he was starting out, but he was often in Leeds. He always knew where to go, where to park ... Oh, the car must still be in the multi-storey off Woodhouse Lane."

"Don't worry about it. We'll see about it. The SOCO people will want to go over it."

"I see."

She gave him the Mercedes's number, then they went back to the police car and began the drive home. Caroline was still in that slightly hysterical, talkative mood, and she hardly needed asking before she began filling Charlie in on the background.

"Guy's mother is called Sheila, and they're still married. In name only, but he lives with her, and she sometimes goes with him to events that interest her ... I'm sorry, I must use the past tense, mustn't I? Marius came up to Alderley every weekend, and that suited both of us rather well."

"Are you still acting?"

"No, that's a thing of the past, thank God."

"Is Guy an only child?"

"No, there's a daughter, Helena. Guy's twenty, she's only fifteen. I met her once, and she and my brood got on very well, as they do with Guy. I never wanted to destroy Marius's home arrangements, though we've had to talk about things recently."

"Oh? Why was that?"

"Sheila seems to have got herself some kind of boyfriend, and she's pregnant by him. That made Marius wonder a bit, naturally – I mean there were questions like whether he wanted to bring up someone else's child as his own."

"Yes, I can see that. So what about you? How many children have you got?"

"Three. The eldest, Olivia, is twenty-nine and she's an opera-singer:

that's why we were at the Grand Theatre last night. She was singing the lead soprano role in *La Forza del Destino*. The other two are much younger – Alexander's sixteen, Stella is fourteen."

"Not the same father as Olivia's then?"

"No. Olivia's by my first husband, Rick Radshaw. Actor, with a reputation of sorts for musicals. He was there last night with his ... *current*. The younger ones are from my second husband Evelyn Cottle, who is always abroad at some embassy or consulate in some insignificant part of the globe where his total witlessness will not do too much harm ... Sorry about the cattiness. If you can't be catty about your former husbands, who can you be catty about?"

"So your name is a stage name, is it?"

"That's right. And it's also my maiden name. The children have all taken that too."

"But now you've retired, and don't miss the life."

"Miss it like you miss an aching tooth. Of course if something absolutely unrefusable turned up, I suppose I could be persuaded, just for the one thing. My giving it all up just like that does worry some people. Jack – that's my best friend in the village, Sir John Mortyn-Crosse, *Bart* – he insists on that last to distinguish him from a mere knight, though I don't know the difference so it's lost on me – Jack thinks I'm forsaking my Art, or some nonsense like that, and is always encouraging me not to regard myself as retired, to maintain all my contacts and that sort of thing. I tell him I have the most wonderful feeling of *peace* in that house, and it comes from having severed all links with the theatre ... Though whether that will be quite the same without Marius, who can say?"

She paused for a moment, but then the hysterical impulse to talk and talk took her over again, and Charlie heard all about the opera the previous night and the party afterwards, her life with Marius, the idyll of country living, her joy at having so much time with her children, how she had been welcomed by the people of Marsham – and on and on. Charlie listened, because he needed to pick up all the background information and atmosphere that he could. But with another part of his mind he was picking out the things that were of most interest, planning possible future moves.

Jack, for example. Sir John Whatsit-Whatsit. He sounded of interest. Was he the sort of concerned friend who could be counted on to have a cool outsider's view of the situation at Alderley – a view that might counter, or at least augment, the rather rose-tinted account of it that he was getting from Caroline Fawley? He hoped, and rather suspected, that he might be.

Caroline directing him, he drove through Marsham and drew up outside Alderley. He got out and opened the passenger door for Caroline, and since she seemed uncertain whether to say goodbye to him, he began to escort her into the house. When the children heard the front door open they came to the sitting room door, and Stella threw herself into her mother's arms. After a few seconds Caroline disentangled herself from her youngest child and drew them all, Charlie Peace following, into the room behind.

"This is Sergeant Peace. He's very kindly brought me home. This is Guy, Stella, Alexander ... Now, could someone make us all a cup of tea?" And when the tea was brought in Caroline told all the young people, in a low voice drained of all emotion, the facts of Marius's murder. Charlie put in a word here and there, realizing that Caroline had asked him no questions beyond how Marius had been killed – presumably because the mere fact of his death was more than enough for her to absorb in the hour or so since the body had been shown to her. He stood by the window looking out over the long garden, its lawns and rose bushes, its sheds and green-houses and tennis court. This was gracious living, Charlie thought.

"So you see," Caroline was saying, in that flat voice which seemed so unnatural coming from her, "we're all going to have to learn to live without him." She took up her cup to her lips for the first taste, but then, suddenly burst into a passion of sobbing and fled from the room. Stella showed signs of running after her, but Charlie slipped swiftly over to stand against the door.

"I think she'd rather be alone," he said. "Wouldn't you, in her situation?"

They looked at each other.

"Probably," said Alexander. "We've only known Granny Cottle dying, and she wasn't close."

Charlie looked at Guy, who simply nodded.

"Now, before I go and leave you to yourselves for a bit, perhaps you'd all tell me what you did last night."

Again, and rather surprisingly, it was Alexander who spoke.

"Oh, we just watched a bit of television."

Charlie left a second or two's silence after this.

"Well, well," he said silkily, his eyebrows raised, "the oldies go off for the evening, and you use your freedom by just sitting in front of the box, eh? What was it that got you so hooked? Cilla Black? Michael Barrymore? The National Lottery draw? Come off it! Saturday night television – it's crap! Only idiots and invalids can watch it. Here are all you bright young things off to university this year, next year, some time in the future, and the best you can think of doing is to sit watching a pile of infantile rubbish."

"It was pretty childish," said Alexander. "So after a bit we played a game."

"What game?"

"Monopoly. We hadn't played for years."

"Really. Where did you find the box?"

Alexander looked around him a bit wildly, then pointed to the sideboard. Charlie went over to it and opened the door. Files, boxes of place mats, old silver, a few letters, an unopened Christmas present all fell out on to the floor. No Monopoly set. The sideboard clearly hadn't been opened since they moved in to Alderley.

"So," said Charlie, "you're lying. I'd guess that Mrs Fawley has a car in the garage. She'd need one in an out-of-the-way village like Marsham. And I suppose you, young man –" he looked at Guy – "have a driving licence. So where did you decide to go? Doncaster? Sheffield? *Leeds*?"

There was silence.

"We went to Leeds," said Stella.

Chapter Nine

Paradise Lost

Charlie left Alderley pondering. So the children had all been to Leeds the previous night. The two younger ones had been more specific about where they had been than the dead man's son, but that was perfectly understandable: it was Guy Fleetwood's first time in the city, and a vagueness about its geography was inevitable. What had they all been doing, as they went their separate ways? Their tale was one of pubs, burger bars and cinemas. Natural, in themselves convincing – so why was Charlie dissatisfied?

He put his finger on the cause as he was driving through the gates of the house: there was something about Guy – perhaps it was his very confidence, or the outer carapace of it – that repelled trust, and this affected his view of the other two. Though they all claimed to have done their own thing, only meeting up in time to drive home and be in bed well before their elders could be expected, somehow nothing that any of them said quite rang true. All of them had something to hide, including the youngest, Stella, who had never made eye-contact with Charlie at all. But the one he was convinced was holding most back was Guy Fleetwood.

The rich man's son who'd had everything he wanted, Charlie asked himself? Or one who'd been kept on a tight financial rein, and wanted more?

As he drove through Marsham, a fairly typical mixture of the picturesque old and the mass-produced new, an idea occurred to him. Seeing a man in a dog-collar emerging through the gates of the churchyard, Charlie slowed to a stop beside him and lowered his car window.

"Excuse me, sir: I'm a police officer." He dived into his pocket and produced his ID.

"Ah – have you come from Alderley? I do *trust* that the news is not bad."

Charlie raised his eyebrows.

"Why do you assume it may be, sir?"

"Ah well, the son of one of our oldest communicants was at the Opera North party in Leeds last night, and he'd rung his mother this morning to tell her – he knew she'd be interested, with him living at least *partly* in the village – that Marius Fleetwood didn't appear there as expected, and that Mrs Fawley was very worried."

"I see. So it's all round the village?" The clergyman nodded. "Well, it will be on the news by tonight. I'm afraid Mr Fleetwood is dead – found stabbed to death not far from the Grand Theatre."

"*Really*? How terrible!" It was a much-practised response.

"Mrs Fawley of course is extremely upset at the moment. I'm sure at some point soon she would appreciate a call. She has no adult to talk to up at the house."

This was received less than whole-heartedly.

"Ah – I appreciate your concern, but I don't find calling *too soon* after a death is a sensible thing to do. In fact the best thing would be to wait for her to contact me. Mrs Fawley and Mr Fleetwood have been to church here – and of course have been made very welcome – but it hasn't been *quite* clear whether they are regular churchgoers or have just been making some kind of *gesture*."

"I see," said Charlie, who did. A more obvious tactic of distancing he had seldom met with. Were there many places in England where the minister could afford to look gift worshippers in the mouth? "But it wasn't Mrs Fawley I stopped you to talk about. She mentioned a friend – Sir John Something-or-Other, double-barrelled, I think, who seems to live locally."

"Sir John Mortyn-Crosse. One of the *old* Marsham families. In fact *the* big family in the area at one time."

"Could you tell me where he lives?"

"Oh yes. He lives with his sister – who is, well, let's say quite a character – in the Dower House, which is all that's left of the old manor lands. Go back the way you came, then where you'd turn right to get to Alderley, turn left. You can't miss it: the Dower House stands out, because there are lots of ... modern houses around it."

So Charlie turned his car around, left the pusillanimous cleric, and went in search of this lost paradise, the desecrated manor lands. He found it quite easily, on the edge of a wilderness of brick boxes

87

like gingerbread houses. He left his car on the road, near the solitary stone house. It had obviously been built for some widowed Mortyn-Crosse for whom her eldest son was willing to go to some expense in order to remove her from the manor house itself. It was solid and unpretentious – by no means small, yet perhaps too small to live in comfortably with a sister who was, well, quite a character.

The bell was a large iron circle in the wall, and you were directed to turn it clockwise. A fearsome clatter ensued, followed by a set of footsteps. Bolts were tugged at, and the door was then opened by Sir John, who looked at Charlie benignantly.

"Yes?"

"Sir John Mortyn-Crosse? I'm Detective Sergeant Peace. Here's my ID. I've just come from Alderley –"

Sir John's face crumpled in genuine distress.

"Oh *dear*. I heard rumours after church. You'd better come in."

He led the way down a dismal hallway and into a larger, better-lit sitting room furnished with pieces Charlie couldn't decide about – perhaps they had once been "good", but he thought not very good. He sat in the fat easy chair that Sir John had gestured him to, and looked at the concerned, worried baronet.

"I don't know what you heard at church," he began.

"Merely that Marius had not been at the party last night, and had somehow ... disappeared."

"I'm afraid he has been found, dead."

"*Dead*?"

"Yes, stabbed to death in a little piece of open ground not far from the Grand Theatre."

Sir John opened his mouth to express shock, but he was forestalled.

"What's *he* doing here?" came a voice from the door. Turning his head Charlie saw a woman built like a trailer truck with an expression of puffy outrage on her face. She could have been a Tory spokesman on law and order matters.

"Sit down, Meta," said her brother. Irritation had entered his voice and a pungent smell had wafted in Charlie's direction. "Sergeant Peace has some terrible news, I'm afraid. Marius has been found murdered."

"That doesn't answer my question. What's he doing here?" Charlie had a sense – one he had quite often – of being the first black person ever to have entered the house. The reaction in Meta Mortyn-Crosse was clearly one of outrage.

"I came to see you, particularly your brother, because Mrs Fawley mentioned him as her best friend in the village, and she has only children or young people with her now –"

"I'll go up and see her tonight," said Sir John. "And I'll get the rector to call."

"I just tried to, but I met with a certain ... reluctance."

"He'll call," said Sir John. "Sorry, we were interrupted. You were telling me about Marius."

"There's not much more I can tell you at the moment. But there was something else, and I may be reading an awful lot into a simple thing, so just stop me if I'm talking nonsense. Mrs Fawley mentioned that you were always trying to persuade her not to give up the stage, always to keep her contacts there, not to regard herself as having retired from it."

"Ye-e-es." A loud report and another smell came Charlie's way. He farts when he's worried or upset, he thought.

"I wondered if you *knew* something – something that suggested to you that Mrs Fawley's position was less permanent and settled than she imagined."

Sir John opened his mouth, shut it, then opened it again.

"Smart, very smart," he said appreciatively. "Yes, I'm afraid, very much afraid, that I do."

"You never told me!" snapped his sister from the door. A different smell wafted Charlie's way – that of brandy.

"Because I didn't want it all over the village, and in no time at all back to poor Caroline," snapped her brother, showing backbone Charlie might have guessed he didn't have.

"But you think you were right?" Charlie asked.

"I know I was. I suppose there can't be any harm in telling you now – all the affairs of poor Marius and Caroline will be round the village by week's end. You see, I happened to be in Hornsea ..." He shot a look at Charlie, then amended his account before he had even started. "No, I'd better be honest, or you'll only find me out. I'm not used to sharp detectives' brains. I went to Hornsea specially."

"Why Hornsea? Is there someone there that knows about Fleetwood's past? His record with other women?"

"Oh no, not at all. I wasn't *snoop*ing – well, not much. Hornsea is where Alf Beck, the former owner of Alderley, retired to. Dear old boy, it was much too big for him alone, and anyway he couldn't afford to run it, even when his wife was there to rattle around in it with him. I just felt like having a word with him, and though I hadn't got his address I knew he was as regular as clockwork, and he gave his dog a little walk after breakfast and a good long one after lunch, about two. So I drove over there, had a bite to eat in a pub –"

"You swine. You haven't taken me for a pub lunch in years," said Meta.

"Why should I, when I see you every minute of every hour as it is? Anyway, I knew he'd be either on the beach or in that little park place, and I heard the dog Laddie barking at the waves before I saw them. Anyway, to cut a long story short – but I'm not, am I? –"

"Take your time. You never know what may be of use."

Sir John looked gratified. Compliments were rare in his life.

"Well, I brought up the subject of Alderley, and dear old Alf came straight out with it. 'I'd've preferred to sell it,' he said, 'and cut all my ties, but Fleetwood's paying a very fair rent, so I'm quite happy.'"

"Ah!" said Charlie. "But Mrs Fawley thinks –"

"Caroline things that Marius owns it, and it's left to her in his will. And a substantial sum so she can keep it on."

"What made you suspicious?"

"It had been on the market for a long time. That's the sort of situation when people consider letting. And to tell you the truth I don't consider that millionaire businessmen are inclined to hand out whopping sums in their wills to women who've been their mistresses. Of course I've little or no experience of them, but I'm not entirely naive."

Charlie thought for a second or two.

"When I said he was dead, you were surprised, weren't you? I suppose you had been expecting some kind of desertion."

"Yes, I had. It's what he's done to others, by all accounts."

"Mrs Fawley seems to think she was something more special to him than 'the others'."

"I know she does, but his mistress is what she is, or was. Before the law, and in his eyes too, I wouldn't mind betting."

"I've heard rumours of others –" began Charlie.

"Scores of them!" said Meta, forgetting her distaste for Charlie in her enthusiasm for scandal. "He was a serial polygamist, was our Marius."

"Meta's exaggerating," said Sir John, "but still ... I wouldn't want to speak ill of the dead –"

"This is a murder enquiry," put in Charlie. "That means you do it sooner rather than later."

"Well then, apparently he had had mistresses before, quite a string of them. Did Caroline think he bought them all big houses and provided them all with assured incomes?"

"Have you ever put this to her?"

"No. Couldn't bring myself to. Couldn't burst the bubble. She was so happy – the happiest she'd ever been, she often said. All I could do was urge her to keep the acting – her stage and television contacts – in the background as an option." He shook his head. "I don't think she ever understood why I was so persistent about it."

"I don't think she did," agreed Charlie. "Unless there was some little cranny in her mind that registered that you were sceptical about her dreamboat man. Maybe we should hope that there was. Then the reality may come as less of a terrible shock."

"Remember we don't *know*," said Sir John. But he and Charlie caught each other's eye, and both of them thought they did know.

"Well, all that this amounts to is that Caroline is a bloody fool," announced Meta. "And I don't think that's any great news bombshell. Whoever expected an actress to be an Einstein? I tried to tip the wink to that hopeless son of hers, but I don't suppose he had the gumption to pass it on."

"Did you like Mr Fleetwood?" asked Charlie, turning back to Sir John.

"Yes ... Yes, I did."

"Did you trust him?"

"No. Not that. I'm not sure I always believed what he told me, even on small, quite unimportant matters."

"Would you have any idea where he might have gone to fill in time – two or three hours – in the evening in Leeds?"

Sir John roared with laughter.

"You've come to the wrong man to find that out! I haven't been in Leeds for fifteen years of more. When I last went there there was Schofield's and John Lewis's and the Classical Record Shop and the men in the market called everybody 'love' and 'my darling.' Now I hear it's all wine bars and restaurants I couldn't afford to go to, and probably political correctness reigns in the market as well."

"No it doesn't," said Charlie. "But lots of the old stalls have gone because the holders couldn't afford the rents, and you get mobile phone stalls and video stalls instead." He got up to go. "Well, I'd better be getting back to Leeds to see what my boss has come up with."

"Oh, there is someone senior in charge of the case, is there?" asked Meta. "I'm glad of that."

Charlie smiled at her sweetly and turned back to Sir John.

"If anything you haven't mentioned comes back to you, or if you hear anything that you think is relevant however small it is, will you give me a call on this number?"

Sir John took the card.

"I will. I'm glad we've had this chat, because I might have been agonising over whether to mention my worries to the police. Oh, and thank you too for telling me about the rector. He's not a bad man, but –" He shrugged.

"He's not a very good one either," said Charlie, grinning. "Thanks for talking to me."

As the door shut on him he lingered on the step for a moment, and heard the voice of Meta saying: "Well, you made a great fool of yourself, telling that nigger how sharp he was, and practically fawning over him as if –" Charlie didn't wait to hear more, but went on his way smiling. It is always pleasing to have one's judgments confirmed.

Back in Leeds he found that Oddie had had a day of mixed fortunes. An attempt to blanket interview the inhabitants of the new block of flats overlooking the murder scene had yielded only very patchy results. Sunday was a bad day, and many of the single residents of the CASPAR flats were obviously home with Mummy, or elsewhere with girlfriends or boyfriends. Those who were interviewed had seen nothing of interest, but nevertheless Oddie had scheduled Monday evening for a second attempt to get a reasonable percentage coverage.

Where he had had better luck was in ferreting around in Fleetwood's background. Here Sunday opening proved a blessing. He walked up to the Merrion Centre Morrison's, found a deputy manager in charge for the day, and told him of the murder. Local news bulletins being sparse on Sunday, this was a complete surprise, and, feeling in some way privileged, the man was co-operative.

"Of course we know about Fleetwood. It's a *name* in the retail trade, and everyone knows he started with us. I'm too young to have had anything to do with him, and so is my boss here. But there *is* someone ... someone who trained with him ..." Eventually it came to him. "Cranmer. Dick Cranmer. He's at the Shelf branch."

"Any chance of his home phone number?"

"I should be able to find it. He's a right old gossip, so he won't be bothered about my giving it to you." He rummaged in his desk and pulled out a dirty and dog-eared little book. "Here we are: it's 01422 341 060."

Back at the station Oddie had got his approach ordered in his mind. He suspected that Cranmer would already have got warning of his interest (the deputy manager's words had suggested one young gossip recognising his elder and better) and he was right.

"Leeds police, eh?" said a fruity voice at the other end. "Well I've been waiting for you to ring. So old Marius has got his comeuppance, has he? I'll not pretend I was expecting it, because I wasn't. You don't, do you? People like him don't get murdered, except maybe casually by maniacs in the street. Now then, what was it you want to know?"

"I gather you were trainee managers around the same time."

93

"That's right. There was no trainee managers' school or anything like that, but we met up pretty often for special sessions and for pooling our experiences and observations. So I did get to know him, up to a certain point. Marius – he was Bert then – was a star, and no two ways about it. You knew he was going to the top, and in his own way and as head of his own company. People here sometimes say we trained him and then he took all we'd taught him and used it for his own purposes. Well, true, but again only up to a point. Everyone knew he wasn't going to be with us for very long, but it was exhilarating having a business brain like his around, and frankly he gave in new ideas as much as he took from us."

"When was this?"

"Oh, late 'sixties, early 'seventies. His last year with us he was deputy manager in one of the less important Leeds stores. They didn't want to give him one of the more important places because there might be too many ideas and practices around for him to take with him. When he took off, around 1975 or 6, he took a lot of our principles and policies with him, but he was very fair: he set up his stores in the South, where we don't operate. And with a different clientèle any ideas he took with him he had to adapt. I believe Fleetwood stores nowadays have a lot more organic produce, every one has a delicatessen counter, the London stores keep the ethnic mix very much in mind, and so on. He has the reputation of being fair, but very smart."

"That's interesting. I wouldn't rule it out, but I rather suspect that this murder has got nothing to do with the business side of his life."

"You never know though. They do talk about cut-throat competition, don't they?" A fruity laugh at this tasteless joke came down the line.

"Heart," said Oddie.

"*Really*? Anyway, what you want is more personal stuff, I take it?"

"Yes – in fact, anything about his private life that tells us anything about the man."

There was a pause for thought.

"He was one for the ladies, that's for sure. I expect you know that already. Mind you, we all were, the trainees: we were the age to be a bit randy. But he was more than most."

"Any names?"

"Oh, some of the other trainees served as one-night stands, but they weren't more than that, and I'm certainly not giving you their names. There was a mistress, and rumour has it a child, by someone in Leeds, but by then we'd lost touch, because I was in an equivalent job in Bolton."

"Know anything about his family background?"

"Not much. Father was a train-driver, lived in Pontefract. There was him and a sister. Give him his due, he'd come a long way, hadn't he? Millionaire, chain of stores with a first-class reputation, nice mistress tucked away in a classy village in South Yorkshire. I wouldn't mind being in his shoes."

"You know about the mistress?"

"Oh yes – Caroline Fawley. Used to be in one of those fairly funny sitcoms whose name I can't remember. Gossip gets around, you know. He may not still be with Morrison's, but he's remembered, and he's still – *was* – in the trade."

"You mentioned he was called Bert when you knew him. What was his full name?"

"Bert Winterbottom. You couldn't make much of 'Winterbottom's Superstores' as a selling name down South, could you? He did right to change it.

When later that afternoon Charlie got back, Oddie gave him a pretty full summary of all that he'd learnt. At one point Charlie's brow furrowed.

"You say he worked in the Leeds area for a time, during which he seems to have acquired a mistress and a child."

"Apparently."

"Caroline Fawley says he never worked in the Leeds area. It's not necessarily important –"

"Not necessarily a red herring either. At the very least we might get some clues about how he treated women."

"And at best a discarded mistress and a twenty-something child with long-standing grudges," said Charlie, his eyes lighting up.

Chapter Ten

Monday

Caroline found it impossible to settle. She told herself that this was the predicament of bereaved people through the ages: what could be important enough to *do*, that it could displace the real duty of grieving? She wandered around the house, registering so many things that had memories of Marius, so many places where she could remember standing with him, or sitting, or making love – all *with him*. It was as if her weekdays without him were dream interludes, and reality only came with his arrival on Friday evenings. When Mrs Hogbin came and started in on a routine which centred entirely on how she had heard the news, how she was gobsmacked, what she had said to her daughter, and what her daughter had said to her, Caroline called on her powers as an actress: the monologue made her want to escape rather than cry, but in the event she did both by turning on a display of theatrical waterworks and bursting out of the house.

I'm naughty, she thought, as she wandered round the garden, but really the thought of being immured in Alderley, the shrine to the love of Marius and herself, and having to listen to Mrs Hogbin's inanities was more than she could bear. What use was theatrical training if it couldn't come to one's aid at such a time? The garden began to work its cure on her. She was glad the children had decided to take the bus to school as usual. Both of them went to state schools in Doncaster – very good ones. She and Marius had had this in common too – an aversion to using private education for their children. Marius had just said tersely that he didn't like the product. What they would have done if there had been no good state schools in the vicinity Caroline couldn't imagine. But the children had, without saying anything, gone down to catch the bus as usual, and Caroline didn't blame them: no reason why they should take the death of Marius as hard as she had. Guy had returned to London to comfort his mother, with the promise to come back on his way up belatedly to take up his place at St Andrews. Leaving her, gratefully and blessedly, on her own – apart, for the moment, from Mrs Hogbin.

The garden had always been hers to tend and develop, but it held as many memories of the man she had lost as the house did. Marius had loved wandering in it, being shown the new shrubs and flowers she had planted, the little forgotten nooks she had found a purpose for. "I'll pay for any help you need," he used to say to her, with a cheeky grin that was the only remnant of his working-class upbringing, "so long as you don't expect me to work here myself. I'm a destructive force as far as gardens are concerned." And she had been quite happy with that arrangement. The blissful week-ends with him were not times to be spent toiling in flower beds with rakes and hoes.

She stopped by one of several huts in the garden, the one where the tools and implements were kept. She frowned. The rusty old padlock was defective, and needed to be pushed in very firmly to lock it. It hadn't been, and it was now hanging loose. Yet she was quite sure it had been securely locked by her when she had last gardened. She tried to remember when that was. Wednesday, she thought: three days before Marius had died ... *been killed*.

She became aware of shouting. It was Mrs Hogbin calling from the kitchen door. Running closer she caught the words "It's that Guy." It seemed no time since she had driven him to Doncaster to catch the early train to London. Now it was one o'clock – he would be well home. She hurried through the kitchen into the hall. "Mr Fleetwood's son," explained Mrs Hogbin. Well, she hadn't thought it was Guy Fawkes or Guy Ritchie.

"Hello, Guy."

"Hello Caroline. Just to tell you I'm home."

"I thought you would be by now. The trains are bad, but not that bad."

"Yes, well, Mum's taking it very well, and I thought you could tell the police that I can be back there tomorrow or Wednesday if they want to talk to me like they said they would to all of us."

"Right, I'll tell them. I believe they're busy in Leeds today, but

Sergeant Peace said they wanted to 'do' us, if that's the word, as soon as possible. Shall I phone them and give them your home number?"

"Yes, please."

"I'm sure it's just a formality."

"Yes ... Oh, one more thing. My mother said she'd like a word – is that all right?"

Caroline, in her surprise, left a second's pause, and wished she hadn't.

"Yes, of course it is."

Sheila Fleetwood had obviously been standing right by the phone, because she came on at once.

"Mrs Fawley?"

"Caroline please. And Marius always called you Sheila to me."

"Yes, he always does. I know it's too early to talk about the funeral, with the police and the coroner and so on involved, but I just wanted to say, Caroline, that I do hope you will come –"

"That's very kind."

"I didn't want there to be any embarrassment about it. *Of course* you should be there. He would have wanted it, we both know that. I shan't actually be ringing anyone else, I mean any of his earlier girlfriends, because I wouldn't want it to become a sort of circus, but we'll expect to see you."

"Thank you. Perhaps the children would like to come too – I don't know."

"Alexander and Stella will be very welcome. I feel I know them already."

Caroline thought she needed to make some kind of return gesture.

"How are you coping?" she asked.

"Just about. It's so totally out of the blue, isn't it? And there's the complication of the baby on the way. I feel I'd like someone adult around the house, at least until it comes. Some really competent au pair, perhaps. Not like me to feel so nervous and uncertain."

"It's totally understandable."

"And then there's the daunting thought of bringing it up without

98

a father ... I'll get used to all these things before long, but at the moment ... Well, I expect you can guess how I feel."

"Yes, I think I can – something of it, anyway."

"Anyway, I must go. So sad that this has spoiled your excitement over *Forza*. It sounds a fabulous début. I'm determined to see it, but I think it will have to be on tour in Nottingham or Hull now."

"Good. I hope you enjoy it. I thought she was very good, but then I would, wouldn't I."

When she had put the phone down Caroline felt rather dissatisfied with the conversation. Going through it as she might go through a playscript she realised she had first felt unease when Sheila had said "He always does," which was compounded when she had mentioned that she wouldn't be ringing any of her predecessors as Marius's bedpartner. Perfectly reasonable things to say, but both things bringing it home to her rather brutally that she was the latest in a long line. Well, she was, wasn't she?

No, she wasn't. She was special. Though, trying to be fair, she could understand that Sheila might not want to see it like that.

Then there was the bit about bringing up the new baby without a father. Well, she had been planning to bring it up without its real father before that, even if she'd been unaware that Marius was not sure he was willing to treat the baby as his own. Perhaps she hadn't realized how much Marius had told her, Caroline. But why bring it up at all?

Caroline wished she hadn't *thanked* Sheila for saying she would be welcome at the funeral. She wished she had just gone.

"Was that Guy's mother?" asked Mrs Hogbin from the kitchen passage.

"That's right. Marius's wife."

"Mr Fleetwood's *widow*. You could have been that."

Big deal, thought Caroline.

She got rid of Mrs Hogbin eventually, explaining that she couldn't drive her to the bus stop because the police had put a seal on the garage and the car. This was news to Mrs Hogbin, who opened her eyes wide and then looked ominous. She obviously was conceiving the idea that the police were about to arrest *someone* in the house.

The thought made her day, and she trotted off to make the most of this information in Marsham, and then in her home village.

When the children came home from school Caroline told them about the phone call from Sheila, and when she mentioned the funeral they said they'd think about whether they wanted to go. That means no, she thought. What child or adolescent *wants* to go to a funeral? A thought struck her.

"Have either of you been using the garden tool-shed?"

"No," they both said.

"Only I found the padlock hanging open, and I know I locked it securely when I last put tools away."

"Alex has probably been using the tool shed to smoke in," said Stella.

"Sneak!" shouted Alexander. "How did you know?"

"I saw you up a dark alleyway in Leeds. I thought you were peeing, but you turned out to be smoking. I expect you've been skulking out to have a quick drag in the garden shed for months, haven't you?"

Caroline felt obliged to chip in.

"Alexander, I *am* disappointed in you! Smoking is so bad for the voice, you know."

"Mother, I'm not thinking of becoming an actor or a singer."

"Well no, I don't suppose you are. But what a habit to take up nowadays! So old-fashioned!"

"Mum, don't you ever look at young people? We're all smoking these days. It's a way of living dangerously. But I haven't been smoking in the tool-shed. I'd probably set fire to something and get myself incinerated. Anyway, it hasn't rained for ages, so I've just gone to the little bit of lawn under the apple trees, where you can't be seen from the house." A look passed between brother and sister that was not one of hostility. "I think you should tell the police about it."

"The police?" said Caroline. "Oh, surely not. It can't have anything to do with Marius's murder. It was probably just some rough-sleeper finding shelter for the night."

"The rough sleeper would have had to get into our kitchen and find the key if you really shut it properly."

100

"I'll ask Mrs Hogbin if she's been out there for something. Or perhaps Wilks has been up while we've been out. He sometimes borrows tools from us for his other gardening jobs."

"Mum – *tell the police,*" said Stella.

* * *

P.C. Omkar Rani was used to getting racial abuse in his job. He got more than if he was working in a corner shop, though rather less than if he had been a traffic warden. Words like "wog", "blackie" and "Paki" (this last no longer geographical, merely a synonym of the others) could be heard in the police canteen as well as in the street, in spite of all the pious words and intermittent efforts of chief constables. In this matter Detective Sergeant Peace had been his role model, though Rani had not always found his advice easy to follow. "Just smile, as if you thoroughly enjoy being racially abused," he had said, when Rani had asked him how he coped. "Then, if the opportunity arises, thump him in the bollocks as hard as you're able. Metaphorically speaking, of course."

P.C. Rani had asked what he should do if it was a woman, and was told it was perfectly possible to thump a woman in the bollocks metaphorically speaking.

"And remember, you'll probably only be able to do it to one in five of the bastards who've abused you, but the feeling is so sweet you can forget the other four you've had to let get away with it."

But that Monday night Rani's problem was quite a different one. He was one of the team trying to do blanket coverage of the people in the CASPAR flats, and the woman he was currently talking to was just too nice for words, pressing coffee on him, talking as if he was her oldest friend, praising his courage in going into the police, and generally trying to make him feel he was the answer to all the country's ills and woes. She has a problem with me, he said to himself. If I was white she would treat me politely, but she would be cool and businesslike. Her name was Rhoda Moncrieff, and she was the third tenant he had interviewed on the floor he had been allotted after the team had penetrated the wire gates and the staff security men. Miss Moncrieff was assistant manager of one of the big stores in Briggate, and Rani wondered what it was like to be black and one of her counter assistants.

"Just tell me what you want, give me time to think because I only heard of this awful thing today, and I'll try to tell you what you need to know." The gush was less in the words than the manner, and she capped it with a winning smile from her end of the long white leather sofa. "I want to do my best for Mr Fleetwood, because really we were both in the same trade."

"Saturday night," said P.C. Rani. "From 7.40 onwards. What were you doing?"

"Right," said Rhoda Moncrieff, and she really did think. Then she reached over to a coffee table and took up a copy of the *Radio Times*. "I'm ashamed to say I ate a risotto off my lap watching *Blind Date*. Are you a bachelor? Can you understand?"

"I am, but I live with my parents."

"Of course. Now *Blind Date* was a bit later than usual, and I finished my meal and switched it off before it ended. That would be around 7.30."

"Good. And what did you do then?"

"I took my plate to the kitchen, put it under the tap, then poured myself another glass of wine, and went over to the window."

She pointed to a wide window, with a view over to North Street. Rani had taken a peek while she was pouring him his coffee.

"Why did you go over to the window?"

"Why? Well, I often do. I'd switched on the television again because there was a concert on BBC2. You can't say I'm not catholic in my tastes, can you? Simon Rattle and the Berlin Philharmonic. I wasn't interested in the first piece – the *Daphnis and Chloe Suite* – but I wanted to watch the next one, which was Beethoven's Seventh."

"So you were at the window, watching what?"

"Not the stars, anyway! I like people. I watch them. In a way it's my job. *You* must understand, Constable. It's your job too, isn't it?"

"It certainly is," said Rani, feeling that the false sincerity in his voice was almost as bad as the gush in hers. "Is this area good for people-watching?"

"Not really, no. Not as good as my last flat. It's *near* to places – lots of clubs, and the Grand Theatre, and of course the main shops – but it's not on the way to anywhere. Around here there's really nothing much, is there? So you see a few drunks, taking the air and not really sure where they are – but that's later on as a rule."

"What about when you were watching: seven-thirty to eight-ish?"

"A bit betwixt and between. Earlier you'd see the shop people and the office people leaving work, some of the residents in these flats coming home. Those are regulars, and after a time you don't notice people you see regularly any more. There'd have been a few of our residents coming back on Saturday, those in the retail trade probably, though we must have a few workaholics in all sorts of jobs, but mostly from restaurants, trips to London or Manchester, visits to elderly mums and dads. So those would be the sort I wouldn't particularly notice ... I do remember a courting couple, very sweet and swoony and old-fashioned they looked –"

"Young?"

"Oh yes. Late teens I should think .... Then there was a roughly-dressed young man – weather-beaten, in jeans, open-necked shirt, though there was a nip in the air, and a long coat. I thought he might be one of those that beg outside the theatre ... Then there was – yes! this might be it, I think – there was an older man, who I noticed because he was wearing a very swish suit."

"Yes, this could be it," said Rani. "When?"

She thought.

"It was when the Ravel was ending and the Beethoven was about to start. Because I watched him: he was walking up North Street, and he seemed to be about to cross the road – towards where the Crescent Hotel is – come and see." She drew him to the window. "There."

"Right," said Rani, looking towards the shabby establishment on the far side of the street below.

"And I thought: 'He's not going to be staying in a dump like The Crescent,'" said Rhoda Moncrieff, "and he stepped back on to the pavement, probably because a car was coming, and at that point

103

there was applause on the television, so I came away from the window for the introduction to the Beethoven, and I didn't see anything else."

"Pity – but not your fault," said Rani, not wanting to seem to criticise so obliging, and so potentially valuable, a witness. "So you stayed on this sofa for however long the Beethoven is, did you?"

"Yes – say between thirty and forty minutes."

"And did you go back to the window after that?"

"Yes. Yes I did. Say by then it was around half-past eight." She took up the *Radio Times* again. "Yes, the concert ended at eight twenty-five. By then the light was definitely poor. And I'm afraid I didn't see the smartly dressed man again though I stood here, watching and sipping, for some time." She saw Rani's face fall, and fell over herself to make up for his disappointment. "But I did see something funny. This time it was a woman. Smartly dressed again – oh, definitely: long fur coat down to the calves – possibly not real fur these days, of course, even if she was really fashionable. Long dress underneath, I could just see that, and I think heavily made up. There was an operatic first night at the Grand, so I thought she might have come out at interval time. And she really *did* go to the Crescent Hotel. Because I thought it must be going up in the world. Or getting a reputation for a certain sort of assignation."

"Let's be quite clear about this," said Rani. "You actually saw her go in?"

"Oh definitely."

"And she didn't come straight out, having found out she'd gone to the wrong place or something?"

"She didn't come out in the next twenty minutes."

When Rani gave a detailed account of this interview next day to Charlie and Mike Oddie he found receptive ears: they even made a tape of his account, to make sure that nothing was missed.

"What can a fashionably-dressed lady do in a hotel that takes twenty-minutes plus?" asked Charlie cheekily.

"Borrow my copy of Alan Clark's diaries," said Oddie.

Chapter Eleven

Probing

In the car from Leeds to Marsham on Tuesday morning, with two uniformed constables male and female in the back, Oddie and Charlie talked of strategies for the coming interviews.

"You've seen more of Caroline Fawley than I have," Oddie said. "What's your opinion?"

"Too contradictory and all-over-the-place to summarise easily," said Charlie, keeping his eye on the road, but trying to visualise her. "On the plus side: intelligent, perceptive, civilised. On the minus side: a dead loss where her own emotions are concerned. They paralyse her judgment. Presumably the two marriages are evidence of this. During all her talk about Marius I had this feeling of rose-coloured spectacles: the wife being pregnant by an unknown boyfriend – couldn't be Marius because it had been a marriage in name only for years. Smell of stinking fish there. *And* in his supposed ownership of Alderley, as I found out from Sir John: he was renting it. This was a temporary affair for him, not a 'Till Death Do Us Part' one. So the intelligence, the human understanding, aren't operative in certain situations. Unless of course she's acting. I think she's doing that a lot. She emphasizes words as if she's in a play."

"And the children?"

"Oh, that's even more difficult, because I didn't see enough of them to judge, and of course I've never met the eldest. Alexander and Stella are mid-teens, unformed – anything could happen to make them quite different people."

"You don't believe the child is father to the man?"

Charlie thought.

"Sometimes maybe. But often they change when they go out into the world – having independence, making their own decisions, makes them new people. Not surprising, is it? Dear old Wordsworth – yes, I *do* know who wrote that –"

"Of course you would. Married to an academic."

"Ex-academic, aspirant novelist. Dear old Wordsworth may have felt the childhood him in the adult him, but other people look back on their early years and think: 'Who the hell *was* that?'"

"Fair enough. What are these children like *now*?"

"The boy is quiet – far from the unbuttoned type. Computer geek. Likes secrets, I think. Whether he hugs them to himself or whether he can be persuaded to give them up through flattering his self-importance I suppose we'll find out. Also whether he's interested in *using* them. Stella is more outgoing, I think. Starting to be very interested in men, something of a tease, with a mind of her own. Close to her mother, but I would guess she understands the situation there."

They were approaching Marsham, and Charlie concentrated on finding the right roads. From the back of the car the middle-aged P.C., Stan Hargreaves, let out a *cri-de-coeur*.

"I 'ope you're right that the child isn't father to the man – when it's a woman anyway. Because if my daughter as a woman is anything like my daughter as a child, she's goin' to make some poor man the stroppiest wife in 'istory!"

They split up when they got to Alderley, Mike Oddie interviewing Caroline in the big sitting room, with W.P.C. Dutton at his side, and Charlie talking to the children individually in a small, under-used study, with P.C. Hargreaves as his lieutenant. Stella went first, and marched in with no obvious shyness or fear of incriminating herself. Charlie introduced Hargreaves, but felt no further need to pander to her youth or make chat before the main business.

"Now, I want you to go over what you did on Saturday night as if you haven't talked to me about it at all. Talk to P.C. Hargreaves here if that will help: he hasn't heard it and hasn't been told it."

Stella turned to the middle-aged P.C. with a dazzling smile, as if rehearsing for a career as a vamp. She's going to be a stunner, both policemen thought simultaneously.

"Right," she said, ticking events off on her fingers. "Parents go off to Leeds around six, I think. Guy immediately suggests we take Mum's car and go off too. Seems like a good idea to us, so we go off to Leeds as well."

"Why Leeds, when there was a danger you'd bump into your parents?" asked Hargreaves.

"Most of the other towns we could go to are a drag at weekends. Leeds is big enough for us to be able to keep away from the sort of place Marius might go to. He was the only one we had to watch for. Mum and Olivia – not that *she'd* care – would be busy in the theatre."

"And when you got there?" prompted Charlie.

"Right. We drove around, and finally found somewhere to park down near the Law Courts. Then we separated and went off to do our own things."

"And what was your thing?"

A tiny shadow crossed her face and was gone.

"Well, farting around for the first hour or two. Just looking at places, seeing what was going on. You can't actually get into anything much if you're only fourteen." She looked at them with a hint of provocativeness. "I can look a lot older if I try, but Ghastly Guy sprang it on us, this trip to Leeds, so I didn't have the time I needed. Anyway I walked around, had a coffee and a bite to eat, caught my brother smoking up one of those little ginnels off Briggate, had a horrible cheeseburger down near the station somewhere, then got rather fed up with the time I still had to waste. I made my way up to the Grand Theatre, though I'd intended to keep away from there. The interval was well over, so knowing Mum was in the stalls I slipped up to the Dress Circle and told the attendants there I was Olivia's sister. One of them said I had the look of my mother, and she let me slip in with her at the back of the Circle and watch for a bit. Olivia wasn't on, but her Colm was, with a baritone. It really wasn't bad. I thought Colm was hot when he came to Alderley, and he looked marvellous on stage. Olivia goes through them like paper handkerchiefs. I don't think she notices whether they're hot or not. They're just notches on a stick for her."

"How long were you there?"

"Oh, twenty minutes maybe. I think it was about quarter to ten when I went out again. I decided Leeds wasn't much fun for someone my age, so I just went to the Odeon and sat through a bit of a film till it was time to start back to the car. I didn't even see the end of the film – not that it mattered, because it was dead boring." She perked up a fraction. "But I can tell you the plot, roughly, to prove I was there."

"Do you read detective stories?" asked Charlie. She drooped.

"Yes. Is it that obvious?"

"Let's just say it wouldn't be much use you telling us the plot, since Mr Fleetwood probably died in the early part of the evening, so far as the preliminary report would suggest."

"So he was already lying there? ... Poor old Marius. He was a bit of a bullshitter, but he didn't deserve that."

"What was your opinion of Mr Fleetwood?"

"Well, let's just say that if your colleague is talking to my mother, he should be taking several pinches of salt: knock off the halo she puts around his head, throw a few handfuls of mud at the pure whiteness of his robes, then the picture might be closer to the truth."

"In what ways did he pull the wool over your mother's eyes, do you think?"

"She was just his bit on the side." She made an attempt to look worldly wise, and came within an inch of succeeding. "He was accustomed to having one, and she was his latest. She wasn't the centre of his life, and she'd have been dropped the moment he was tired of her. He set her up in this place because *he* liked a bit of luxury and elegance. He wouldn't have wanted to spend his weekends in an old semi – quite apart from the fact that Acton, where we used to live, would have been too close to home for him."

"Have you any evidence of all this?"

"No. But would you care to bet on it?"

"No, I wouldn't. What about his son?"

"Ghastly Guy? He was back at the car when I went back to the Law Courts. I don't think he'd found the swinging Leeds scene as riveting as he'd hoped."

"I meant what did you think of him?"

She paused before replying.

"You'd better ask Alexander about Guy. He knows a lot more."

"But you must have an opinion."

"I think he's a pathetic little twerp."

* * *

"It was love at first sight," said Caroline. "I know that sounds corny. *All* this is going to sound corny. That's how it was, though."

"How did it happen?"

"I was eating in an Italian restaurant with a friend. Female. I'd just been in an awful comedy that flopped in the West End – taken off after only three weeks. The friend had to leave early to get to the theatre – she was in a quite successful transfer from the National. I was on my own, just ordering coffee, when this man came over, said he was sorry about the play, that I deserved better, and could he order both of us a brandy and could he drink his with me."

"And after that?"

She shrugged, and smiled tearfully.

"After that the next thing I knew was he was in bed with me, and I wished we never had to leave it."

Oddie wondered how many women had similar stories about Marius Fleetwood.

"And then quite soon after that you were here at Alderley, and the arrangement was an established thing?"

"That's right. Within a month or two. That's nearly a year and a half ago. I still had some television work to do, but I could commute, and one of the things was *Heartbeat*, which is filmed here in Yorkshire, so it all worked out beautifully."

"But now you've given up your career – I suppose that was your own decision?"

"Oh, very much so. I think Marius would have quite liked it if he was associated with someone who was on the television a lot of the time. But as soon as I saw this place, and got settled in, I thought 'This is it.' Being *with* the children all the time, there when they needed me. And having Marius come up every weekend. Those days were just – I can't explain – *wonderful*! The crowning point of my life. They made me feel that all those years as a moderately successful actress had been a waste of time."

"And it didn't worry you that you were – to put it bluntly – a weekend mistress, and he also had a five-days-a-week wife?"

"No. It had become a marriage only in name: they lived entirely separate lives. But he never tried to run Sheila down, make her ridiculous in my eyes or tell nasty demeaning stories about her. He was *tender* towards her, and concerned about how I should regard her, and I thought that was nice, chivalrous. It said a lot about how he regarded women, how he thought they should be treated."

Oddie changed the subject.

"There hasn't been any problems with people in the village? I would guess there would have been plenty, twenty or thirty years ago."

"Probably there would have been. I don't think the swinging 'sixties made much of an impact in places such as Marsham. But over the years, almost without people noticing it, things do change, and attitudes. I've been made *very* welcome, and the children too. My big friend in the village is Jack – Sir John Mortyn-Crosse, a *lovely* man. He tells me your sergeant has already talked to him. I hope he didn't regard him as some sort of rival for my affections, who stabbed Marius in the middle of a quarrel over me."

"No, not at all."

"Because we're just good friends. There's another whopping cliché for you. But we really *are*."

"I gather from my sergeant that there had been some talk recently between you and Mr Fleetwood, as to whether things should go on quite as they have been doing."

"You mean Sheila's pregnancy? I have to admit that that did come as a bolt from the blue. I mean, knowing how things were between them, and not knowing her age: I'd assumed she was about Marius's age, that is probably beyond childbearing, and if not that, then too sensible, if you get my meaning. It's all a bit of a *mystery*, who the boyfriend is. But we decided – at least for the moment, but probably long-term as well – to let things go on as before. The present set-up ... sorry, the set-up as it was until Saturday, suited us, suited our lives and routines. So in the circumstances it didn't seem to us that something that we had nothing to do with needed to change it. The baby actually coming, and Marius not wanting to be its nominal father, might have made a difference, but somehow I don't think either of us thought that would happen, or if it did that it would alter things. We so wanted things to continue as they are ... were. They were so *perfect*."

Without the slightest sense of any snake in the Eden under-growth, Oddie thought. And P.C. Dutton was barely able to keep the scepticism she felt from showing on her face.

*   *   *

Alexander came into the little study, rather nervous, rather uncertain, but also rather, under the surface, pleased with himself. He's got something for us, Charlie thought. Whether he's going to give it up easily, or only after I've played him for hours, is another matter.

"Basically I just wandered around," he said, when Charlie got down to the matter of what he did on Saturday night. "Seeing what it was about Leeds and its club scene that everyone says is so fantastic."

"And did you find out?"

"Not really. I think it only takes off when the pubs close, and we had to leave too early for that. I saw a lot, had the odd drink in the sort of place where they don't ask any questions about age, but that was about it, really. Anyway I'm not sure I'm ever going to be a clubber."

He was practically asking to be asked, Charlie thought.

"You say you saw a lot," he said. "Anything in particular?"

"Well ..." If there was any desire to string it out longer, the desire lost. Alexander had found one occasion when broadcasting a secret was better than hoarding it. "Can we go forward a bit?"

"Of course, if it will help."

Alexander sat for a moment, putting his thoughts in order.

"The next morning, Sunday morning, I had to get up early to go to the loo. I was on the landing when I heard a noise downstairs.

There were no lights on, but there was enough light to see by coming through the hall windows. I saw Guy come in from the door to the back garden, lock it, then go into the kitchen with keys in his hand – two keys."

"I see. And what do you make of that?"

"Yesterday Mum noticed that the shed for the garden tools had been opened and not shut properly. It's a stroppy old padlock, and you have to really click it in to lock it securely."

"I see. So – again – what do you make of that?"

"Right. Go back to Saturday night. I was going around, just looking, seeing where the popular clubs were, casing the pubs where the younger people hang out. That was interesting, because a lot of the pubs are down little alleyways – ginnels or snickets I think they call them. And you can hang about in the darkness outside and watch."

Charlie sat there wondering who he had seen. Marius Fleetwood? Guy? His sister Olivia? No, of course she'd been on stage, or in the theatre anyway.

"Go on," he said.

"I saw Guy, working his way in with a group of six or seven young people. I think he'd had somebody pointed out to him. Because after a bit he started trying to work this bloke out of the group. He seemed rather older, this man, closer to thirty than to twenty. They got a bit aside, and were talking low. Like they were negotiating. Then the other one looked at his watch, nodded his head in the direction of the Gents, and left the pub. Ten minutes later Guy headed in the direction of the loo, and a minute or two after that the man came back to the pub and went straight to the Gents as well."

"You're suggesting a drugs transaction?"

"That's what it looked like."

"Half the young people in Central Leeds will be taking something on a Saturday night."

"I'm looking at it in conjunction with the early morning trip to the garden. It wasn't something he was going to take himself. It was something he was going to *hide*. He was already in the car when

Stella and I got back to it in the Law Courts area. We got there five minutes early, from different directions. He was there, comfortably in the driver's seat, looking as if he'd been there for some time. He wanted to be sure he could put something in the boot or the glove compartment – no, that would be too dangerous – without our seeing. It must have been the boot, so he went and retrieved it next morning, in case the car was used, and rather than keep it in his bedroom, he concealed it in the garden shed. There's a lot of old sacks and packets of compost and stuff, and nobody ever gardens while Marius is down. There was no chance of its being found – and anyway if it was he'd have denied all knowledge of it."

"That's easy enough to check, isn't it? said Charlie" ... I take it you and your sister didn't much like Guy."

"Condescending git," said Alexander, without a great deal of obvious animosity. "Shows off the fact that he's got all the right clothes, all the right software, all the right everything except brain. But it's not that. We want to find out who did this. Otherwise it will be hanging over Mum for the rest of her life. It will be difficult enough to persuade her to put Marius behind her without an unsolved murder holding her back."

"That makes sense," said Charlie, mentally reserving his judgment. "I take it, then, that you'll want to pass on any other information you might have – so that we can look at it, decide whether it has any relevance to the murder."

"Yes. Yes I would," said Alexander, with increasing conviction. "I can't say I've got any *information*. I mean, Stella and I had had our suspicions about Marius. He was the great love of Mum's life, but was she the great love of his? He was a serial adulterer, and we thought Mum was going to turn out to be just one more episode. But you'll be thinking along those lines too, I suppose."

"We're keeping the possibility in mind. Was there anything else you wanted to tell us?"

"Well, there was something. Not something secret or anything, but I bet Mum won't have told your boss about it."

"Why would she want to keep this thing secret?"

"Because she doesn't want anyone connected with him to be the murderer. She doesn't want that sort of hatred to have any place in her beautiful picture of Marius. I expect she hopes it will have been done by some passing tramp – or passing schizophrenic's more likely these days, isn't it? But in fact everyone says it's usually somebody close."

"Usually. Close in one way or another. Who are we talking about?"

"A boy. His name is Pete Bagshaw, and he's about twenty or so. He came here three or four weeks ago. Mum invited him in, fed him, let him have a bath ... The thing is, he looked exactly like Marius. A young Marius."

Charlie digested this.

"Let me get this right. A young man – someone none of you had ever met before, is that right?"

"Yes."

" – came here, and your mother invited him in and so on, and – well, did they discuss Marius and his resemblance to him?"

"Not while we were there, and I don't think before that. I suspect *he* saw she registered the resemblance, she saw he realized this, and the whole subject was not raised openly. But as he was leaving Mum suggested he come again, when Marius was here. And he said 'Better not', or something like that."

"That's pretty bizarre."

"Well, maybe. But she raised it later with Marius, and he said he'd never lived in Leeds, but he'd had a scapegrace brother who did – now dead."

Charlie blinked, then tried to keep his face neutral. Was this another of Fleetwood's lies?

"I see. This young man lives in Leeds, does he?"

"Yes, Armley."

"Anything else you know about him?"

"Doing a computer course at Leeds Metropolitan University. Mother works in a supermarket. He's got a bit of a thing about her. How she's slaved away for a pittance for years, and how he wants to get a good job, earn loads of dosh, so she can live in comfort."

"I see. Well, thanks for all the information. Maybe it's time I went to have a look at the garden shed. Perhaps it would be best if you pointed it out to me and found me the key, then made yourself scarce. Guy Fleetwood is supposed to be arriving this afternoon, isn't he?" Alexander nodded. "Best if he doesn't associate you with any find we might make. Ah – is that the living room door?"

They all went out into the hall. Caroline was emerging from her interview. She smiled at Charlie waterily as she walked through and up to the bathroom. Charlie put his head around the door of the living room.

"Could you come with me for a moment, sir?"

Oddie nodded, and together they went to the back door. Alexander came out of the kitchen with a key, pointed to a shed at the far end of the garden, then scuttled off.

"Get anything out of her?" asked Charlie as they walked across the lawn.

"A lot of stuff about her beautiful relationship with the deceased. I wouldn't call it sub-Barbara Cartland, but it wasn't more than a notch or two better. I got a detailed account of everything that happened on Saturday night, though, and that could be useful. What are we expecting to find here?"

Charlie opened the padlock with some effort.

"Wait and all will be revealed. Now – nothing visible to the naked eye, but that wasn't to be expected. But these sacks and plastic bags look as if they have been moved around a bit, don't they? Carefully does it ... *There*. I think that must be what we're looking for."

There, wrapped in plastic, exposed by the removal of several smelly packages, was a white block – solid, substantial, and very valuable. They were just about to move closer when Oddie's eye was caught by a movement on the lawn. He turned back to the door, and saw a young man approaching at a fast rate. When Charlie too appeared in the doorway he registered their presence and pulled up sharply, then turned and began to run. He only noticed P.C. Hargreaves a second before the burly policeman, who had followed him through the house, appeared in the back door. It was too late, and he was brought down by an efficient rugby tackle just as Oddie and Charlie ran over.

"Guy Fleetwood, I presume?" said Oddie, standing over him.

*   *   *

"You can knock off for the night," said Oddie to Charlie, when Guy Fleetwood was safely banged up in a custody cell. "Go home and play tickle-toes with young Carola."

"Young Carola is way, way beyond playing tickle-toes. She is already weighing up her various career options."

"No chance of her choosing the police force, if she's as intelligent as you claim."

"Not a chance in hell ... What are you planning to do?"

"I'm going up to the Grand Theatre. Margaret is there for *Forza*, so I know the eldest Fawley is there. I thought she might be willing to talk to me, either at interval or after the performance. Then we can say we've done all the Fawleys, at least for the moment."

But when he put the same request to the stage door keeper the man raised his eyebrows, then scribbled the request on a bit of paper and sent his junior off with it.

"Bit of a tartar when the fancy takes her," he said with a wink to Oddie. "I didn't want her blasting my ear off down the phone with you standing by listening. Between ourselves I don't give much for your chances before the thing ends at ten-fifteen or so. The talk is she likes to have it off with someone in Interval. Says it does wonders for her voice. Someone said Dame Nellie thought the same, but she had to pay them or lasso them. This one doesn't have to. Quite tasty for an opera singer."

Oddie heard the five-minute warning bell when the boy came back with the expected response: she would see him after the opera, and definitely not at interval time. He nodded to the stage doorkeeper, and on an impulse went round to the main entrance, where the last stragglers were hurrying to their places in the stalls. He flashed his ID at the woman on the door and the woman selling programmes.

"It's the Marius Fleetwood murder enquiry," he said.

"*Really*! We wondered if you'd want to quiz us!" said one. "Everyone's talking about it," said the other.

"Saturday night, the first night: you were here then?"

"Oh yes! Very exciting. Best first night in a long time," was the collective response.

"Were you around here when Mr Fleetwood left the stalls?"

"Oh yes, if we've got the right one. Very smart man, well set up, someone you'd notice. He hurried down the corridor, smiled at us, then out towards the street. We commented on what a shame it was when tickets were at a premium. We didn't know of his ... connection, you might say, with Miss Fawley."

"And did anyone else leave, maybe soon afterwards?"

"No one else left," the programme seller said emphatically. "Not from the stalls, nor from the Circle or Gallery. We've been talking about it among ourselves. If anyone left it would have to have been during Interval, and I doubt anyone did. No one spotted empty seats in the second half. It was such an exciting night everyone stayed."

"Well, I hope tonight's the same," said Oddie, calculatingly. "My wife's there."

"Would you like to stand at the back?" asked the programme seller. "You being police it would be perfectly all right."

So Oddie let her lead him up the corridor, then through the door into the stalls. As he took up his position he could feel the excitement in the house, become part of it, even though the overture was still being played. And when the dumb-show finished and the scene started he shared in the thrill of hearing a gorgeous voice: fresh, expressive, of seemingly limitless power. He was no expert, but no expertise is necessary to respond to the human voice in full flood. By the time the scene ended with Don Alvaro's flagrant disregard of elementary firearms precautions, a dying father and the lovers escaping separately into the night, Oddie was hooked, on the opera, on the voice.

But he looked at his watch. Twenty to eight. That was when Fleetwood had slipped out of the theatre, then.

By Interval Oddie was half in love with Olivia Fawley. The scene with the Padre Guardiano and the monks was like a benison after a gruelling day, but the cheers of the audience set the adrenalin flowing again. He slipped out to be the first at the bar, and eventually found his wife Margaret, having a quiet cigarette with a friend in Briggate.

"What on earth are you doing here?"

"Watching the opera, as it's turned out. Actually waiting to interview the star. I've been allowed to stand at the back because I'm a policeman, and therefore not like ordinary mortals. Can I borrow your programme to discover what's going on, or do I have to buy one?"

"Borrow mine – they cost the earth."

So when the curtain went up on the tenor agonising, as he was to do for much of the rest of the opera, Oddie was clued up on the tortuous events which made up the plot. Some twenty minutes into the second half a thought struck him – a possibility. Twenty minutes after that the possibility was becoming a conviction. He slipped out into the corridor and read the programme again. Then he scribbled a note to Olivia Fawley telling her he was called away and would talk to her the next day. He slipped round to the stage door again, and left it with the keeper.

Coming out of the stage door he turned towards Briggate, then strode in the direction of the Crescent Hotel.

Chapter Twelve

Love Nest

Oddie dallied as he began up North Street. To his left were the CASPAR Apartments, with perhaps half of the visible windows lit up. Beyond that circular block were the sloping lawns, at the top of which, among the ill-kempt bushes, Marius Fleetwood had been found dead. There were no police there now, but the occasional street lamp showed some straggling lengths of police tape near where the body had been. Oddie continued along to where Rani's witness had seen the smartly-dressed man about to cross the road. The traffic, by this time of night, was spasmodic. Oddie was able to cross towards the dingy exterior of the Crescent Hotel without difficulty.

All you could say for the hotel was that its name was not totally mendacious. North Street, at that point, did form a sort of curve that might be dignified as a crescent. But the wooden sign that announced the name was cracked, the paint on the letters peeling, as it was too on the window frames and door. Through the window he could see the foyer. At the desk a man was reading the *West Yorkshire Chronicle* with his feet up on the shelf behind it. When Oddie pushed open the doors the griminess of the foyer almost choked him, as if a dusty grey blanket had been thrown over his head. Maybe the place appealed to you if you were a connoisseur of Leeds Rugby League teams of yesteryear. The team photos, replete with self-satisfaction and thuggish glares, glowered at you from all the walls. But other than these there was nothing to attract anyone even of the oddest tastes to the place.

The man behind the desk folded his newspaper without haste.

"Want a room? I can do you one for thirty-seven, fifty."

His dirty white shirt was open at the neck, and he wore trainer bottoms to cover his lower half. His teeth were stained and gapped, and strands of his hair had been half-heartedly combed over his pre-vailing baldness. Oddie reflected that the rate for the room was probably no worse value than the hundred and fifty pounds charged by some very ordinary London hotels.

"No thanks," he said, taking out his ID. "Police."

The man screwed up his face, but Oddie would have betted that he knew what was coming.

"Police! Well, that's a bleedin' turn-up. We've never had much 'assle from the police before."

That at any rate was true. Oddie had checked, and the computer had only showed three suicides and a natural death in the last five years. The suicides he could understand.

"You mean the police haven't had much hassle from you," he said. "I knew that."

"Is it that death over near the CASPARS?" asked the man.

"Yes, it is. And you are? –"

"Les Cartwright. I own this place, worse bleedin' luck."

Oddie nodded.

"We're checking the last hours of Marius Fleetwood, the dead man. He had a chain of supermarkets down south. We think it possible he came here, or to one of the shops or offices near here. Swish, well-set up man of around fifty."

"Doesn't sound much like our customers, does it?" said Les Cartwright. He paused as if he was awaiting Oddie's next question, but when he spoke it was obvious he was considering his own position. "I suppose I better come clean. No, I never seen a swish, well-set-up man 'ere on Saturday night – that is when we're talking about, isn't it?"

"Yes. Towards eight o'clock."

"Well, the fact is, like I said, our customers aren't great dressers, so I've never had in 'ere the sort of man you described, so far as I can call to mind. Still, to tell the truth, I was half-expecting someone like that on Saturday night."

"Half-expecting? What do you mean?"

Cartwright looked straight at him, for almost the first time, cunning and guilt mingled in his face.

"I don't know how I'm gunna make you believe this. Maybe the best way would be to show you. Come wi' me."

He raised the flap of his desk and came out into the foyer, heading towards the stairs. Oddie noticed there was a sign saying LIFT, but it looked as if it had been out of order since the days of Harold Wilson. Cartwright walked boldly up the stairs, automatically avoiding all the places where the carpet was worn through to the boards. Oddie followed more cautiously. On the first floor they proceeded along a landing which had clearly not known the feel of a paintbrush in decades, and whose carpet was in a state of such decrepitude that its one-time pattern could only be guessed at. From one or two of the rooms came the sounds of transistor radios. At the end of the corridor Cartwright selected a key from the bunch in his hand.

"Prepare for a surprise," he said, and put his hand into the room to press a switch.

Oddie's first impression was of a flood of light. He blinked, then took a step from the dimness of the corridor into cascading brilliance. The room he entered was larger than he would have expected the Crescent to possess, with a massive bed covered by a blue and cream silk eiderdown, with an imposing bedhead in the same colours, a thick green carpet on the floor, a wonderful Art Deco table, chairs and occasional tables, most of them with vases, ashtrays and cigarette or jewel boxes in the same style. It was a wonderfully stylish room, almost like a stage set, and the impression of taste and imagination at work was supplemented by a sense of fun, of tongue in cheek. Whoever had designed this room had seen it as a challenge, perhaps, but also as a big joke.

"Bathroom in similar style," said Les Cartwright. "But I suppose you get the idea."

"But how – how come –?" began Oddie. "It all looks so new and –"

"Well, you won't need me to tell you this wasn't dreamed up by me as part of my regular renovation and redecoration programme," said Cartwright.

"No," said Oddie.

"Sit down. Might as well make use of the place. Can't see it getting much bleedin' use in the future."

Oddie eased himself into a sofa of nice clean lines in immaculate aquamarine linen covers. Les Cartwright perched himself on a similar chair opposite.

"It was three weeks since, and even then half of me said I was dreaming, and the other half said: 'Ang on – this is too good to be true. There's something funny 'ere. Maybe something that could get me into trouble.' And I was right. It was, wasn't it?"

"Not necessarily," said Oddie. "Go on."

"Well, it all started wi' a phone call, and that was a funny one too. Man at the other end asked how large was my biggest bedroom, an' I said they were all much of a muchness, give or take a foot 'ere and a foot there. And the man said that was a shame, because he'd 'ad it in mind to make me an interesting offer. I perked up at that. And that's when I remembered this place. 'Asn't been used in years, 'asn't this one. Not in my time, any road, and not for years before, I'd be willing to bet. All the rooms at one time were pretty much of a size wi' this one, but they were all divided up into two, even three, and for some reason this one was left."

"Money run out?" suggested Oddie.

"Story o' this 'otel, that would be," agreed Cartwright. "So I told him we had this disused room we used as a store, and I estimated it at about twenty by fifteen. I was near enough, too. I've been a builder in my time."

Cowboy variety, Oddie said to himself.

"So anyway, he came along to look at it, this chap: Mr Fairlie 'is name was, Walter. And he saw this room, and said 'Ideal', and put the proposition to me."

"And that was?"

"That Fairlie would redecorate the room, furnish it, put in a new bathroom, all the works, and it would be available to 'is employer for three weeks starting last Saturday, and after that it would be mine to let as I saw fit, on a par with the other rooms."

"And the catch?"

"There was none that I could see. Still can't. There was to be no cost to me. You might say a room like this will be precious little use in a hotel like the Crescent, but it's a sight more likely to make me a bob or two than a bloody box-room."

"Fair enough. So you said yes."

"'Course I did. He 'ad the builders and painters in next day, first putting in the new wall for the bathroom, then the plumbing, then a swish new bath and shower – bit too fancy for my liking, but there you are: it was meant to appeal to a lady, that much I could guess, slow on the uptake though I might be. Then the painters did this room, then Fairlie moved in to furnish it. I tell you, it was like a dream. I used to come up 'ere every evening – late, after they'd knocked off, which often was nine, ten, even later, and I couldn't believe my luck. The 'ole thing was finished last Tuesday, with two days to spare."

"You were always given to understand that Fairlie's employer would be using the room last Saturday?"

"Oh yes."

"And a woman?"

"That was mentioned on Fairlie's last visit. I winked at him to show I'd guessed that, but 'e just smiled vaguely. The arrangement was, I 'ad to 'ave two keys made for the room as well as my own: one for each. They wouldn't be arriving together. Beyond that I wasn't told anything about either of them – just one man and one woman. The classic formula, you might say."

"But it didn't take place, did it? Tell me what happened on Saturday."

"Saturday. Well, I thought it was in order to make a bit of a fuss. I got out the suit I was married in, and wi' a bit of holding in and straining of the buttons I got meself into it, even bought a cheap tie at the supermarket, something bright but dignified, if you get me. Then I waited."

"No one came."

"Not at first. 'Some time towards eight' Mr Fairlie had said, so I sat here, reading the paper, just like when you came in, but a bit more on the watch, if you catch my meaning. For a long time no one came."

"You didn't see anyone outside that fitted the description?"

"I wasn't looking outside. It's a while since I cleaned them windows any road. I was on the watch for that front door to open so I could get to my feet an' salute, in a manner o' speaking. Nothing 'appened. Then about – oh – a quarter to nine, in came this bird, and

I thought 'This must be 'er.' And it was. Asked for the key to Room 118 cool as you like and went upstairs."

"What was she like, this woman?"

Les Cartwright scratched his chin.

"Not my line really, describin' people."

"Take your time. What age, roughly?"

"Say towards thirty."

"Face?"

"'Eavily made up. Lipstick, powder, the lot – more than most women would use nowadays. Eye colour? 'Aven't the faintest. Don't spend my time looking for the colour o' people's eyes. Full cheeks, strong voice."

"Dressed in?"

"Long fur coat over long black dress. 'Some classy bird who's at the Grand Theatre,' I said to meself, an' I bet that's what it was. Tells 'er bloke she's at the opera, then slips away first chance she gets. Anyway she comes up 'ere, finds a room several grades above what she's been expecting, but no man to go with it."

"You're quite sure of that? No back entrances or anything like that?"

Cartwright shook his head.

"Back door I'd've 'eard, fire escape maybe not, but 'e 'adn't got a key, remember. I'd got the keys at the desk, to be called for. Anyway, when she went out she wasn't best pleased, that I can tell you."

"Did she say anything?"

"She did when she tripped on a bit o' frayed carpet 'alf way down the stairs. 'Fuckin' 'ell!' she said, loud as you like, lady though she was or tried to pretend she was. Then she threw the key at the desk, muttered something about 'aving been made a fool of, and marched through the foyer and out. And that was the last I saw of the two who this room 'ad been dreamed up for."

"So what are you going to do now?" asked Oddie.

"I'm going to phone that Walter Fairlie, if you tell me this was all up to that Fleetwood character."

"I'm telling you nothing as yet, but you can give me his number."

"'Ere, 'ave 'is card. I've got it by 'eart. Apart from that, what can I do? I've got a tarty room, but I haven't the first idea what to do with it."

Oddie shook his head. "It's not tarty. It's what people call tasteful. Could be very convenient for people appearing at the Grand. You could charge so much for a quick naughty, so much for all night. They'd probably find it amusing. Slip the stage doorkeeper a tenner every time he got you a customer."

He had meant it as a joke. But as he left the room he saw the slow spread of enlightenment and calculation over Cartwright's face. This could be the saving of the Crescent Hotel. Putting the thought from his mind he went back to the Grand Theatre and saw the last half hour of the opera.

The next morning, when Oddie related his discovery to Charlie, the younger man sat for some time hunched forward in thought.

"So you think this man, if he had appeared, would have been Fleetwood?"

"It's the best explanation we've had so far for his being in that part of the town. You don't go there unless you've something specific to do there."

"You don't think he did in fact turn up at the hotel, something went wrong, and Cartwright helped dispose of the body?"

"I'll keep it in mind, but no, I don't."

"Next question: who was the classy tart?"

"She was – may have been – a lady having an assignation. These days that doesn't make her a tart."

"Things were so much easier when it did," sighed Charlie, and he went off to follow up the matter of Peter Bagshaw, unenlightened about Oddie's guess at the identity of the woman. Guesses in Oddie's view are always best left unshared until they can be rejoiced over.

Meanwhile there was the postponed interview with Olivia Fawley to be got through. When Oddie rang the people at Opera North they said they'd see what her plans for the day were, then rang back ten minutes later to say that she was coming into town anyway, and would talk with him in her dressing room. So at eleven o'clock she received him there – rather as a queen might receive someone she was about to award something rather special to, though in Olivia's case it was nothing more than her time.

"It's the matter of your mother's friend, Marius Fleetwood," Oddie began.

"Of course it is. Let's say 'lover' shall we?"

"Her lover. As you know, I suppose, he came to the theatre on Saturday but left after the first scene, about seven forty."

"Marius never pretended to be musical," said Olivia.

"But you got on well with him?"

"Perfectly well. Much better than with someone who *did* pretend to be musical. He ranked high on my mother's list of husbands and lovers."

"Is it a long list?"

"Is that relevant? ... Oh well, I suppose it could be. It's a quite moderate list for someone who is on the stage. But she's not as a rule a good picker, as she would be the first to admit. Marius was generous, considerate, tolerant – all the things she'd never had, certainly not from my father, nor from her second husband."

"Your father was this Rick Radshaw, was he?"

"That's right. He was here on Saturday, probably to claim any credit going for my success, and his current joined him for the party afterwards."

"So when Mr Fleetwood met his death – let's say the earliest would have been a bit before eight – what were you doing?"

"Oh, second scene. Scene at the inn. In view of the baritone, mezzo and the whole of the chorus, not to mention the audience."

"Yes – actually I know. I was there part of the time last night. Wonderful."

"Thank you," she said, all queenly again, after a sharpish spell.

"But the latest time he could have been killed – say nine, half past. What would you be doing then?"

"Well, if I wasn't on stage I would be in my dressing room."

Oddie's voice gained an access of silkiness.

"But there's no question of 'if' is there, Miss Fawley? The soprano has no part in the second half of the opera until the last ten or fifteen minutes. You weren't on stage from the moment the curtain came down for the interval until the very last quite short scene."

Olivia looked daggers at him.

"That's right. She becomes a hermit and not part of the action. You will know this if you were there. So at that time I must have been here in the dressing room."

"For the whole – what? hour and a half, is it? – until you're on again?"

"Yes."

He looked at what now seemed a hard, obstinate face. A fool, he thought. A talented, lovely-voiced fool. With a libido of stratospheric proportions.

"Miss Fawley, do you own a fur coat?"

She looked as if she was about to lie, but pulled herself back. Too many people at the theatre had seen her in it.

"Yes. I get a lot of flack about that, but I don't give a f – about that kind of thing. They should mind their own businesses. Anyway it's just the jealousy of the little people."

"It's a long coat, isn't it, down nearly to your ankles?"

"Yes."

"That would nearly cover the hermit robe you wear in the last scene before the interval – make people think you had an evening dress on under it."

Olivia shrugged.

"So?"

"So I think you should tell me why you went to the Crescent Hotel in North Street at around eight forty-five on Saturday night, and stayed there until nearly ten."

"The Crescent Hotel? I've never heard of it. Why would I go to a dump like that?"

"You know it's a dump then?"

"If it's not one of the well-known ones it must be a dump."

"And you are going to continue to deny that you went there on Saturday?"

"Certainly I am. Will you go now please? I've got to practice, and shopping to do after that, and all kinds of people to meet. Leave me alone."

"Certainly. But I shall be back. And you would be very unwise to refuse to see me, because you might find yourself under arrest. And arrest in connection with a high-profile murder would be no good at all for your burgeoning career, would it?"

And Oddie went, rather eagerly, out of the presence.

* * *

The Rector went on his own on Wednesday morning to visit Caroline Fawley, to administer what comfort his presence and his religion could afford her. His wife had declined to accompany him. Sir Jack had volunteered, but the Rector had tactfully turned down his suggestion. Jack's presence, he felt, would be inhibiting.

Mr Watters had a collection of phrases for the consolation of the bereaved – different phrases for each sort of loss: husband, mother, daughter and so on. He also had a number of vague phrases for when the nature of the loss was less clearly defined. He found these particularly useful when talking to parishioners whom he knew had lost someone or other but couldn't quite remember who. This happened more often that might have been expected, since his parish now comprised three villages. It was these phrases he used with Caroline, because after all nothing could be vaguer than the nature of her loss. In fact, legally speaking, she had not suffered any loss at all. So he used the sort of phrase that could have been called forth by a dead friend, or even a dead dog.

"I hesitate to say that time heals," he said in a calm, gentle voice he had perfected for such visits, "but it really does dull the pain, it really does enable us to turn our thoughts to the future. We must remember, surely, that the deceased would not want us to stop living life fully and fruitfully."

Caroline let him go on. She, who had spent her life mouthing the words of Shakespeare, Ibsen, Coward and Agatha Christie, could not object to people who worked to a prepared script. The truth was, Mr Watters's words seemed to have no relevance at all to her loss of Marius. The hard, searing pain that seemed to stab her every time her thoughts were brought back to him was a world away from his threadbare comforts. Fortunately he apparently expected no response, as if he thought he was talking to a statue. It was only when his words became a little more specific that Caroline thought she should intervene.

" ... and it will certainly be a great loss to Marsham if you decide you don't want to continue living here, with all those memories around you."

"Oh, but I do, Mr Watters," said Caroline. "They are wonderful memories, beautiful ones. I certainly don't intend to run away from them."

If Mr Watters was disappointed he was too experienced to let it show.

"That is excellent news. And it's a tribute to Mr Fleetwood that you cherish his memory so warmly."

"It is. I shall never feel any other way."

"And will you actually be able to stay on at Alderley?"

"I feel sure I will, yes."

"That is very good news for us all in the village. And I'm sure it will be pleasing too for Mr Beck."

"Mr Beck? Who? – Oh, the former owner. Alf Beck, isn't it? I don't get the impression that he cares much what happens to Alderley."

"Oh, but I don't think that's true," said the vicar. "Alf cares a lot about Alderley and the village. He'd lived here for more than forty years when he moved to Hornsea. He's a dear friend to many of us here – I phoned him only yesterday. But what I meant was he'll be pleased still to have the income from the house coming in."

Caroline was unable to suppress the impact his words had on her showing in her face. She did manage to stop herself from asking questions, from showing still more unmistakably that she did not know the house was rented. What aroused not just shame but anger was the feeling that Mr Watters had planned this conversation, had designed it to reveal this fact to her. And that he was pleased with her discomfiture.

But even as her desire to get rid of the Rector became overwhelming, her natural good manners and charm saved the situation. Smiling, she stood up.

"I really must be getting on. There's always so much to do after a death, isn't there? Distressing things, but ones you want to get done. I hope I shall see you in church on Sunday."

After he had gone she sat down and wept with pure rage. It was brief, but somehow purifying. When it was over she sat and thought out what she should do. She had a shrewd suspicion that if she were to ring Jack Mortyn-Crosse he would be able to confirm authoritatively what the Rector had just made her aware of. Suddenly many of Jack's odd or funny remarks seemed to make proper sense. But somehow she didn't want to ring him. It would be to lay bare her shock and revulsion at Marius's behaviour to an unendurably kind scrutiny. In the end she rang Directory Enquiries and got the number of Alf Beck in Hornsea. Soon she was speaking to a man with a gentle kind of Yorkshire accent.

"I was so sorry to read about it," he said. "A real gentleman, Mr Fleetwood, in all his dealings with me. I only met him the once, but I could tell he was a very pleasant man as well."

"Thank you so much," said Caroline, uneasy that the sentiments coincided rather embarrassingly with her own until that day. "Of course I'm having to think forward now. I was wondering how far ahead –"

" – the rent is paid. Of course you were. It's to the end of next month. But you're not to worry, my dear. A week or two beyond then is neither here nor there, and I wouldn't expect you to pay, not good tenants as you've been, and not after the awful shock you've had with this murder. I've been delighted to have you in the house, someone I almost feel I know from the television. And it's been a relief knowing that the furniture has been in responsible hands."

Caroline said weakly that she was very grateful, and that everyone was being so kind she didn't know what to say.

Her voice belied her mood. When she had put the phone down she felt a great rage swelling within her. It was a rage such as she had not known since she had been married to Rick. Her second husband had been too much of a nonentity to merit it, and none of her occasional lovers had measured up to it. This, she registered in the back of her mind, was not a theatrical rage, half assumed for effect and for self-satisfaction: it was the real thing. She looked around her, at the sofa with its memories of love-making, at the dinner table with its memories of intimate meals, at the garden in which he had appeared to share her pride and joy.

Sham! Everything that had happened between them was soiled. Suddenly beautiful moments could only be seen as vile deceptions. She took up the decanter from which she had always poured him his favourite Amontillado and threw it against the wall. Frustratingly the heavy glass failed to smash. A red rage possessed her, seemed to colour everything she could see with the colour of blood. She ran into the kitchen and seized the sharpest carving knife. Upstairs she found that Marius's wardrobe had been denuded of most of its contents by the police, but she took out a pair of casual trousers and slit down the legs, then cut criss-cross patterns through all the area of the crotch. Then she found his favourite shirt which had somehow got hung in her wardrobe. She seized it, and had just begun to slash it when, holding it as she was by the front, with its pocket, she realized that there was paper inside it. Taking it out she found it was a letter.

At the same time, nearing the end of his walk back to the Rectory, the Reverend Vernon Watters prepared to tell his wife the details of his visit to Mrs Fawley, aware of how eagerly she would be awaiting them, and conscious that he had achieved all he had set out to achieve. He was less conscious, perhaps, of the fact that this was the first of all his visits of condolence to the bereaved that had actually made a difference – had indeed changed a whole way of thinking and thus, potentially, a life.

Chapter Thirteen

Sons and Daughters

Guy Fleetwood was one worried boy. That was how Charlie thought of him, though he gathered he was twenty. His age manifested itself in swagger rather than maturity, and Charlie remembered that he had had the disadvantage of a successful and forceful father (something he, Charlie, had certainly not been encumbered with in his own distinctly more confident early twenties). And Fleetwood had been rich to boot. Perhaps that had been most inimical of all to a successful growing-up process for his son.

But at least the self-made wealth of Marius Fleetwood had bought his son a good solicitor: Martin Adcock – the best money could hire in the Leeds area. And honest with it. Even humorous, though not with the usual lawyer's humour.

"Let's start," Charlie began when the interviewing formalities were entered on tape, "with the packet of heroin found in the garden shed at Alderley."

"Excuse me, Sergeant, but is there any reason to connect my client, a mere visitor to the house who only arrived the day before, with the package?"

"I think the connection can be made immediately," said Charlie. He turned to Guy. "You went to Leeds on Saturday night, and one of the pubs you went to was the Shorn Lamb. Is this true?"

"I didn't notice the names of the pubs I went to. Should I have?"

"This one's in a little snicket off Briggate."

"If I understand the word snicket correctly, that description could apply to a lot of the pubs off Briggate."

"You've done your research, and in a remarkably short time. You did go to one such pub, then, in the part of Briggate between the Headrow and Boar Lane?"

"Yes." It came after a second's silence.

"We have in fact established that someone resembling you did, that you attached yourself to a group of mainly students, and that finally you had a private conversation with a man – a man well-known to us."

"The police know so many charming characters," said Guy, his upper lip curling, though shakily. Charlie noticed a nudge of reproof from Martin Adcock.

"We do – you're quite right," he said. "And it seems that you have been pretty keen to make their acquaintance too. We've also established that you approached this man after being advised he was a source of drugs."

"I would like a break in this questioning so that I can consult with my client," said Adcock.

"Willingly," said Charlie, seeing a change of policy towards one of coming clean and pleading youth and a spotless record. Twenty minutes later he was reading the usual formula into the tape again.

"My client would like to make a full statement about the events of Saturday night in the Shorn Lamb in Briggate," said Martin Adcock.

"Very well," said Charlie. "Let's start with his going in there."

Guy cleared his throat.

"Well, I went in, and I got talking to this chap who was on his own, and I asked him about getting hold of drugs, and he told me to go over to a group near the window, and talk to a man with a scarlet shirt on. So that's what I did. I muttered 'Can we talk?' and soon he separated off from the rest, and I went with him and we made a deal."

"This was a deal for a substantial amount of heroin, not a mere fix or two for personal use?"

"Yes."

"Why were you suddenly setting yourself up as a dealer?," asked Charlie, who knew a greenhorn drug dealer when he saw one.

"Sergeant, I think you're jumping ahead –" Martin Adcock began.

"Well, I was going to Scotland," said Guy, some of his jauntiness returning. "St Andrews – the sticks! I reckoned there was a wide

133

open market there, and I could muscle in and corner a good share of it."

His solicitor put his head in his hands.

"I was going to say that you were jumping ahead of the evidence," he muttered in Charlie's direction.

"If you think St Andrews, which is 50 miles from Edinburgh, is going to know even less about drugs and the supply of them than you seem to, you really should stick to your father's retail trading," said Charlie. "Edinburgh is a drugs capital, Glasgow is the same, and St Andrews is close to both and draws its students from both. You were sold a packet of rubbish, and if you had tried to get rid of it you'd have been out of pocket, probably beaten up, and out on your ear from the University. You should be damned glad you're going to be arrested. It will be safe-keeping for you, and a lesson not to wade in way, way out of your depth."

Guy looked at him. By now the fires of swagger and aggression were all but burnt out. It was time for him to put his head in his hands.

"Thank God my father's dead," he said.

* * *

There was only one supermarket in Armley that really deserved the title. When Charlie rang them on Wednesday afternoon to see if they employed a Mrs or Miss Bagshaw they came up with the information straight away: yes, they did. She was a woman in her mid-forties, they told him. Her address they had to go to their computer for, but eventually they told him: fifteen, Diamond Street. She was on duty until three.

The Metropolitan University of Leeds, Charlie suspected, might be rather more chary about giving out information, so he drove out there, flashed his credentials at someone really high-up in Administration, enlarged on the progress of the Fleetwood murder enquiry, emphasized that what he was doing was merely eliminating suspects (which was what, following eminent example, he called being economical with the truth) and got from them Pete

Bagshaw's details: he was twenty-one, beginning his third year of studying computer science, having done well in his first two years in this and the related subjects of Higher Mathematics and Information Technology. He was not in one of the halls of residence, but lived at home. His address they gave him as fifteen, Diamond Street, Armley. Bingo!

Charlie timed his visit for three-thirty, by which time Mrs Bagshaw (if Mrs was what she called herself now) should be home from work. Diamond Street turned out to be a road of small four-roomed terrace houses, no doubt built in the year of the Diamond Jubilee. They were probably several times better built than most houses going up today, but they had a mean look, and were clearly not regarded as desirable. The front door of number fifteen was a modern import, with a bell beside it. When the door was opened Charlie was disappointed to see a young man. He'd wanted to save the son till he'd spoken to the mother. He'd intended to get the background clear in his mind first, then delve into the past.

"Is your mother in?" he asked. The young man shook his head.

"No. She probably will be soon. I should think she's gossiping on the way home." Charlie pulled out his ID and put it close to Pete's face. "Oh that," the young man said. He turned without inviting him in, but led the way down the hallway to the living room. It was a small, comfortable room which opened directly into the kitchen. There were lots worse houses to be brought up in, Charlie decided.

"What did you mean by 'Oh that'?" Charlie asked him.

"The Fleetwood business," said Pete Bagshaw. "That is what you're here for, isn't it?"

"The murder, yes."

"Well, there you are. I knew someone at Alderley would have told you about me. That silly girl, probably."

Pete Bagshaw had sat down. In the afternoon sunlight Charlie got a good look at him. His resemblance to the dead man was striking, but Charlie also noticed that he was moderately tall, and was getting quite a physical bulk on him. Not that you needed much of that to stab anyone, he thought, but the interim post mortem had spoken of considerable force. Without being asked Charlie sat down opposite the young man.

"Not the girl, the boy," he said. Pete looked disappointed, as if there should be honour among computer geeks. "Why did you think it was the girl?"

"She was interested in me, but didn't get anywhere. I think she'll be a right little sex maniac in a few years' time."

"I think that position in the family is already taken by her sister," said Charlie.

"Sister? I didn't know there was a sister. I only saw the one."

"And you saw the mother, of course. Was it her you really went to see?"

"In a way ..." Pete considered, and gave the impression that he'd never really thought the situation through before. "I suppose it was mainly curiosity. My girlfriend had told me about this TV actress living near Marsham – that's where her flatmate lives. And she'd told me who she was mistress to. My girlfriend only knows I've got a father who walked out on Mum and me, not who he was."

"So what did you decide to do about it?"

"I decided to do some walking in the area, with a sort of cover story about the Duke of Edinburgh Awards, which actually I did five years ago. And that's what happened. All perfectly innocent and legit. I went past the house, and she – Caroline that is, not the daughter – noticed me. I think she thought I hadn't seen her in the garden, but I had. I felt sure she had spotted the resemblance. Then I went back, and was invited in, and we both knew who I was – we neither of us needed to say anything."

"You said it was mainly curiosity. What else was it?"

"I suppose ... it's difficult to find a word for it ... maybe the nearest is spite. I wanted to tell her how her precious lover had treated my mother. I wanted to say: 'Watch out. Soon it will be your turn.' But when it came down to it, I couldn't. The children being there made it difficult. And she was too nice. My quarrel was never with her. The nicer you are, the more easily fooled, as Mum was. And I sensed she wouldn't believe me in any case – that she was at the stage where she'd accept anything he told her as gospel, so I'd just be banging my head against a wall."

"You mention how your natural father treated your mother. What –"

But they were interrupted by the sound of a key in the door.

"That's Mum now," said Pete, getting up. "She'll tell you."

The woman who came in had evidently once been very striking – a beauty, perhaps one with a strain of fragility. She had neither now, but Charlie felt drawn to her warm personality as she put an arm round her son's shoulders. She smiled at the visitor.

"I think I can guess who you are," she said, but Charlie went through the routines all the same. "I'm Betty Bagshaw," she said when he had done. "Please sit down."

"Mum can tell you how Fleetwood treated her," Pete put in, insistently.

"Yes, but I think we'll talk on our own," said Charlie. "One thing before you go: where were you on Saturday evening?"

"I was here all the time. Partly working, partly watching television."

Charlie didn't repeat his scorn at the idea of an intelligent young person watching Saturday television. He could have watched it just to be companionable with his mother. Or he could have been doing something else entirely, elsewhere. Betty Bagshaw had blinked during her son's answer, and looked as though she was committing it to memory.

"I've got an early evening lecture, Mum," said Pete quietly. "Can you wait my tea till I get home?"

"O' course." She waited till he was gone, then sat opposite Charlie. "He's a good lad."

"I'm sure. I'm not suspecting him of anything." Though he was suspecting him of not telling the whole truth about his Saturday evening. "I want to talk to you as much as anything to get background. That's one thing we lack for Mr Fleetwood. We've had someone tell us how he got started in business up here with Morrisons, but we know almost nothing about his personal life."

"Best say as little as possible about *that*," said Betty Bagshaw. "But now he's been murdered I suppose that's not on the cards."

"No, it's not." Charlie started her gently on the way he wanted her to go. "Tell me how you came to get involved with him."

She left a few seconds' pause and then took a deep breath.

"I was very young, just out of school. I was on a traineeship, just probationary – not a trainee for anything grand, just working on the tills. He was older, of course. He was a *management* trainee – much grander. We met at a disco, and found we both worked for the same firm." She blushed, rather prettily. "I think in fact he'd noticed me before we met up."

"And how long ago was this?"

"Twenty-seven – no, twenty-eight years."

"A long time."

"Yes. Another world almost. Well, you won't need me to fill in the gaps, will you? We started an affair, he was a wonderful lover, and always seemed a wonderful person." She paused. In skating over the early days of her affair with Fleetwood she seemed to have aroused memories that were less than idyllic. "Though the truth is," she resumed, "I was never entirely easy."

"Why not?"

"I never felt part of his life, part of his circle, his friends. I never felt I *belonged* there. Do you sometimes feel that, being black, like?"

"Most of the time," said Charlie cheerfully. "It has its advantages. Not being on the inside you don't *accept* things – don't assume your ways and values are everyone's ways and values."

"Maybe," she said sceptically. "But I didn't like it. It was like I was in a side compartment of his life – in fact talk about someone's 'bit on the side' always makes me feel uneasy, even now. He didn't mean to make me feel like that, maybe, but I did. And to add to that, my family never accepted him. They were very straight-laced, Methodist stock, and they regarded Bert Winterbottom – that's what Marius was called then – as their lovely and promising daughter's vile seducer, which he was in a way. Mind you, I was never promising in the way they thought I was. I was never going to get anywhere on my own. And in the end the affair just fizzled out. A long period when he got less and less interested, then the end. I was relieved in a way."

Charlie pondered the story.

"You say this was twenty-eight years ago when you two met. It must have gone on for a fair while, with your son now twenty-one."

Betty Bagshaw looked embarrassed.

"Well no. That was later. I feel such a fool. And I *was* a great big fool, and everyone who told me so was right."

"What happened?"

"We met up again, several years after we'd split up. On Leeds Station it was. I'd been visiting my sister in Sheffield, he was off the London train. He'd branched out by then, started his first two supermarkets. We saw each other as we were going towards the ticket inspection barrier. Somehow everything clicked again. We both knew it. He marched me straight into the Queens Hotel, booked us into their best suite, and that was it for a couple of nights. Luxury like I'd never seen. He loved pampering and surprising people."

"I think that stayed with him," said Charlie.

"I suppose it would. I know that the very first time we – you know – he'd booked this lovely cottage in Northumberland. That wasn't luxury, it was loveliness: just mountains and moorlands and forests. He was so romantic in a way."

"But when the baby came?"

"Oh, he never acknowledged it was his. Said it could be any-one's. He knew I wasn't the Sunday School type – and hadn't been even when I was sixteen. Father could have been anyone, he said. Offered me a sum of one thousand pounds as a one-off gift. No acknowledgement of responsibility on his part." She smiled as she sighed. "Like a fool I signed on the dotted line. I don't know that I'd have been any happier if I'd fought him in the courts, but even in 1980 a thousand didn't go far."

"I don't suppose it did," said Charlie. "These romantics can be surprisingly hard-headed, can't they?"

* * *

Thinking things over on Wednesday lunchtime, after the Rector's devastating visit, Caroline could see no option but ringing Marius's solicitor and finding out her position from him. It was a Cardiff firm, dating back to the early days of the Fleetwood chain, and she had met the man for a moment when she had been down there for the weekend with Marius. To call him was embarrassing, but she told herself she had to get beyond and above embarrassment. As soon as she had finished a merely toyed-with lunch she rang him.

"Mr Pritchard I *am* very sorry to bother you, but it is rather difficult for me to make plans, not really knowing how I stand. I know the rent on Alderley has been paid up until the end of next month, but beyond that ..."

"Yes, yes. I do understand the difficulties of your position, Mrs ... Mrs Fawley. In fact, Mrs Fleetwood has instructed me to answer all such questions."

Caroline didn't quite like that "all such".

"That's very kind of her," she said.

"Yes, it is. Now, the codicil to the will instructs me to pay rent for a further two months after the period already covered, should that be your wish, and leaves you in addition the lump sum of ten thousand pounds, deductible from the estate."

His voice faded into silence. That was it then.

"I see. It's good of you to make things clear. Now I can begin to make plans," said Caroline. Then her voice too faded into silence, and she put down the phone.

Oddly enough the thing that rankled most keenly was that "two months". Why not three, or six? She had never thought of Marius as small-minded, but he certainly thought small when he made wills. Only a *petty* man could have specified two months. And she knew perfectly well how far ten thousand pounds went in this day and age. No distance at all. Perhaps this was some kind of standard settlement, something Mr Pritchard always had ready – something Marius had up his sleeve for all his women.

Damn him! she thought.

Meanwhile she had another dilemma, a moral one, and one very close to home. Since she had removed the note from the pocket of

Marius's shirt the whole affair it revealed seemed to have been burning a hole in her brain. She reached for her handbag and took it out again.

"OK. Crescent Hotel ca. 8.45. Looking forward to it.

The eternal O."

Christ! The eternal O! The human bike more like. And Marius had ... Marius had been on his way to ...

She looked at her watch. Three o'clock. She could probably catch Oddie or Peace if she drove to Leeds now. She scrawled a note for Alexander and Stella, took out the keys to her newly-restored-to-her car and got on the road. Her rage did nothing for her driving, but it fuelled her determination.

Oddie and Charlie were both busy when she arrived at Millgarth, and it was nearly five o'clock before she found herself sitting in Oddie's office, with Charlie standing by the door and Oddie behind his desk. Her wait had screwed her up psychologically, and her mixture of emotions suddenly found an outlet.

"I feel disgusted with myself."

Oddie looked at her compassionately.

"You haven't done anything disgusting yet."

"No, but I'm going to."

"Do you want us to be discreet about the source of any information you're about to give us?"

Caroline's chin went up.

"No. I definitely don't. If I'm behaving badly it's because they nauseate me with their – with their farmyard behaviour!"

Oddie continued to look sympathetically at her. By the door Charlie's expression was more cynical. Caroline rummaged in her bag again.

"I was ... going through my wardrobe, and found that I'd put one of Marius's shirts there by mistake. I found this in the pocket. It's been washed with the shirt, but it's still readable."

Oddie read the note, called Charlie over and handed it to him.

"It's an assignation note," Oddie said finally.

"Yes."

"For Saturday, probably."

"I looked in the Leeds directory. There's a Crescent Hotel there, near the theatre."

"Oh, we know all about the Crescent. And the handwriting is your daughter's, I take it."

"Yes. Without a doubt ... There is a long period in the opera when her character is off-stage."

"I know. Luckily I saw a performance. Before I did I'd assumed your daughter was out of the picture. In fact she has nothing to do from around eight-thirty to around ten. A long time with nothing to do."

"Oh, Olivia will always find something to do. She's well known in the profession. No one would think of going to her dressing room in the course of a performance. She says her voice needs it ... Oh God! I've not been a good woman, not by old-fashioned standards, not even by my own, but I can't think what I've done to account for my daughter being a nymphomaniac who thinks nothing of stealing her mother's man."

"I have to say, so you don't feel too guilty at bringing this in to us, that I'd guessed about this assignation before you came," said Oddie.

She looked at him, her forehead furrowed, her mind working.

"I think, you know, I'm not feeling guilty at landing my daughter in it. She landed herself in it. What I feel guilty about is producing such a rapacious *horror* of a woman!"

She leapt to her feet and ran to the door. Charlie ran after her to escort her from the building. With prompting from him she made it to the staircase, then down them and through the outer office, where Charlie let her through the electronic doors into the public area.

Sitting there was a smart, intelligent woman of maybe forty-something, regarding them both. Caroline didn't see her and was blundering through towards the main door. The woman got up, however, and went over to her.

"Hello. It's Caroline Fawley, isn't it? I'm Sheila Fleetwood."

Chapter Fourteen

Widows Together

"Are you all right?" Sheila Fleetwood asked.

"Yes. Yes – I'll be fine." Caroline was doing the plucky little wife. It had been a frequent role for her, but her choice was ironic in the circumstances. "The drive home will do me good."

"You should *not* drive in that state. It would be asking for another tragedy. Look, I was thinking of going back to my hotel for tea. Why don't you come along and share it with me? You don't have to talk if you don't want to, but I always find that tea and scones work wonders."

Caroline nodded miserably. She had no particular desire to go with this woman, nor to like her. But somehow it already felt as if she had known her for a long while.

Sheila had obviously registered the taxi rank just around the corner from the Police Headquarters, and she bundled Caroline into the back of the first waiting one. She was staying at the Queens, and when they got there she gave careful orders for their tea at the desk and took Caroline up in the lift without pestering her with talk or fussy attentions. Her suite on the third floor turned out to be rather grand.

"Marius always insisted on the best. Part of the image, part of selling himself. Actually I think he used to bring totty to this place from time to time."

The old-fashioned word seemed to unite them, but Caroline looked around her uneasily, sensing a weight of adultery in the walls and furnishings of the suite.

"Oh dear," she said. "Things *ought* to be so difficult between us. The wronged wife always seems to have moral right on her side, but being the wronged mistress doesn't pack much moral clout."

"Oh, I don't know," said Sheila. "It depends on what you were told."

"Told?"

"By Marius. What kind of assumptions you lived under. It's

many years since I had any illusions about my place in his life, so I ran out of indignation and grievance long since. You, I suppose, have only just learnt the truth about him."

"Well yes, that's true. But that wasn't entirely what upset me, made me rush out of the police station like that."

"What was it?"

"Olivia."

Probably Sheila could guess what was coming from that hint, but she thought it would be salutary for Caroline if she was forced to spell it out.

"The great singer in the making?" she asked.

"Great whore more like," said Caroline bitterly. "Oh, I feel so – so *soiled*. That they could do this to me."

"She and Marius?"

"Yes."

They were interrupted by the arrival of tea. Little sandwiches, bread and butter, toasted teacakes, scones, fruit cake and biscuits. Caroline hadn't known that afternoon tea still existed outside the tea-shops in places like Harrogate or Cheltenham. She would have said she had no appetite at all, but when she began on the large tray she found quite soon that she was tucking in, and that the array of old-fashioned favourites was genuinely restorative. Sheila was tucking in with an equal heartiness.

"The question is," Sheila said, when they were beginning to slacken, "was she just totty?"

"Olivia? Just totty as opposed to my successor?"

"Yes."

Caroline thought.

"I should think that for her it was a matter of a night or two only. For him – I don't know. I realize now that I never knew him. *And I don't give a bugger!*"

Sheila was silent.

"OK, that's silly," admitted Caroline. "Of course I give a bugger. Several buggers. But I hate them. Hate them for what they were doing, or going to do. Hate them for doing it to *me*. If you think I'm a raging egotist, so be it."

"Oh but I don't. I couldn't. Your reactions are pretty much the same as mine, when I first got to know about his activities. That was quite early on in my marriage." She looked quickly at Caroline. "I suppose you think I should have left him."

"I'm not the one to give marriage guidance. But yes – I think I do. The word 'farmyard' keeps coming into my head."

"Yes ... I suppose staying with him was a sort of seduction: I let myself come round to keeping the marriage together because I didn't want to give up the sex, the lifestyle, the security. And I thought the children needed a father, and at that point he seemed a good one. These may be excuses, but there's lots of truth in them. I do love my children, with all their ... weaknesses."

"Guy?"

"Yes, poor Guy. Currently in a custody cell. He's always felt overshadowed, kept down, undervalued. I shouldn't have said 'their' weaknesses. Helena is fine."

"Is Guy in serious trouble?"

"Yes. Dealing, not just use."

"I think that's what my children suspected."

"Typical of Guy that he never got beyond the *intention* of dealing. Thank God, of course. I intend to be around for him. The fact that he's weak, trying to make a splash without an ounce of commercial nous, doesn't make the slightest bit of difference."

"No – why should it?"

"I intend to be around for him," she repeated.

"For all I know Olivia may be in trouble too. I intend to do nothing at all for her."

"She's a lot older. You expect some kind of moral sense to develop during their twenties, if it hasn't before."

"Moral sense? She doesn't know what the term means. I feel such a failure. I can't even blame Rick, her father. He wasn't in the picture for more than her first two years. And I don't believe in bad blood or nonsense like that. It was how I brought her up – though God knows I never went in for conduct like *hers*, so it wasn't example that turned her this way."

She seemed to be heading back towards her old mood of self-flagellation, and Sheila pushed the cake-stand in her direction and said "Have one of these. You'll feel better." Caroline almost laughed at her faith in confectionery.

"This is the end for me," she said. "No more men, no more affairs, not even stable ones. That's what I thought Marius's and mine was. I thought 'I'm lousy at marriage. This suits me better.' But the truth is, it has nothing to do with marriage. I'm just a lousy picker for any sort of relationship."

"I expect you'll change your mind."

"I will *not*! What about you? Will you marry the baby's father?"

Sheila looked at her for a second or two, then burst out laughing.

"Is that what he told you? That's a new one! Let me tell you the truth. I have had the odd fling during our marriage, two to be precise. The last one was ten years ago."

Caroline gaped.

"You mean Marius was –"

"Of course he was. My baby will be his posthumous child. He wanted another son. I resisted for ages, because I thought it was just disappointment with Guy. Not a good basis for bringing a late child into the world. In the end I gave way. Marius always got what he wanted ... I say, I do hope it's a girl."

"That will be a slap in the face for him. I think he really despised women, don't you? Like Mr Dombey. I once played the first Mrs Dombey in a television adaptation. I died in the first five minutes of the first episode. But Marius was different to Dombey. He despised us even as he made love to us."

"I must say it never showed."

"No. But I bet he never thought of a daughter – or of any other woman, come to that – as his successor. I should think you'd be good at running a big firm though."

"I've certainly never thought of myself as a businesswoman," said Sheila. "I quite like sitting on the boards of arts bodies: galleries, museums, orchestras, that sort of thing."

"Oh God! How can you! All those ghastly people – control freaks on ego trips ... Still, if you can bear the sheer awfulness of that kind of person you would probably do well as a High Street tycoon."

Sheila shook her head.

"I've got this bulge in my belly to take care of, and for the next few years it will be a full-time job."

"We both have burdens. You've got a baby – and I don't pretend to envy you. I've got to find somewhere to live, and start sucking up to people to revive my flagging – or currently non-existent – career."

"Did you make any friends around Alderley?" Sheila asked, genuinely interested in the social position of a mistress in the twenty-first century.

"Oh yes. Best of all, Jack – Sir John Mortyn-Crosse. He is a *really* good friend, and tried to warn me. Then there's the Rector – well, I *thought* he was becoming a friend, but I begin to think he was just a time-server."

"Is Sir John unmarried?"

"Widower. But no, there's no romantic involvement. He would be a financial drain on me rather than vice versa, and he farts the whole time."

"I can't see that's an insuperable problem. In an age when organs and combinations of organs are transplanted wholesale, flatulence must be curable."

"Perhaps none of the great medical minds have taken it up. Anyway I've told you: I've done with men."

"Then you'd better get your finances in order. What provision had Marius made?"

"Ten thousand pounds and two months' rent. That *two* hurt. I never thought Marius a cheapskate."

"He was though – always excepting where his own comfort and convenience were concerned. And of course he would never compromise his reputation as a rich and successful entrepreneur."

"Oh, if only I had him here, to give him a piece of my mind!"

"To be fair to him he did take account of inflation. The last one got a pay-off of ten thousand too, but the one before that got eight. That's on a par with the two months as a sign of – let's be kind to the dead and say 'caution'. So you're going back to stage and TV work, are you?"

"If I can get any. What other career options are open?"

"I believe the Little Theatre in Doncaster is looking for a manager."

"Manager? Be the big panjandrum? I don't know if I could do that. It would mean orchestrating all the giant egos into one harmonious whole – draining, I should imagine."

"If you don't have faith in yourself nobody else will. The point is, you'd be in charge so you could shun the giant egos – not give them engagements."

"True. So no job for Rick."

"Who's Rick?"

"My ghastly first husband. Exists on a diet of self-love. He was around last Saturday: he was at the performance, and he and his awful partner were at the party afterwards. I wonder if the police have been on to him."

"Should they be?"

Caroline thought, clinging on to the idea, but not wholly convinced.

"Perhaps he found out about her and Marius. Though if he bumped off everyone who deflowered – or should that be deadheaded? – his precious daughter he'd be a serial killer of Harold Shipman proportions." But another thought had lodged in her mind. "You know, a small theatre company in Doncaster doesn't sound such a bad idea. The children could keep at the same school. And South Yorkshire has quite nice houses within my price range."

"Doubtless that was why Marius chose Alderley," said Sheila dryly. "I'll put in a word in the right quarters. Can't promise anything. I'm only a London gadfly in the Arts scene. They'd want an actor Manager, of course."

"I'd prefer that myself ... Isn't it odd, us two getting on well like this?

Sheila shook her head.

"Not odd for me. I got on well with all the mistresses of Marius that I met. I was going back and forth in the Police Station – seeing Guy, his lawyers, various policemen, and I saw you sitting in the waiting area. When you rushed out I was hanging around on the off-chance of meeting up with you, after I'd had a not-very-satisfactory talk with Guy. I thought you might have been living with Marius under an illusion – all his women were – and I thought from your look that you might have learnt the truth. Since it was unlikely that I'd see you at the funeral –"

Caroline erupted.

"Unlikely? Bloody impossible! Since I don't like making scenes, and since I couldn't sit silent when hypocrisies were being spouted, I shall stay well away. Actually, I can't understand why you don't do the same."

"You forget, I loved him."

"Once."

"Still. Always. Why else would I be having his child at the age of forty-two? Why else would I have stayed with him, through all his affairs and adventures? It wasn't really the stability and the sex and the perks of marriage. I loved him, and I think he loved me. Perhaps it was that that always made me curious about his women ... Could you do something for me?"

"I'd like to. You've been very kind to me."

"Do you have any clout at the Grand Theatre? Could you get me a ticket for the next performance of *Forza*? I'd like to see your daughter."

"Olivia? For the voice? That's wonderful. Or because she was his last mistress?"

"Or intended to be. That more than anything, I suppose. Saturday was one of the few times that Marius failed to get what he wanted."

* * *

Coming back to the Station on Wednesday evening after a long and serious interview with the manager of the Shorn Lamb – one of many he had had over recent years about drug-dealing in his pub – Charlie pulled up when he saw a smart and substantial car arriving. It was the profile of the woman in the passenger seat that struck him: it reminded him of the picture accompanying a profile of Olivia Fawley that had appeared a couple of days before in the

Times Arts Section. When she got out of the car he was sure: a calf-length fur coat (a touch of bravado this, under the circumstances) and a handsome but hard face. The driver leapt out of his side, and bustled round to usher her towards the public entrance to the police headquarters: he was a bulky young man whose manner was protective, as if he was professing an exclusive right in the young lady which the lady herself in no way accepted or acknowledged.

When Charlie went through the waiting area she was shaking hands with her solicitor and telling her companion, in the tones people used to use with servants, not to wait.

"The new Callas is awaiting us downstairs," he announced to Oddie, when he got to the detective squad's office. "Come to make a full confession and explanation."

"Hmmm. Callas went for tycoons too, didn't she?"

"At the highest possible level of course. But Onassis looked like a toad in smart gear. Fleetwood was a prince beside him ... So why didn't you share your theories about Olivia Fleetwood, eh?"

Oddie looked his sergeant straight in the eye. He was prepared for this one.

"Have there never been times in other cases we've shared when you've hugged a theory to yourself, to bring it out triumphantly when you've had time to test it and find that it stands up?"

"Well, just possibly, from time to time –"

"In those cases it was a young detective earning his spurs by making a bit of a splash with a bold theory. In my case it was an old hand showing that the grey cells haven't entirely given up functioning."

"You had the distinct advantage of having seen the bloody opera," grumbled Charlie. "Run it past me, will you? Why is she off-stage for so long?"

"She and her lover get separated at the end of the first scene. They each think the other dead, and at the end of the first part, at interval, she becomes a hermit in a cave near a monastery. After that we don't see her until the very end, when she and lover-boy and vengeful brother all meet up again. I checked up on most of the later parts of the opera on CDs. Thirty-five quid they cost me. I can see what they mean about the record companies running a racket."

"So this Olivia, now awaiting our pleasure, as she waited for Fleetwood's, had – what? – an hour and a half for hanky-panky with him, if he'd turned up?"

"Almost, if you include Interval. Over an hour if she left it till the second half before she slipped out."

"Interesting."

"Let's go and hear her own account of it, shall we?"

Olivia greeted them with regal aplomb and marched with them to the interview room, leaving her solicitor scuttling along behind them like a stressed-out poodle. Olivia took possession of a chair, slipping out of her fur so that it provided her with a decorative surround. Her lawyer, normally one of the city's more effective and conscientious practitioners, sat nervously beside her, conscious, as were all the others in the room, that nothing he was going to say was going to have any influence with the star of this interview.

"I gather," said Oddie, "that you want to amend your account of last Saturday night."

"Yes," said Olivia, in a hard, neutral voice. "Marius and I had a date. He had organised it at the Crescent Hotel. I went along at around twenty to nine. I waited until half past nine, then I went back to the theatre. I was put out, of course. But now I know why he didn't turn up."

"Maybe you do," agreed Oddie. "Time of death is still a rough estimate, and will probably remain one. But can we go back a little? How was this assignation set up?"

Olivia gave a magnificent shrug, as if she was about to put a shot.

"Does it matter? We both knew we were interested, from looks. I was at Alderley regularly from the time rehearsals started, and almost always at weekends. There were plenty of looks. It was only a question of who made the first move."

"And who did?"

"Oh, Marius, of course. It's always best to let the other make the first move. And then if Mother found out and kicked up rough, I'd just point out that it was Marius who propositioned *me*."

"It didn't worry you, taking your mother's lover?"

"I didn't take, I *had* him – or would have. It was never going to be anything else than a bit of short-term fun. Why should it worry me?"

"Some people might have been concerned about the morality of it."

"I don't think it's a sphere where morality enters in."

Oddie kept hold of his eyebrows, for fear of a stratospheric ascent.

"So tell me about his first move, and how the thing was set up."

Olivia pouted with boredom.

"The first verbal move was one weekend, three or four weeks ago. We passed each other on the landing, and he just said 'When is it to be, then?'' I just said I'd let him know. I thought about it, then wrote to him at his office. I said the first night would be appropriate, and gave him an approximate time. Sex during the performance does wonders for my voice – thinking about it before, remembering it afterwards. I said I'd leave all the arrangements to him. He told me the details on the phone; 'Don't judge by appearances' he said, and well he might! I confirmed them in a note, because he asked me to (typical businessman). After that I was sent a barrage of love-letters – including one sent to Alderley when he knew I would be there. He loved living dangerously, that I guessed. Frankly I wasn't so impressed by the letters themselves, because I suspected he'd sent similar letters to all his women. Some of the phrases didn't seem to apply. I'm not a 'beautiful and subtle English rose.' And anyway I don't go for that sort of crap."

"What do you go for?"

"I'm in it for the sex. If that's good, I'm happy."

"I see ... Well, that leads us naturally to Saturday night, doesn't it?"

"I've just told you about Saturday night."

"We need a little more detail than that." Oddie suspected she had found the evening embarrassing or shaming at the time, and he was glad to force her to go through it again. "Let me take you through it.

You say you left the theatre at about twenty to nine. By which door?"

"The big side doors used for scenery."

"So no confirmation from the stage-door keeper?"

"No. And I came back the same way. There's a small inset door that's usually unlocked."

"You knew the way to the Crescent?"

"I've got a Leeds A to Z, for shopping purposes. I'd looked up North Street. I was surprised when I saw the Crescent."

"Pretty run-down," said Oddie.

"That doesn't begin to describe it. Seedy. Scungy. Positively creepy. And the awful jerk in Reception spilling out of his suit didn't do much for it. But I remembered Marius's remark about not judging by appearances."

"So you got the key and went up to the room."

"Yes. I unlocked the door, then just stood in the doorway and laughed for joy. I heard a stair creaking, and realized that creep was listening to see how I reacted. So I went in and shut the door. It was fabulous – just like a stage set for *Intermezzo* or something like that." Oddie and Charlie both tried to look as if they knew what she was talking about. "It was so smart, so in period, and imaginative. He'd really been clever."

"I believe he liked to find something rather special for the first time," said Charlie.

"Did he?" said Olivia, unfazed by being one of a long line. "Only if the circumstances were right, I suppose – if there'd been a bit of a build-up. Mum and he just left the restaurant where they'd met up and were at it in Acton within half an hour."

"So when you finished admiring it, what happened?" asked Oddie.

"Nothing. I'd been half expecting him to pop his head round the bathroom door, burst out laughing, and then get down to business. I went and opened it, but there was no one there. I even opened the wardrobe. I felt such a fool. Then I sat down. I was beginning to get angry. There was champagne in a bucket. I opened it and had a glass – no more: drink does nothing for my voice. The point is, there was nothing I could do but just sit there getting angrier and angri-er."

"When did you decide to leave?"

"Much later than I should have done. I was a fool. This was a dis-aster for the voice – not just no fuck, but *absolutely* the wrong frame of mind for the final scene. I only have ten or fifteen minutes in that scene – Verdi was a bloody fool – but they're good ones, and Marius had spoilt it so that everything was just *wrong*. Anger was absolutely the wrong mood for it. I wished I'd had a quickie with Colm in inter-val. Better than nothing. Anyway, I just banged out of the room, down that nasty corridor and stairs, threw the key to the creep, then marched out into the street and back to the theatre."

"What was going on on stage?" asked Charlie.

"Preziosilla doing her bloody Rataplan with the chorus."

"So you went straight to your dressing room, and saw no one till you got your call for the final scene?" asked Oddie.

"That's pretty much right. I saw one of the stage-hands, but I did-n't proposition him, if that's what you're interested in. I was too angry for that to do any good."

"And when you heard of Mr Fleetwood's death, you decided to conceal the assignation at the Crescent?"

Again she shrugged that field athlete's shrug.

"Nobody's business but mine. I don't like being stood up, and I didn't know when he was killed. Mum's in no position to cast any first stones, but on the whole it was better if the thing didn't come out. Let her live with her illusions. It's what she's always done, until the feller proves to be yet another louse in her eyes."

"So – no shame?" said Oddie.

"Are you a policeman or a bloody clergyman?"

And that was all they got from her. Charlie escorted her and the solicitor out to the main office and into the public area. She dis-missed her legal adviser with a curt "Thanks". When he had slunk off she turned to Charlie. He wondered whether she was going to proposition him, and didn't know whether to feel miffed or relieved when she didn't.

"Does my mother have to know about this?" she asked.

"She knows already," he replied. She nodded, unfazed.

"I'd better keep out of her way for a bit," she commented, and sailed serenely through the glass door.

Outside Charlie could see waiting the swish car that had brought her there. As she appeared at the top of the steps, the large young man leapt out of the driver's seat and went to open the passenger door. Charlie slipped outside.

"What the hell have you waited for?" Olivia demanded. "I told you not to. I'm not fucking *help*less. You don't fucking *own* me."

Chapter Fifteen

Backstage

Thursday morning Charlie had off, and Thursday afternoon was filled with tedious and backbreaking formalities connected with the Fleetwood murder. It was close on seven when he arrived at the Grand Theatre. The audience for the evening's performance was arriving and greeting each other: the atmosphere was friendly because many of them were subscribers, and they saw each other at every performance. Charlie however slipped down the side lane that led to the stage door. As he descended the five or six steps he saw that the stage door keeper was in close conversation with a gangling middle-aged man in tight jeans and a baby-blue sweater. They were both bent forwards, and the keeper had been writing something on a piece of paper, which he now handed to the other, who slipped it into the back pocket of his jeans and straightened up.

"My best thanks as always," he said to the keeper. "My visits to Leeds wouldn't be the same without you, Syd."

As he left the window Charlie came forward, flashing his ID.

"Detective Sergeant Peace. It's about the Fleetwood murder."

He was conscious as he said it that the middle-aged man in the blue sweater had suddenly stopped on the steps leading out. He turned towards the exit on to the street, but only in time to see the man's feet disappearing through it.

"Oh yes, Mr Peace. I've talked to your boss – Oddie is it?"

"It is. Before I get down to business, who was that?"

"That? Oh that's Rick Radshaw. An actor and singer. He's been with us in *The Mikado* and *Yeoman* – with the Doyly Carte and a company that calls itself the Carl Rosa. Nice little tenor voice, they tell me."

"I see. And the father of Olivia Fawley."

"That's right. She took her mother's name. More recognition potential, her mother having made a nice little career in television."

"Never misses a trick, Miss Fawley," commented Charlie. "Has he been visiting her now? Or did he want her address?"

"No – this was something quite different – personal," said Syd. "Now, what can I do for you?"

Charlie decided to let the matter slide. For the moment.

"I wanted to talk to one of the stage-hands. Nothing too important. Just confirmation of a time – alibis and suchlike, you know."

The keeper waved his hand through towards the theatre.

"Be my guest. Be a bit careful where you go, though. Curtain up in five minutes' time. Don't want you suddenly appearing on stage."

Charlie rather fancied himself on stage – had once considered applying to drama school. Opera, though, didn't appeal. He went into the maze of corridors with caution through what seemed to be a building-site of activity, with costumes being adjusted, stage mechanism given a last-minute testing, and people rushing hither and yon on missions that no doubt seemed to them important when they set out. Gaining the wings, and treading gingerly as if at any moment he might be whisked up into the flies, he caught a glimpse of a set that looked more like a cartoon than the background for a Verdi opera.

"Isn't *Forza* being done tonight?" he asked a passing stage-hand.

"No, not till Saturday. You have to have at least two days' rest between performances, preferably more. It's punishing, that's what all the singers say, and I can believe them. It's *Love for Three Oranges* tonight. A doddle for the voices, a bit of a nightmare for us."

"I'm looking for one of the stage-hands who may have seen Olivia Fawley arrive back in the theatre during the first night of *Forza*."

"Policeman, are you?" Charlie nodded. "The one you're after will be Simon Neely. That's him over there, with the fair-to-brown hair. I saw her leave, by the way."

"You did?"

"Yes – I bet she thought no one did, didn't she? She left about half way through the interval, when everyone was busy getting the stage ready for the second part, and all the performers were hovering around the stage. I was fetching something, and I saw her slipping out the big doors into the side lane. I suppose that would be about twenty/quarter to nine."

"Right," said Charlie. "That could be useful. And that's Simon Neely is it?"

"Yes. Wait ten minutes until the opera's started, then he'll be free."

Charlie nodded. But instead of standing around he slipped away from the stage, found a payphone in a nice private area backstage, and rang Oddie's home number.

"Mike? Charlie here ... Backstage at the Grand Theatre. Just waiting to talk to that stage-hand. They're not doing *Forza* tonight – something about oranges ... Mike, this is just a hunch – not a brilliant guess based on a sensitive reading of masses of evidence, but a hunch ... Yes, I'm sure you've had them, Mike. Now, didn't you say that when you were talking to the owner of the Crescent you made a joke at the end?"

"Yes," came Oddie's voice. "He could think of nothing that swish room in his dingy hotel could be used for, and I suggested that he let it out as a knocking shop for the highly-discriminating. People like the performers at the Grand Theatre, for example. I had a feeling he might have taken me seriously."

"I have a feeling he did just that," said Charlie.

Back in the wings Charlie was deafened by brass, but things seemed to be going to plan on stage, and there was a good deal of audience laughter. He started looking around for his quarry, but someone came up behind him and touched him on the shoulder.

"Are you looking for me? I'm Simon Neely. Dick said you wanted to talk to the man who saw Fawley arrive back."

Charlie registered the brutal use of the surname.

"Yes, I did. Anywhere where we can talk and actually hear each other?"

The man nodded and let the way back from the stage area, ending up in a little alcove in the middle of a long corridor.

"It's not really worth your trouble all this," Neely said. "I could have told you what I know in ten seconds. I saw her coming in through that door over there, the one cut into the big doors for the sets. That was around twenty to ten. End of story."

Charlie nodded, looking at the immense square area through which the sets had come.

"Know what was going on at the time on stage?" he asked.

"The soldier's moll was doing her number," said Neely. "They call it rataplan or something like that."

"Right. Now where's her dressing room?" he asked. Simon Neely gestured down the corridor in the other direction.

"Five doors down. She's there now."

"There now? She's not in this opera as well, is she?"

"Good Lord, no!" said Neely grinning wickedly. "Not her cuppa at all. A bundle of laughs this one."

"Why's she here tonight, then?"

Simon looked him straight in the eye.

"You're on this case, mate. Your guess will be as good as mine, if you're doing your job. It'll be exactly the same as mine, though I'm more up in who she'll be doing it with. My guess is that it's the cook."

"The *cook*? Does the theatre have a cook?"

"The cook in *Oranges*. He's a fantastic figure about seven feet high (stilts of course) and he rages about wielding a great cleaver in the second act. I should think he's using his chopper now."

"I get you."

Neely looked at him, his face twisted, but apparently in some effort to understand the woman he was talking about.

"She's not subtle or choosy, you know. Her contract gives her the use of the female star's dressing room every night while *Forza* and *Oranges* are on the bill. *Oranges* has no real female star, so no hair has been flying. She can use the room whenever it suits her, and *for* whatever suits her."

"You don't like her. Did you and she by any chance have words on Saturday night when she arrived back here?"

"Not then." Neely pulled himself up. "Oh, wait: she muttered 'You're bloody useless' as she went past."

"Flattering."

"I'd better explain. She did send out clear signals in my direction a fortnight or so ago, when stage rehearsals started. I just said: 'I'm sorry, love. I'm gay.'"

"Are you?"

"Oh, I'm a happy chappie most of the time. But no, I'm not gay in that sense. It just seemed – I dunno – more final than saying that I wasn't interested."

"It certainly worked. Why weren't you interested?"

"Does that need an explanation? You are or you aren't. I just wasn't. I'm not into being eaten alive. There's something – I don't know – unhealthy about her. Twisted. Perverse. I don't know the right word, but she seems consumed with getting what she wants. Anyone who goes with her must feel like a sort of machine. You get a few like her in the theatre. In fact, I've been with one or two of them. You don't feel good afterwards, and that's putting it mildly. You feel like a dirty used rag."

"What did she say when you told her you were gay?"

"Word for word it was 'Christ, just my luck to fancy a bloody faggot.' I think political correctness has passed La Fawley by. Though I rather suspected that she didn't actually believe me, but had to pretend to because anything else would be less than flattering to her ego. She preferred not to think I was straight, because then she would have had to work out why I'd knocked her back."

His eye caught a figure at the other end of the corridor.

"There's boyfriend, or whatever you call him. Use-in-emergency prick is what he really is. It's pathetic, isn't it."

Charlie looked at the figure skulking at the other end of the corridor of dressing rooms – moody, unhappy, uneasy with himself. Suddenly Colm became conscious he was being watched. He turned with military precision, and they heard the sound of his shoes scuttling off.

"Pathetic," he agreed. He asked Neely to keep him informed if anything happened he might be interested to hear about.

"I'm all bewildered by these corridors," he said. "Could you point me in the direction of the stage door? I'd like to have another word with the keeper."

"Syd's not the keeper. The proper one is in hospital at the moment. Syd's just one of the underlings who's got his two weeks of glory."

Neely was very good at conveying his opinion of people without openly stating it. Charlie looked at him quizzically.

"And Syd's reputation is? –"

"A touch on the sleazy side. You want special services, or if you're offering them, Syd's the one to go to."

Charlie nodded gratefully, and went in the direction the stage hand had pointed.

Business for Syd seemed to be brisk. He was in the middle of another hushed conversation when Charlie arrived back at the stage door. It was with a small, youngish woman, growing into fat, and at the approach of Charlie she ended the conversation and slipped up the stairs to the outside world.

"I seem to have that effect on people," Charlie said genially.

In fact he had always found since joining the Force that his presence anywhere got round incredibly quickly, presumably due to his colour. It was a disadvantage more than an advantage.

"Nothing personal," said Syd, with an attempt at geniality himself. "That was Sally Lane: chorus member and bit-part player. She'd done her bit in *Oranges* and was off home. As you are, I suppose."

"All in good time," said Charlie, his grin especially wide. "I'm not really interested in Sally Lane, but I am distinctly interested in Rick Radshaw."

"Ah – the one who –"

"Who stopped on the stairs when he heard I was a detective, then scooted out when I turned to look at him."

"Oh, I think you're making too much of that, Mr Peace. Everyone here is interested in the murder, naturally."

"Oh yes, naturally. Especially when your new star singer has been twice interviewed at length by us."

"Well, I'll not pretend she's a general favourite here."

"Is she not? Rather ungrateful on the men's part, I'd have said. You just said 'Everyone here' is interested in the murder. But Mr Radshaw is not 'here' at the moment, is he?"

"Not at the moment, but like I said, he has been."

"Yes. And when he has, you've been able to be of service to him, haven't you?"

"Well, we try and be of service to all the players, Mr Peace. That's part of a stage doorkeeper's function."

Charlie leant forward, suddenly intimidating.

"Don't give me all that bullshit, Syd. I wasn't born yesterday. I'm not interested in any pimping you may have done for Rick Radshaw in the past, but I am interested in what you're doing for him at the moment. Tell me, fast."

An expression of injured innocence suffused Syd's face. It was well-practised, Charlie guessed.

"At the moment? I'm not doing anything for him at the moment."

"Then why was he here?"

The man swallowed, and in his head he ran through a litany of the lies he used when the theatre authorities decided his activities had overstepped the mark.

"He's in the area because his partner is acting in Bradford. He just called in to pay his respects."

"Pull the other one. He thanked you, and said his visits to Leeds wouldn't be the same without you. Would it help to jog your memory if I mentioned the Crescent Hotel?"

His mouth dropped a fraction.

"How did you know about that?" Charlie stood quite still and waited. "I ain't done nothing wrong." This was said aggressively. "The hotel just rang, said they'd got this very swish room, and it was available for hire."

"Long or short lets."

"Yes."

"Redecorated to the specifications of Marius Fleetwood, lately deceased."

"Well, he did mention that."

"And you'd get your cut for bringing it to people's notice."

"Nothing wrong with that, is there? Nothing wrong with any of it."

"No, there's not," said Charlie, drawing back a little from the confrontation. "An assignation for a quick one is not an offence anywhere except Kabul or Tehran – and maybe Boston. But just because there's something rather whiffy about all this, as I think you realize, perhaps you'd better tell me precisely what you're doing for Mr Radshaw. Otherwise I might have to go a lot higher up to get the necessary muscle to prize it out of you."

Syd looked very sick.

"Well, you might say Mr Radshaw is a bit of a connoisseur."

"Oh yes? What is it? Delft china? Netsuke?"

"Don't come the smart arse with me! ... Oh, sorry Sergeant. No, it's what you might call physical things he's a connoisseur of."

"I thought it might be."

"And I sort of ... suggest people who might provide something novel, tell him about new establishments that have sprung up since he was last in town. Or, as in this case, tell him about new locales, situations for seduction that he might find – you know – stimulating."

"I know. So Mr Radshaw, at your suggestion, has probably by now been along to arrange the hire of a room that his own daughter was to have been bedded in on Saturday by a man who was stabbed nearby by a person unknown. Seems Mr Radshaw has a pretty strong stomach, doesn't it?"

"It sounds worse the way you put it."

"Pardon my crudeness. And I presume the lady he is taking there is not his present partner."

"That's his fucking business, isn't it."

"Couldn't have put it better myself," said Charlie, taking his leave.

Talking it over with Mike Oddie on Friday morning, Charlie conveyed his strong sense of the awfulness of the assistant stagedoor keeper and his customer, but then said with a shrug:

"Can't see that it's relevant."

"Maybe not. But it's an interesting indication of character. And it's just possible it could be useful as a lever."

"If he knows anything we would want to know. By the way, I

have the impression from Caroline Fawley that his present partner is a pretty formidable character."

"This case is littered with them," said Oddie wearily. "Anyway, Radshaw is one of the unexplored possibilities – likewise his partner, though she was probably on stage at the time he was killed. There's one other aspect we haven't made a great deal of headway on."

"Where did Fleetwood come from?"

"Right."

"Family, parentage, education. What was he kicking *against*?"

"If he was. It tends to make a good story if someone who was a serial adulterer comes from a strict Methodist background. But it's just as likely that he would come from a background of similarly randy males. Randy females, come to that."

"But the thing is that we don't know," said Charlie. "I wonder if his wife knows. Sometimes wives and husbands are ignorant of the most basic things about each other."

"Sheila Fleetwood is supposed to come in this morning. There's the hearing and the bail application for her son. Perhaps we could ask her. And we've had a call from a sister that I haven't had time to follow up. I don't get the idea that Fleetwood was worried by the fact of having a working-class background, do you?"

"No. But there may be something in that background he was keen to conceal."

When Sheila Fleetwood came in at ten in the morning she had her daughter with her – a bright, lively fifteen-year-old with a sparkle in her eyes and an obvious kinship with her mother.

"Wigged school just for the day," Sheila explained to Charlie. "Came up on the early train to give me moral support at the bail hearing."

"Nice of her," he said, giving her a smile. "I don't think there'll be any problems though. There certainly will be conditions. Make sure he sticks to them, or he could be in deeper trouble. I don't get the impression of a very strong character, I'm afraid."

"He's not. We'll do what we can, me and Helena."

"Oddie and I were wondering if we could have a few words about your husband's background."

Sheila looked uneasily at her daughter, who caught the glance.

"Oh Mum, for heaven's sake! I've known Dad has another little woman tucked away somewhere since I was seven, and I've known that he changed her regularly like a library book since I was eight. You can't tell the policemen anything worse than that."

"Well –"

"He's the Unknown Father. I want to know about him."

"I suppose you're right." So five minutes later, in Oddie's office, she turned to him and said. "You want to know about Marius's background. Really I'm almost as much in the dark about it as you are. What in particular do you want to know?"

"Background. Family background, for a start," said Oddie.

Sheila marshalled her thoughts.

"Birthplace, Pontefract. Original name: Albert Winterbottom. I must say I'm very glad he changed it. He only told me when he had to produce his birth-certificate for something or other. Father a train driver, mother a housewife, as they all were in those days. Marius got to grammar school, and went straight from there into retail trade."

"Trainee at Morrisons," put in Charlie.

"That's right. Stayed there for five years or more, learning the basics. He could have gone to university, but he always said he already knew at the time he left school that he wanted to go into retailing, so university would have been useless to him: 'No point in farting around getting a degree,' as he usually put it."

"And did you have much to do with his family?" asked Oddie.

"I had nothing to do with them."

"I'm guessing that wasn't your own choice."

"It wasn't." Sheila paused and thought for a moment or two. "Quite early in the relationship, when he was getting to know my family, I brought it up. 'You don't want to know about them,' he said. Of course I brought it up again when the wedding list was compiled, and later too, but Marius always brushed me aside. Eventually I stopped."

"What was your own father?"

"Something in the City. That sounds almost as vague as Marius was about his, but that's because I was never interested enough to find out in detail. He was pretty high up in some insurance company – that's as much as I know to this day."

"And you don't think it was snobbery, social shame, whatever you call it, that made him cut himself off from his background?" asked Charlie.

"No ... No, I don't ..." Sheila thought again for a while. "I *think*, knowing Marius, that he cut himself off from his family because they couldn't be of use to him any longer. He could be very ruthless, and he would be pleased rather than ashamed to hear me saying that."

"Anything else you can tell us?"

"Mother dead ... Oh, all this should be prefaced by 'I think.' Marius was always ready with a lie if it suited him. So I think his mother was dead by the time we married. There is or was a sister. *I think* his dad is now in some kind of home."

"I've got another grandad then," said Helena.

"Not one that's much use to you, I'm afraid. Marius did say not so long ago 'I don't think he knows what time of day it is, let alone what month or year.'"

"That would suggest some kind of occasional contact," said Oddie.

"Yes, that's what I thought. Quite probably he was paying nursing home bills, perhaps through his sister. And really that's all I know – or all I think I may know."

"Not much at all," said Oddie to Charlie later, when Guy had been released on bail into his mother's care.

"Nothing much to go on from our point of view. Nothing in the way of motive for murder. Total neglect, a 'couldn't care less' attitude, which had been going on for years."

"Still, it's got to be followed up. Toss you for who does Radshaw and who does the Winterbottoms."

They tossed, and Charlie got Rick Radshaw and Oddie the Winterbottoms.

Chapter Sixteen

Proud Father

The terminal state of decline of the English breakfast could be illustrated by the habits of the Mortyn-Crosses. The Dower House, where traditional habits and values were clung to as if they had the efficacy of prayer beads or jujus, indulged in the full caboodle on one day a week only, a Sunday. Otherwise the first down to the kitchen cut white and brown bread and made toast, and marmalade and jam was put on the dining-room table. And that was it. Traditional breakfast dishes – the full fry-up, scrambled, poached or boiled eggs, kippers or kedgeree – might be cooked at lunchtime, but breakfast was whatever cereal Jack or Meta might prefer that day, and toast.

Mind you, Meta took a lot of it. And each piece called for a great deal of butter before it was topped with Frank Cooper's Oxford Marmalade. Jack had always regarded his sister's eating habits as being in the nature of a healthy appetite, a jolly girl's hunger. Recently however it had suddenly assumed the aspect of outright gluttony. That Friday morning he averted his eyes from the knife applying the butter as a brickie does cement on to a wall, and from the spoon thrust into the marmalade pot as if it was diving into a bottomless lagoon. Really, he thought, Meta had never grown out of the nursery: greedy, petulant, childish. He suddenly thought she was a burden heavier than he could bear.

"I'll go down to old Patel when I've finished breakfast," Meta announced, "and pick up the *Telegraph*."

"Why have we changed from the *Times*?" complained Jack.

"I've told you, the *Telegraph* is better for juicy court cases and murders," Meta pronounced. "It's well known."

Jack, who could subject statements like that to pedantic scrutiny when he was in the mood, today merely sighed.

"Is it the Fleetwood murder you're still interested in, or has another of our friends been killed?"

"Of course it's the Fleetwood one. It will be in the news for weeks yet, and then again at the trial, if they ever catch anyone. I don't pin much hope on your blackie pal, but the older one who's been on television may have a brain in his noodle. Though he did say yesterday that they hadn't ruled out the possibility of a mugger who took fright, or a shizo ... schizo – you know."

Jack sighed again. Meta must be the last person in Britain who found the word schizophrenic beyond them.

"You sound as if you'd feel cheated if it was a mugger or a schizophrenic," he said.

"Not so interesting as if it's someone we know," Meta said, munching. "Any of the children could have done it. Or one of Caroline's husbands or old boyfriends. Or one of those theatre people, or someone from Marius's past. People are saying his past is littered with old girlfriends and look-alike children. They say there was one seen in the village not so long ago – a boy."

Jack felt he had to protest.

"You're talking as if this was just any old murder case. But Marius was a friend."

"He wasn't a friend of mine."

"Well, I do have to admit that I had reservations about his intentions," Jack weakly conceded. Meta sniggered.

"You're talking as if they were Victorian lovers."

"But I looked on him as a rather scapegrace nephew, who I was always pleased to see."

"It was *Caroline* you were always pleased to see, you oaf."

"Of course it was. Caroline is a wonderful acquisition to the neighbourhood – a delight to see and to talk to. I have the highest respect for Caroline."

It was said emphatically, but Meta snorted.

"You're deceiving yourself. You're in love with her. Anyway, I think it's pretty funny to talk about having the highest respect for a kept woman. And the vicar and his wife feel the same."

Jack flinched, but kept his glance on her.

"The vicar must take whatever line he feels right. Naturally he has to uphold the Church's beliefs. But I won't have Caroline called names in this house."

Meta snorted again.

"Kept woman, floozie, piece on the side, tart." She realized she had gone too far when Jack rose in anger, and she pushed back her chair and said "Off to the village."

Casting a regretful glance back at a half-finished piece of toast she bounced out of the room and out of the Dower House, banging the front door behind her. Jack sat for a second or two in thought. Then he got up and went to a tall cupboard built into the hallway. From the top shelf he took down two old suitcases, dusty and falling apart from long disuse. He started up the stairs with them, then, as an afterthought, went and bolted the front door. Once on the landing he went into his sister's bedroom and threw the suitcases on the bed, sending up a cloud of dust. Then he opened the wardrobe and, higgledy-piggledy, put skirts, suits and coats into one of the cases, stuffing them in and forcing it shut. He went to a chest of drawers, pulled out petticoats and knickers, stockings, bras and nightdresses, and threw them into a case. He could hardly bear to look at them, though they were all familiar to him from the weekly wash. Then he fastened the clasp and took both cases downstairs. Having looked out of the living room window to see that his sister was not arriving back at the house, he unbolted the front door and put them outside. Then he got a piece of paper and wrote on it

"META. THIS IS THE END. WILL SEND ON REST WHEN YOU HAVE AN ADDRESS."

This he pinned on the front door, then went inside, bolted it, and went to the kitchen to make a cup of tea and wait.

It was ten minutes before he heard the inevitable Meta commotion. There was banging on the door, and then the constant ringing of the bell. It was a real brass bell, and Jack didn't see how he could disconnect it without ruining it, so he tied a wet tea-towel around the clapper and this at least lessened the nuisance considerably. He knew that Meta would come round to the back eventually, so he moved, tea-cup in hand, into the hall, and just in time. Maddened by the silence the bell-ringing produced, Meta strode round, banged on the back door, then peered through and banged on the window. Jack was not tempted to peer back through the crack in the hall door. He knew that the unattractive sight of her pudgy, blotched face could produce in him a pity that might induce him to let his sister back into his life, where she had occupied a prime position for so long. No more. Never again. Those days were over. Pity should be expended with better discrimination.

Eventually – as he knew she must, because there was nothing else she could do – Meta went. He heard her stomping down the path, and, going to the living room window, he saw her plodding towards the village like an invading storm-trooper. She was not carrying the two suitcases. That did not surprise Jack. Meta had never been one (in the long-ago days when they had the money to travel) to carry her own luggage. And she would not yet have given up. Where would she go to resume her campaign? There were not a great number of houses where she was still welcome, so Jack put his money on the vicar.

The call from Mr Watters came half an hour later. He said that he had Meta there, at the vicarage, that she was very distressed, that he was sure their differences could be sorted out, family differences were so distressing, particularly in an *old* and *distinguished* family such as the Mortyn-Crosses, a family with such *deep* roots in the neighbourhood, and if he could be of any use, could act as some kind of mediator in the sad little matter, he'd be glad –

"Best thing you could do," barked Jack, "would be to collect her bags and put her on the train to Peterborough. Give her ten quid for the taxi fare to Aunt Sarah's, and I'll reimburse you when I know she's gone."

There were mutterings of dissent from the other end.

"Your sister has talked about her aunt, but she says they hate each other."

"All the better. It'll give them both plenty of privacy. Sarah's eighty-seven and in need of care. Meta is in need of a roof over her head. It's the perfect solution. So make it clear she's *never* going to come back here."

He put the phone down on some well-intentioned squawks.

Then, exceptionally for him, he went and poured himself a whisky – a triple by pub measures – and diluted it as he liked it, with ice and tap water (Jack was traditional, but not a slave to tradition). Then he sat down, not doing anything, but just thinking – basking, if the truth be known, in what he had just done, and in his new solitude. Another half hour later he heard the vicar's car, unmistakably wheezy, and heard the luggage being loaded into the boot. He sat on while Meta stomped up to the front door, opened the letter-box and screamed through it "Jack, you're a cruel bastard, and you'll pay for this." He felt his happiness well up inside him as he heard the vicar's car drive off for Doncaster station and the train to Peterborough.

He had never felt so happy since his last day at public school.

* * *

Charlie found the village of Abbotsdale without too much difficulty. He arrived there on Friday at lunchtime, after the talk with Sheila. It was five miles from Knaresborough, and the softer end of what the tourist traffickers called The Yorkshire Experience. Gently rolling fields surrounded the village, edging towards the determined flatness of the Vale of York. The village itself consisted of about twenty-five houses and cottages, all probably centrally heated, and all competing in their minds if not in actuality for the title of Best-Kept Cottage Garden. The natives were fairly friendly, however. He had got Rick Radshaw's address from the woman at Opera North who had invited him to the first-night party, and when he had rung three times at the doorbell a neighbour poked her head out of her door and said with grim humour: "Try the pub."

At least there still was a pub. Many of the villages close to Bradford – more convenient for Lauren Spender's acting engagement, but less well-heeled than this one – had lost their last pub, and determined drinkers were condemned (if they took notice of drink and drive laws) to a long trudge to the nearest village that still retained that last bastion of British civilisation.

He heard a voice as soon as he opened the door of The Spotted Cow and felt the warmth of its simulated gas open fire in his face.

"What always strikes me, coming North," the voice said, just a touch too loud, and with the suspicion of a drawl, "is how short everyone is. I mean, down South I'm a fair height, but up North I'm a *giant* because everyone's so short. And round here they're positively *dwarfish*!"

How to win friends and influence people, thought Charlie. His eye picked out the tallest man in the groups around the bar and went over to him.

"Mr Radshaw? I'm Detective Sergeant Peace." And he flashed his ID.

"So?" said the next great soprano's father.

He was half-standing, half-sitting on a bar stool, and his arm had gone around the shoulder of his partner, a hard-faced, over-cosmeticised woman of about forty. Radshaw was wearing jeans, and was still lean enough to do so without exciting ridicule, but his long, thin face was greedy rather than just hungry, and his eyes told of endless morning and evening drinking sessions.

The people who had been around the pair when Charlie came in had spirited themselves away to other parts of the Public Bar, probably not so much from tact or nervousness as seizing an opportunity.

"So I'd like a talk with you both."

"Why don't we grab a table then?"

"I need more privacy than that. Couldn't we go back to your cottage and talk?"

"Go back to the cottage? But I'm still on my second drink." One look from Charlie made him crumble around the edges. "Oh very well ... Fred, another double Scotch please ... I'll just have this, and then we'll get back."

"Bacardi and Coke, Fred," said the fragrant Lauren.

"Look, there's not much point in talking to Lauren," said Rick. "She was on stage all evening in *Loot*, in Bradford."

"On stage all evening doesn't always mean what it seems to," said Charlie. "Still, I did flick through a copy in Waterstone's before I set out. Fay does seem to be on most of the time. If the lady wants to she can stay here, and we can talk alone."

He was fixed by hard, violet eyes.

"No, I think I'll come. It could be quite interesting."

Rick Radshaw, too, now that he'd got used to the idea, seemed to quite fancy being interviewed. He had almost certainly entertained the idea that he might be, because he hadn't asked in connection with what Charlie wanted to question him. He downed in his second gulp his third double whisky, then pulled himself off the stool and up to his full height (about five foot ten, Charlie estimated).

"Come on. I'm ready for the rack and the thumbscrews."

"You've done *Yeomen* once too often," said Lauren dismissively.

Charlie had the impression as they all three did the two minutes' walk back to the cottage that the eyes of Abbotsdale were on them from behind closed windows. Clearly if so there must be something about him that marked him off as "copper". What a humiliating thing to realize about himself! Rick and Lauren seemed impervious to the attention, either because they didn't notice it, or because they accepted it as their due, they being Thespians. Rick threw open the cottage door, and they were greeted by an agreeable centrally-heated fug. Rick went straight to the drinks cabinet, took out an opened bottle of red wine, and sloshed two glasses full.

"I'm on duty," said Charlie, knowing that neither glass was for him. Rick looked at him as if wondering at this conversational irrelevance.

"Fire away," he said at last, holding out a glass to Lauren, who was standing against the kitchen doorpost in a pose familiar in theatre productions.

"Obvious question first," said Charlie. "What were you doing on Saturday evening?"

Rick had sat down, and now began his spiel with copious use of his hands, either a bad stage habit or the result of alcohol.

"Round about six, maybe a bit before, we left to take Sweetie here to the theatre in Bradford. Dropped her off about half past six, then drove on to Leeds. Parked the car near the Merrion Centre, then went down to the Grand. In the run-up to the start of the thing –

Forza del Destino, I mean – I saw the dead man and my ex-wife Caroline Fawley, and we had a few perfectly amicable words. Then I took my seat, which was on row S, several rows behind Caroline because I'm only the bloody father, aren't I? And there I was for the rest of the evening until curtain fall – hooked! She was fabulous. I've got a very nice voice, but somehow I've managed to pass on one that's not just that, but something miraculous. It makes me very humble, I can tell you, and –"

"You sing yourself in musical comedies and operettas, I believe?" Charlie slipped in.

"That's right. I could have done opera, the voice is large enough, but I had this fabulous success early on with Freddy in *My Fair Lady*, and after that the offers kept rolling in, and they were all in the same line. I've done plenty of Gilbert and Sullivan, but I suppose the closest I've come to legit opera is Offenbach. Paris in *La Belle Hélène*, and Orpheus. That was a fabulous production, but a bit too risqué for some English critics. The producer made Euridice into –"

"You left your first wife not long after Olivia was born, didn't you?"

"Only wife. And she left me. Faults on both sides, I suppose. Don't be taken in by Caroline's romantic heroine airs. She can sleep around with the best of them."

"High class whore, if you want my opinion," said Lauren from the door.

"And how much contact did you have with your daughter after that?"

Rick Radshaw spread out his hands.

"Oh, you know how it is: a visit to the Zoo, then months later it's Madame Tussaud's ... Well, not that much, actually. Of course I loved her – loved her to bits. Still do, actually. But somehow things get in the way, don't they? Caroline's in something at Bexhill-on-Sea and I'm in something in Harrogate. The logistics are almost unworkable. It seemed sensible to scale things down."

From what? Charlie asked himself. He thought of his daughter Carola, now determinedly crawling and tottering to her feet. He decided in a flash that he was never going to get a divorce. He also put this particular rotten father on his blacklist.

"So if Ms Spender hadn't been acting in this area, you probably wouldn't have been at your daughter's first night at all?"

"Oh, I wouldn't say that. No – I think that, granted I wasn't in anything myself, I'd have been there. And particularly as word gets around about anything special, and that's what I was hearing. From my agent, for a start, from all sorts of people in the musical theatre, as you might call it. Oh, I think I'd have come up. Olivia is heading for something big, and I'd have wanted to get a sl – " He pulled himself up. "I'd have wanted to be there for the beginning of it all."

Charlie could have sworn he was going to say "a slice of the action." He surely had had an idea that there might be something in it for him in his daughter's approaching fame. Drink was leading him into revelatory mood, though caution was still reining him in. He was glad when Radshaw got up and splashed more red wine into his glass.

"Opera singers earn fantastic sums these days," Charlie commented.

"Absolutely bloody fantastic! Pop star earnings."

"That's right at the very top, of course."

"That's right. And that's where she's going to be. All the people at the very top at the moment are men. There's plenty of space for a woman up there."

"Let's hope she makes it ... You said you were in the theatre for the rest of the performance, but you didn't tell me about the Interval," said Charlie, looking at him closely.

"Interval? Ah yes. Oh, I was in the bar, of course – accepting the congratulations of anyone who knew I was Olivia's father. Caroline will tell you. She was nearby doing the same."

Charlie risked his arm on a lie.

"She says you were close by for the first part of the Interval."

"Oh well, I – er – " He ground to a halt.

"Where did you go, sir? Was it backstage?"

Collapse of lean party.

"Well, of course I shouldn't. But as you know Syd and I are good friends, so I tipped him a nod, and –"

"And you went to your daughter's dressing room, didn't you, sir?"

"Yes. Well, I knew the opera, and I knew it was a long time before she was on again."

"But you hadn't heard that she likes to have sex at some point during the performance?"

His eyes opened wider.

"Does she, b'God? Syd never told me that. Chip off the ... Well, anyway, that does explain one or two things."

"Oh?"

"The tenor was leaving as I came near the door. I recognised him by his costume – great-coat over jeans, typical modern production touch. He was looking put out – distressed really. I suppose he'd been given the brush off?"

"Quite possibly. I have the impression that he's used now and then, but only when something newer and more exciting isn't on offer."

"Well, probably it was. Because when I'd knocked and gone in, Olivia was in a long fur coat, and it was obvious she was on her way out. I started to make apologies, but she just said 'I'll talk to you at the party afterwards,' and swept both of us out. I slipped back to the front of house, and had a quick second drink."

Charlie pondered this.

"When she said 'I'll talk to you at the party afterwards,' it sounds as if you had something definite to talk about – not just party-talk."

Rick screwed up his face. The drink was removing the last of his inhibitions.

"I did. I'd sent her a note a couple of days before, wishing her well, saying how proud I felt ..."

"And?"

"And suggesting that what she needed was someone around her – like a combination of agent, protector, PR man, and general dogs-body, getting her to her hotel, to the airport, the opera house – that kind of thing."

"And the person you thought of for this role –?"

"Well, the voice isn't going to last forever, though it's still in *pretty* good nick I can tell you. And you'd need someone *absolutely* devoted to your interests, and who would be more likely to be that than her father?"

"And did you get to talk to her at the party?"

"Yes ... *Bitch!*"

His face was dark with remembered fury.

"What she actually said to him," said Lauren from the kitchen door, "was 'Get lost, you creep. You've never given a fuck about me till now, and I'm not having you anywhere near me in the future.'"

"I see."

"Charming, wasn't it? Tells you something about the way that bitch Caroline Fawley brought her up."

Charlie's reaction was that it was the only thing he'd heard said by Olivia Fawley that gave him the slightest respect for her. He got out of the cottage without even mentioning Rick's interest in the Crescent Hotel. Why jeopardise the relationship of Rick and Lauren? It had the supreme virtue of preventing them from making anyone else unhappy.

Chapter Seventeen

The Ones He Left Behind

Oddie had rarely had professional reasons to go to Pontefract, and he had a good knowledge only of the centre of the town. On the way up there he pondered idly on the sort of suburb the Winterbottoms would have lived in in Marius's childhood as Bert. Back-to-backs or terraced late-Victorian houses with their own back yard, he would have guessed.

Where they lived now might be another matter. There had been no problem tracing them. The dead man's sister had rung the Leeds police on Monday, saying she was getting pestered by the local press, and she thought she ought to talk to the police – if they had any reason to look at her brother's background – before she gave way to the reporters' thirst for details of the dead man's early life. Oddie wished he could have made the journey earlier, but at least he had given the sister, Hester Brierley by name, notice of his visit the day before. She would take the day off work, she said. Her father was in a nursing home two streets away, and she would take the policeman to call on him, though if it was one of his bad days there wasn't a lot of point, she said.

When Oddie had been through the centre and started out towards Cranbourne Road, it became clear that he was penetrating into one of the "nice" areas of the town. Good quality semis and detached houses with well-kept gardens, paintwork and stonedash all in good nick. Number twenty-six was like all the others, with plentiful lead-lighting of floral and geometrical design in the windows and front door. As he was getting out of his car, the front door opened, and a woman came out.

"I've been keeping a watch out for you," she said, coming through the gate. "Shall we walk to the nursing home now? It's no way, and they say it's one of Dad's fairly good days, so best to do it as soon as possible, because you never know if it's going to last. I'm Hester Brierley, of course."

"And I'm Detective Superintendent Oddie, if you want the full mouthful," said Mike. "It's very good of you to take all this trouble. Does your father know his son is dead?"

"He's been told, but he hasn't taken it in, and I don't want to tell him again. I shouldn't be trying to teach you your own business, but I think if you start talking to him about Bert he'll just chat away and won't ask you *why* you want to talk about him."

"That sounds like a good idea. Were your father and ... Bert close?"

"Yes. Maybe close in a superficial way – men's things: cricket and football matches together. Pontefract Town were our team, of course, until Bert decided they were born losers, and he started to support Newcastle United. And they'd go to Test Matches in Leeds over the summer sometimes, and Dad took him to the Railwaymen's Club for his first pint."

"So he was a father's boy?"

"Yes, but like I say, in superficial ways mostly. It was Mum who was the mover in our household. She was the one with the ambition. Dad was pleased when I got into Teachers' College, but it was Mum who pushed me to make the effort, she who made it possible. It's from her that Bert got his drive. And she could be ruthless too, but in a small way – in a domestic context, you might say."

"Are you a teacher still?"

"Yes, I am. It's been my life. And I'm still loving it, in spite of everything ... Here we are."

The street they were in had that suburban similarity to the one Hester lived in. They pushed open the gate of The Wayside Nursing Home, which was the largest house in it, with an annex visible to the rear, and the front door opened to admit them. They were expected, and were welcomed.

"This is Mrs Mackie, who runs the home," said Hester, and he shook hands with a bright-as-a-pin Scottish lady who clearly regarded the Home as the next thing to a stately one. "And this is Detective Superintendent Oddie, who's in charge of the investigation. I expect he's the one you've seen on television, isn't he, Mary?"

"He is that. I'm very pleased to see you. Will you come through to the annex? I'll just show you into Mr Winterbottom's room, then I'll leave the three of you together."

They walked through the communal area, past what seemed at first like a forest of dull eyes, registering and then instantly forgetting their presence. In the midst of them, though, Oddie noticed sharp, glinting eyes observing, knowing who he was, what errand he was on, and relishing such an unusual event, something that gave savour to their day. The little party entered the annex, better lit and painted a bright white, with pictures of sea side and mountains on the walls. Mrs Mackie opened a door.

"Hello, Mr Winterbottom," she said, in a voice without false brightness. "Here's your daughter and the friend of hers I mentioned who's come to talk to you."

"Oh yes ... Come to talk."

There was a sort of residual sparkle in the eye, perhaps a product of this "good day", but it was fighting a losing battle with the prevailing dullness and life-fatigue. Oddie sat down on a chair on one side of the bed, and Hester Brierley on the other.

"That's right, Mr Winterbottom," said Oddie, trying to keep the talking-to-children tone out of his voice as successfully as Mrs Mackie managed to. "I'd like to have a good chat, if you feel well enough. About your son Bert."

"Oh yes. I think they told me that. About Bert ... What was it you? ..."

The voice faded.

"There's a lot of people interested in Bert, you know, Mr Winterbottom. He's a bit of a personality in the world."

That brightened him up.

"He is that! People have stopped me in the street wanting to talk about him for years. I don't know what I did, to have a son like that. Always going to do something, be something, was our Bert. And he did. Not many can say that. And a good son he's been to me. Bought me this house." He looked around and actually registered that something was not quite right. "*My* house," he amended. "Where I'll go home to, soon as they've found out what's wrong wi' me. Oh yes, he's a good son, is Bert."

"I hear that you and he were keen on sport, back when he was a youngster."

"We were that. Went to all the home games, and a lot of the away ones too. Didn't cost the earth, like it does now so they tell me, and they were real footballers on the pitch then, not bloody *stars*. Bert knew them all, read the sports pages soon as he'd got through the business ones ... Oh, he were a champion lad."

"I'm sure he was."

"I'd've been proud of him if he'd gone to university, but I was even prouder when he decided not to, and went into business. His mam was a bit disappointed, but I weren't. He had his head screwed on right. Business is where the money is, not in teaching and all that ... for all that teachers are necessary," he added, directing his words to his daughter. "But you makes your pile in business – and people are always going to need food, aren't they? – and when you've made it, you can do whatever the fancy tells you to do. He could buy that house for me without blinking, could Bert. He could have lived like a Lord, bought football teams, had a string of racehorses – just whatever he pleased! Eh, it makes me proud! I blink my eyes just to think of it!"

"I heard that he's thinking of expanding his business into the North," said Oddie.

"He is! Told me so hisself! He comes back often, you know, back to his home. Came to see me the other day. Stood there in the doorway and said 'By 'eck, you've got a few more years left in you yet, Dad. You look as fresh as a daisy!' It did me good to see him, and his good-humoured face. And he said to me, he said: 'I'm thinking of opening stores up North, Dad.' He were sitting there where you are now when he said it. 'I've held off long enough, not wanting to compete with Morrisons's, where I trained. But they're strong enough to stand a bit o' competition. I'll start wi' a big one in the centre o' Leeds, then I'll have one in Middlesbrough, then one in Newcastle.' Oh, he's going to be big up here! Getting back to his roots is our Bert ..." His eyelids began to blink, and he looked around him uncertainly. "Hester, love?"

"Yes, Dad?"

"Have I been talking a long time?"

"Not that long, Dad. Just ten minutes or so."

"Do you know, I feel tired. I think I'll try and have a little sleep."

He closed his eyes. Hester came over and eased him down into his bed. Then she tucked him up, and the two of them tiptoed out of the room. They found Mrs Mackie, busy with the varied wants and whims of her "guests" and thanked her for making Oddie welcome. Then they walked back to Hester's home in near-silence, Oddie trying to absorb what he had heard. When Hester had made coffee and fetched biscuits they settled down in her airy and comfortable living room for a talk.

"How much did you believe?" Marius's sister asked Oddie.

"I don't know. If I hadn't done a bit of work on your brother before I came here, I'd probably have believed all of it. Your dad seemed so ... lively, on the ball, so proud and full of everything that concerned his son. Was it all fantasy?"

"All the recent stuff? No, it wasn't. Life is never as neat as books, is it? Bert – I can't call him Marius, it sounds so bogus – left Pontefract about 1967, when he left school. He was training with Morrisons, as Dad said, and they're a Northern company as you must know. We saw quite a lot of him while he was a trainee manager – Mum would have had his guts for garters if he hadn't shown up pretty regularly."

"Was he afraid of her?"

She considered.

"Bert was never obviously afraid of anyone or anything. But I'd say he was morally afraid. She had standards, she made sure she passed them on to us, and I think she thought she had done. Bert was always on his best behaviour when Mum was around and watching him. While he was at school she made sure he was in by ten, did his homework and all that, and when he had girlfriends she vetted them. Of course I knew more about what he actually got up to than she did. Once he'd become a trainee manager her nannying him wasn't possible any more, but she still had enough influence to make sure that he came back every other weekend, went with Dad to a game, took us all to one of the good shopping towns, told us what he was doing. Of course, that was a sanitised version. I suspected it at the time, but whether Mum and Dad did too I never knew. He'd been left home two or three years when Mum was diagnosed as having cancer."

"And I suppose he was around a lot of the time then."

"Yes, he was. He was a good son to her up till the time she died, which was about six months later. And it went against the grain. Bert didn't like illness or unhappiness or unpleasantness. He came up to see her in the evenings, passed an hour or so with her, then went back to Leeds or Manchester or wherever. Said he was busy at weekends being relief manager in one or other of their stores. Really I think that weekends were too long to be in the vicinity of pain and misery. A quick evening visit was about his measure."

Oddie seemed to sense a well of bitterness there, or at least cynicism about her brother.

"I think maybe his girlfriends found the same thing in him," he said.

"I can imagine. Of course I knew some of his early girlfriends. One minute he'd be there, the next minute gone. He'd avoid recriminations and emotional mess like the plague. I expect poor Caroline Fawley would have found the same thing before long. Such a nice woman she always seems – but I suppose like everyone else I'm just thinking of the parts she plays on television."

"So far as I can judge she's not so different from her roles ... And after your mother's death, did things change?"

"Yes, but not immediately. No drastic cut-off point. But come the mid seventies, when he started out on his own, then his visits and phone calls (I never recall any letters) became fewer. That was about the time he bought Dad the house he mentioned."

"So that was true?"

"Oh yes. It's about ten minutes' walk from here – a nice house, to our way of thinking, pretty much like this one. Mum would have loved it."

"But your dad wasn't so keen?"

"Oh no, he loved it. You're jumping to conclusions – putting things into typical fictional patterns. Dad was happy as Larry, and *proud* – you've no idea! He was always a good mixer, was Dad, so the fact that he was suddenly transported to a middle class area didn't faze him. He'd always got on well with my friends from teachers' college, and my colleagues at school, and for a long time he had lodgers in the house, usually students at the Pontefract Poly. No, I just mentioned Mum because I was thinking how happy they would have been *together* in it, Mum and he. And perhaps Mum would have kept Bert up to the mark. Dad, I think, misunderstood ..."

"What do you mean, misunderstood?"

She sat for a few moments, gathering together her thoughts.

"You know what sometimes happens when children from pretty ordinary families – I don't like the term 'working class' – get educated, or make money, and move up in the awful English class system. There's not just an obvious gulf between parents and children, there's a gulf of understanding as well as social standing. The children don't really know what worries or hurts their parents, and the parents try to cling to the idea that the children haven't changed, that everything is as it was when they were little ... That house, for example –"

"The one he bought your dad?"

"Yes. I think Dad saw it as a sign. Bert wanted to keep in touch with his roots, have a foothold in the North. And when the visits became fewer and fewer he started ringing him at work – he got the number of the Fleetwood Group somehow or other, maybe just from Directory Enquiries – and he'd chide him about never seeing him, about the fact that he was losing his Yorkshire accent, and so on, and so on. Finally he went too far and Bert snapped and told him a few home truths."

"Because the house hadn't been his way of keeping in touch, had it?"

"No. It had been a way of buying Dad off. And that was essentially the end. No invitation to the wedding, or the christenings. Simple card at Christmas with just a signature – the *new* name. He used Dad's pestering as an *excuse*, I'm sure. He'd wanted to make a clean break for some time, and that gave him a flimsy sort of reason. Dad was devastated."

Oddie sat thinking for a bit.

"And was this break total?" he asked finally. "Did it extend to you too?"

"My card was signed 'Love, Marius'," she said wryly. "And more recently 'Love, Marius, Sheila, Guy and Helena.' That was after we'd seen each other again, had a bit of a talk."

"How did you come to meet up again?"

She clearly would have preferred not to talk about it, but she poured them both second cups of coffee and forced herself to.

"Tom, my husband, died three years ago. We'd had a very happy marriage, a son we both loved and got on well with – he's at Harvard at the moment, doing a doctoral thesis on something I barely understand. Tom was a teacher too – a wonderful one, far better than I am ... He got so depressed with the way education was going in this country: the regimentation, the suppressing of everything that isn't strictly utilitarian, the denial of flair and imagination in the teaching profession – above all the grisly farce of the inspections, which skew the whole school for months in advance."

She left a long silence. Oddie waited.

"During the run up to an inspection of his school he committed suicide. He felt his work had become a gross betrayal of all he'd ever stood for ... I felt so angry. I sent round a letter to all his friends and relations telling them that his death was suicide and why he had done it. One of the people I sent it to was Bert."

"And he came straight up to you?"

"No. In one of the old type of Hollywood film he would have, wouldn't he? But it was months after the funeral and the inquest – maybe three months. It was one of those lonely evenings: one eventually gets used to them, but never quite accepts them. There was a ring on the doorbell, and when I opened it, there was Bert. Twenty-five years older than when I'd seen him last, but unmistakably Bert. He just said 'Hello Hester', and my face was in his shoulder and I was crying all over his expensive suit. And he was putting his arms around me and saying that he'd hoped that I was getting over it."

"What happened?"

"He came in. We had coffee and cakes – funeral bakemeats, belatedly. I had a few little weeps. We talked about Tom – they'd never

185

met – and what a *good* man he was. 'I've never understood good people,' Bert said. He listened, and he understood, and he comforted. It was wonderful having him around again, even though I knew it would be brief. He told me about his wife and his children – just normal family stuff, but I was glad that at last I knew something. He didn't tell me about his other women, of course. When he was showing signs of leaving, towards nine o'clock, I came out and asked him to do something for me."

"Visit his father."

"Yes. I knew Bert, knew his moods, and this was a good one. I felt sure nothing could go wrong. He knew the house, but I walked with him anyway, and left him at the end of the road. When I kissed him goodbye he said 'Aren't you coming with me?' but I don't think he really wanted me to. He knew it would be best with just the two of them on their own. I phoned Dad the next day after school and he was over the moon. Just kept talking on and on about what Bert had said, what he'd told him about his businesses, his family, his houses. I was so glad I'd asked him to do it. I heard afterwards from Dad's neighbour that he'd seen Bert leaving about half past nine, so he wasn't there more than half an hour. But I was so happy for weeks afterwards that he'd made it up with Dad, and that he really felt for me in my loneliness."

"And then?"

She shrugged.

"Does there have to be an 'And then'?"

"You didn't rush to contact us when your brother was killed. I don't get the feeling you'll be at the funeral."

She pondered.

"I want to put this as clearly and simply as possible, but I don't want to seem a complete fool ... I suppose it was naive of me, but I thought his coming to see us would *lead* to something: a bit more contact, a telephone call now and then, even an invitation to stay with him and his family in London. But there was nothing. Just the card at Christmas, signed with the extra names, like I said. The *effect* was cruel rather than kindly – not the intention, I'm sure, but the effect."

"What do you think the intention was?"

"I don't know. You see, I don't know 'Marius', only the young Bert. But I would guess it was just some momentary impulse, one weekend when he happened to be in Leeds and had nothing special to occupy an evening. 'I'll go and see Hester. She's just lost her husband.' Not a *bad* impulse at all. Something left over from Mum's influence, just a trace left of her standards, her feelings about how one should behave. But incredibly skin-deep. Once he'd done that little bit of his duty, it was just forgotten – nothing followed it, not as far as he was concerned."

"But it did have consequences, didn't it – on your Dad?"

"I thought you might have guessed that. You've known people going towards senility, haven't you?"

"Yes," said Oddie, his face twisting. "My mother."

"I should emphasize that you saw him today at something approaching his best. On other days he can just drift in and out of consciousness and hardly says anything with any grasp of reality – those are the days when he's at his worst. But Bert's visit was towards the beginning of the process, and he was so overjoyed by it that it was the start of this fantasy: Bert was a good son, he came back regularly, they went to sporting fixtures together, he said things that Dad could quote to people, he even used to claim that Bert consulted him about business affairs."

"And in fact there was nothing between that one visit and Bert's death?"

"Nothing. But the fantasy cheered Dad up no end, and I never tried to disabuse him of it. I did ring Bert once in the years since his visit. It was when Dad was taken into the nursing home, about six months ago. I found his number by Dad's phone, and I rang him to tell him what had happened and why."

"How did he react?"

"He was quite brief and businesslike about it. I explained that I wanted to keep my job on, and couldn't nurse him during the day, and he said he understood, that he was too busy to talk, but I was to send the bills for the nursing home – the part that was not covered by his pension – to him and he'd see to them. And that was it."

"You were disappointed, I imagine."

"Yes, I was. Again," she added wryly. "The bills weren't the reason I'd rung him. I thought about it, but in the end – I'm a teacher, and there are no rich teachers – I did send the bills to him. They were always paid. But I felt I was doing things on his terms, that he had enclosed me in a world run by his values. And I wondered whether people around him always had to do that."

"I rather think they did," Oddie said. He began to shift in his chair. "Is there anything else about your brother that you'd like to tell me?"

"No, I don't think so." She got up, and they began towards the front door. In the hallway she stopped and turned to him, and surprised him with a question.

"Did you know D.H. Lawrence was called 'Bert' at home?"

Oddie shook his head. That was one odd fact that he had not learned from his wife.

"No, I didn't know that."

"David Herbert Lawrence, known to his family as Bert."

"I think I'd go for 'David Herbert' myself."

"And when he met his sisters later in life, years after he'd flown the nest, and they still referred to him as 'Our Bert' he didn't like it at all. 'I'm not their Bert,' he said, 'and I never was.'"

Oddie stood on the doorstep and looked at her.

"You feel you didn't know him, don't you?"

"Yes."

"And that you never knew the real man."

"Yes. I feel that as a boy he must always have been playing some kind of game or charade with us, waiting to get away to become the real him ... I told you, didn't I, that I knew some of his girlfriends – the ones he had while he was still a boy?"

"Yes, you did."

"They were all strong people – independent, intelligent girls, with a good future in front of them, if they worked and fought. He left them miserable, uncertain, unsure of themselves and their capabilities."

"That's interesting. There may be some kind of pattern in his chosen women."

"And maybe he met someone too strong to be used like that."

Chapter Eighteen

Gathering the Threads

When Charlie arrived at CID on Saturday morning, his boss was just finishing a phone call.

"Yes – that was rather what I suspected. The other information was interesting, but I can't really see it as having any bearing on the case – unless our view of it changes drastically. I'm grateful to you for your time. I know you must be pretty stressed out at the moment." He put the phone down. "That was the manager at the Fleetwood Group's headquarters."

Charlie raised his eyebrows.

"What's our interest there?"

Oddie spread his hands.

"When a rich man is murdered we can't ignore the fact of his riches. We need to know what's going to happen to the boodle. And there are other ramifications, such as whether there were any of his rivals who obviously would like him out of the way."

"A bit mafioso that, isn't it? I don't often want to sound complacently English, but I don't think firms here usually go around getting their rivals put permanently out of business."

"Nor do I, but who knows? There's a school of thought that says we're being taken over by the Russian mobsters. Anyway, the truth as sent down from headquarters is that he was planning a cautious, exploratory expansion into the North – hardly a threat to the dominance of the big boys in this area. And that will go ahead in any case: his death changes nothing – the group is too big for that. And his fortune all goes to his wife."

Charlie chuckled.

"His marriage was far from over, then."

"We suspected that. I wonder if he'd tried that one on lots of his women, or if it was a new one especially framed for Caroline Fawley. I think his marriage and his affairs represent a rather eighteenth-century sort of arrangement. There is the regular mistress, but the wife is the one of real importance. I think at the Fleetwood group they would like Sheila to take on an important role. Apparently she is something of a whizz at getting things done in the Arts organisations she chairs, and also good on the PR side. I gather from my contact that she is insisting that until the baby is born, she can't make any decisions like that, and they'll have to appoint a stopgap chairman. Maybe what she is trying to do is make sure nothing permanent is decided until Guy grows up a bit."

"That might mean a very long wait."

"It might indeed. Anyway, all this is interesting, but not really for us, I don't think."

"Nor do I. What do we do now. Pause for breath?"

"I think so. Do stocktakings, like Prime Ministers do: call together the Cabinet and say 'Where are we at, and where are we going?'"

"And the answer in politics is 'nowhere' as a rule," said Charlie. "We haven't got a Cabinet, though, have we? Hargreaves is a good, solid bloke, but his brain is never going to solve any of the mysteries of the universe. Troops are thin on the ground."

"We could call in Rani," suggested Oddie. "He did a lot of the bystander-witness interviewing, and he's just been talking to Walter Fairlie, who did the work at the Crescent. But mostly he could be useful as an outsider, a sounding-board if you like: someone who knows the circumstances of the murder but not all the psychological network behind it. Having him here will force us to go over all the detail, maybe get a new perspective."

So twenty minutes later they were seated with a bemused but distinctly flattered Rani, with a flask of real coffee, some sandwiches, and a whole case to survey.

"If we begin at the beginning," said Oddie, "then it has to be with the dead man. There's still a possibility of a random slaying, but we've uncovered enough dirt, enough possible motives, to let us put that on the back-burner, at least for the moment. Who was Marius Fleetwood?"

"Bert Winterbottom, for the first twenty-odd years of his life," Charlie pointed out. "And by your account a good son in a solid working-class family."

"But one with upwardly-mobile impulses," said Oddie. "Mostly but not entirely centred on the mother. Dad apparently never had much trouble mixing with any class of person. Was it the upward mobility impulse that made Bert itch to get on? That does come over strongly from my talk with the sister."

"I know how he felt," said Rani.

"Do you?"

"And how. Families are stronger in Asia, and in Asian families here. You really have to fight if you want to get away from the life they've earmarked for you."

"And you wanted to come into the police force," said Oddie with gentle irony.

"I wanted to do something different, and I didn't want to spend three or four years in higher education. I made it – I'm not standing behind the counter of a you-name-it-we've-got-it shop – but it was a struggle."

"Interesting. But with Bert Winterbottom it was rather different: they were behind him all the way. I have the impression that they recognised that the family had produced a boy who was definitely exceptional. They were proud as Punch that people who knew him realised he was, even at seventeen, someone who was obviously going to make a splash."

"So when he kicked the ladder from under him, it was a piece of real ingratitude," said Charlie.

"Yes. OK, his father was pestering him a bit. He could have been dealt with firmly. Instead his sister is convinced that the pestering was used, brutally, as an excuse to cut the bonds entirely."

"Right," said Charlie. "So now we have Bert Winterbottom meta-morphosed into Marius Fleetwood, successful and respected busi-nessman. And deservedly so, by all accounts."

"Oh, absolutely," said Oddie. "Straight, responsible, responsive – founder of a chain that in quite a short time developed a bond of trust with its customers, as the old Marks and Spencer's did, though it took them much longer to do it. Fleetwood's Supermarkets got themselves an instant reputation: they gave value, they told the truth, they were responsive to environmental and ethnic concerns, they were model employers."

"But in private he was a lying two-timer, is that right?" asked Rani.

"That's about it. Seems like he had to let off his immoral steam somewhere, and he did it in his private life. We're not talking here just about him having a wife and a mistress. He seems to have slipped into the convenient lie like a duck into water. He tells his mistress his marriage is effectively over, and when his wife gets pregnant he tells her it's by some younger lover. And when a young lookalike enters the stage who was born and grew up in Armley, he tells her he's never lived in Leeds, but he had had a younger brother who did, a tearaway, and he'd slept around like there was no tomorrow – the said brother being a spur of the moment invention – I could go on. The charming liar personified."

"With a basic contempt for the women he was charming and making fools of," said Rani.

"That could be a much longer list than we know about," said Charlie. "And we know about his wife, his current mistress, and a long-ago lover in Armley. Add to them his own children, who did or could have had grievances against him – Guy and Helena, and even perhaps the Fawley children and certainly Peter Bagshaw. That's a pretty good list to start with."

"And you can add to those his own family back in Pontefract," said Oddie. "I agree with you it's a formidable list, but I don't think we should include Sheila Fleetwood among the women he fooled. Once, maybe, but not for years. They perfectly understood each other, apparently, and she stayed with him on his terms. Comparisons with Hillary Clinton and Mary Archer spring to mind. She knew, I imagine, about all his sexual liaisons. She may well have a motive, but it surely has to be something other than his womanising – something we haven't uncovered yet."

"And did she have an opportunity?" said Rani. "Living in London ..."

"She was at a board meeting of the Gordon Craig Theatre trustees in Stevenage until about five o'clock," said Oddie. "But let's stick with motive for the moment. We haven't discussed yet his new situation, of starting up a liaison with the daughter of his mistress. That was an entirely new factor."

"If it wasn't just a one-night stand," said Rani.

"There was the matter of the newly-decorated fantasy room at the Crescent, which he was to have the use of for three weeks – which is about the length of the rest of the current opera season at the Grand."

"Walter Fairlie tells me he'd done one or two similar jobs – part of the process of wooing women who later became long-term mistresses. On the other hand, it could have been a one-night stand on Olivia Fawley's part," objected Rani.

"That's quite true. And in that connection we have to remember that Olivia brings with her into this case a long list of lovers from her recent past and present."

"And also a father who was ambitious to cling to her skirt-tails if her career takes off as people expect," said Charlie.

"That's right. A decidedly unsavoury character, Rick Radshaw. We only have his word for it that she gave him the brush-off at the post-performance party. It could have been earlier."

"What about Caroline Fawley?" asked Rani. "She could have one of the best motives of all. She's woken up to Marius now, she says, but can we be sure she didn't suss him out much earlier?"

Oddie and Charlie thought.

"No, we can't be sure," said Charlie. "By all accounts they were pretty careless, Fleetwood and Olivia. There could have been mounting anger on Caroline's part as she realized they were panting for each other, and that it was going to climax, in every sense of the word, on the first night of *Forza*."

"But then opportunity really *does* present a problem," said Oddie. "But before we get on to opportunity, just one observation: as his sister said (and she's one herself) he really went for strong, independent women. He deceived them, he played with them, he brought them down, but he wouldn't have had half so much fun if they'd been gorgeous bird-brains. I'd say that applied to Caroline Fawley just as much as to the others – though we've thought all along that she was a bit of a fool to be taken in. So, at one time or another, had Sheila Fleetwood, Mrs Bagshaw, and a whole lot more."

"Maybe the only one who wasn't was Olivia Fawley," said Charlie.

"Fair point. But she wasn't in the market for a long-term relationship. She's only interested in ships that pass in the night. A totally different agenda. His agenda, apparently, was long-term, hers short."

"Maybe that was the problem," said Rani. "Maybe that was the undoing of him."

* * *

"No, no," said Caroline into the phone. "I couldn't think of dragging you out here. In any case it's rather tricky to find. I'll come to the theatre. I very much want to see it again, and I haven't been backstage at all ... Oh, I agree about the potential, provided we can find the sort of repertoire that suits the size of the theatre and suits the patrons too. We'll have to see what's available from outside, as well as initiating productions ourselves, of course ... Yes, I'm glad Mrs Fleetwood recommended me, and please: you don't have to be embarrassed about it. We're not embarrassed, why should you be? When shall we say, then ... No, Monday isn't too early. Ten o'clock. That's fine. Oh, and by the way if you *do* find that I suit, and if we can come to an agreement, I shall need to find a house near Doncaster itself – something quite modest, because I shan't have the children with me that much longer. Do please keep your eyes open ... You are terribly kind!"

She put the phone down, pretty confident that they would find that she suited them. Philip Massery, the Chairman of the Trustees of the Little Theatre, had been trying to suppress his drools at the prospect all through the call. Caroline wished she could remember what it was that she and Marius had seen there. It had made very little impression at the time. Luckily she kept a diary, and could well have noted the title of the play. If the performance was undistinguished, all the more chance for the new broom to improve things.

194

She had not wanted Massery to come to Alderley. She was very conscious of the sort of spectacle she now made, posed against the backdrop of the house: the mistress, set up in a solid, impressive establishment, suddenly finding herself about to be turned out into the cold. It was not quite like the Lady of the Camellias coughing herself to death in a denuded apartment, but it was along the same lines. She had been deserted by Marius in his hour of death, just as any of her predecessors would have been if his death had coincided with their period of tenure as his accepted mistress. The *special* place she had imagined for herself in this line had been a figment of her own imagination. She would have hated it if Philip Massery had come to see her amid the ruins of her hopes and aspirations. He might have appointed her to lead the Little Theatre of Doncaster out of *pity*. She wanted to go there in hope, make the place the centre of her life, and succeed there, both as actress and as administrator.

The sound of an elderly motor car aroused her from her reverie. She knew it was Jack – his first visit since the murder, though they had talked more than once on the phone. As she opened the front door Alex came out of his little computer room and started up the stairs to the lavatory. Caroline had intended to kiss Jack, in thanks for his visit and his tender care of her while she was Marius's mistress, but now she gave him no more than a formal peck, and still got suspicious looks from her son.

"Jack, thank you so much for having come," she said, drawing him into the kitchen. "You've been wonderful to me, and I'm so grateful. Tea or coffee? And what would you like with it? I've got chocolate cake, or some little biscuits I made for Marius last weekend which are still nice and crisp."

"Oh tea. And the biscuits, if the memory is not too painful."

"Not painful at all."

"I usually avoid coming up at weekends," said Jack, "but now –"

"*Now* you're doing me a service. Taking my mind off things. And by *things* I mean anger rather than grief."

She was aware, as she fetched the tin of biscuits and brewed the tea, of a suppressed excitement in Jack. She tried to dampen it down when they went into the sitting room and waited for the tea to brew.

"I've just been talking to the Chairman of the Little Theatre in Doncaster," she said. "There's a chance of a job there, as big panjandrum – a sort of actor-manager."

"Oh Caroline, I *am* pleased! You know I always –"

"Yes, Jack, I know – *now*. And now I know why. You were trying to warn me about Marius, not trying to preserve my dramatic gifts for the English stage."

"Both, my dear – both."

"At least you didn't know about him and Olivia. I suppose you've heard by now?"

"Rumours, my dear. Mrs Naylor's son is very in with Opera North."

"People love that kind of thing. It makes me feel dirty. It's a terrible thing when your own daughter *disgusts* you. I never want to see Olivia again."

"Don't say that. Some day she may have need of you."

"I certainly hope she does!" said Caroline grimly.

"Anyway," said Jack, trying to turn the conversation, "it will be wonderful to see you on stage."

"Oh, I'll only do old-woman parts, and there aren't enough of those to go round."

"If you only give yourself old-woman parts I shall write letters of protest to the *Doncaster Evening News*."

"You're so sweet, Jack. I'm afraid I shall have to move to a smaller house, and one closer to Doncaster. I'm really sorry about playing host to the fête, but it looks as though you and Meta will have to shoulder it again."

Jack bounced up and down in his chair and sprayed biscuit crumbs all over his ancient suit.

"You haven't heard, then?"

"*Heard*, Jack?"

"It's all round the village, but probably no one has told you because you're more or less in mourning."

"Mrs Hogbin is the only one who brings me village gossip, and her day is Tuesday. Tell me, Jack: I'm on tenterhooks."

"I've turned Meta out of the house!"

Caroline's jaw fell open.

"Jack! You haven't! ... What do you mean, 'turned out'."

"I mean I packed her bags, put them outside the front door and locked her out."

"But why? You've lived together so long – all your lives, in fact. What had she done?"

Jack looked down and became cagey.

"Oh, it had been building up for a long time."

She'd been sounding off about me, thought Caroline.

"But where will she go? She's got no money, or so she always says."

"She's gone to Aunt Sarah in Northampton. I had a bitter phone-call of complaint from Auntie yesterday evening. But she's eighty-seven, and needs someone there. They'll shake down."

"But what if she's turned out again?"

"She can't be. Sarah hasn't got the strength."

An awful conviction came over Caroline. Meta had been turned out to make room in the Dower House for herself and the children. She'd realized he was besotted, but she shuddered at such cruel consequences of something that was an illusion, a chimera, something that absolutely never could be. It had to be nipped in the bud.

"Jack, I can see how excited and pleased you are about this –"

"I am!" he said, his mouth stretched in a broad, triumphant grin. "It's like a liberation, Caroline. I haven't been so excited since VE Day!"

Caroline's face assumed an expression of warm but sad sympathy.

"But you do realize, don't you, that though I'm *enormously* fond of you as a friend, it never can be more than that. It's nothing personal. It's just that Marius was *absolutely* the last man in my life, and –"

"Caroline!" He almost shouted. She raised her head and looked at him, and saw that his face was red with a sort of horror. "You misunderstand. I've never for a moment imagined – ... I've wor-

197

shipped you, but absolutely not in that way. I wouldn't have dared! And you know, since Lydia died, and the little baby, there's never been any question, not the slightest in the world, of –"

Caroline had to dash in to retrieve the situation.

"Oh Jack – I am *so* sorry. You must think me an awful fool. *Please* put it down to all the traumas and horrors of the last few days. I just thought your turning out Meta, after all these years, and you always having been so good and considerate to me –"

"Enough said! Dear Caroline, enough said! I turned out Meta because I've been wanting to for years without really realizing it, and I finally plucked up courage to do it. Already I feel as if my life has been transformed. I can spend my last years alone and in peace. You can't think how happy that makes me."

Probably Aunt Sarah would have liked to do the same, Caroline thought. Then she felt she was being mean.

Rather sooner than he might otherwise have done, Jack decided that he had better be off. Ushering him through the hall and out into the September sunshine Caroline was conscious of the eyes of Alex and Stella on them from the stairs. She suddenly had a thought that almost made her laugh. Jack had gone through the whole visit without farts or tummy rumbles. His distaste for his awful sister must have been the thing that upset his stomach, and he had effected his own cure for it. How odd! To cover her amusement she said:

"Jack, I do hope you can forget my stupid, *stupid* mistake, and we can go back to being as we were."

"Of course, Caroline my dear." He paused, then looked at her with a twinkling eye. "And, you know, thinking it over, it's really rather flattering. In fact, truth to tell, I'm chuffed to bits that you could even think of it!"

And, looking at him, Caroline could believe it.

She waved him goodbye, and went back into the house, which suddenly seemed over-large, undistinguished in its architecture and furnishings and even slightly ridiculous as a home for herself and two children. The two children were still standing on the stairs, looking at her in that adolescent weighing-up, judgmental way.

"You don't have to worry," she called up. "I haven't made a fool of myself."

But that, she thought, was exactly what she had done.

* * *

"So what say we go on to opportunity?" asked Oddie. "Can we rule out his two current women on those grounds alone?"

"I'd have thought we had to rule out Caroline Fawley, at least as doing it herself," said Charlie. "There's no doubt she remained in the theatre when he slipped out, no doubt she was around throughout the Interval, and was in the theatre for the second half. Rani and the other uniformed people have checked that very thoroughly, and it's dent-proof. Aside from hiring a knife-man – and a gunman would be much more likely and efficient – she's in the clear."

"But not the wife," said Rani. "Meeting ends at Stevenage at five o'clock. M1 then A1 – you could do it easily by 7.45."

"I've been in a car with you, Rani," said Mike Oddie. "You're a maniac."

"I'm a fast, safe driver," protested Rani.

"In the passenger seat it felt maniacal. I'd put Sheila Fleetwood down as a careful, efficient driver. We'll class her as possible but unlikely."

"All three children have to be classed as possible and not at all unlikely, as far as opportunity is concerned," said Charlie.

"I agree. I can't see Guy as having the guts, and the other two are awfully young to murder a capable, well-set-up man who's also a sort of father-figure to them. But we're not into character – a quagmire area anyway. We're into opportunity. And you're forgetting, Charlie, that there are four children."

"Four children. I stand corrected. Or rather five. Miss Helena has kept herself pretty much in the background of the picture so far as our investigations are concerned. Or should we say six, remembering Olivia? Still a child, with its typical want, want, want. But back to the real, actual child: the one who, so far as we know, has never seen his father. I don't fancy Pete Bagshaw's alibi at all. At home watching television with his mother. Backed up in a too-pat way by his mother. He could have been anywhere."

"Not quite," said Oddie. "If he was with a lot of other people – fellow students, say – he would have told us. But he could have come into Leeds. He could, if he has a car or the use of one, have gone to Alderley to snatch a look at his dad, or to do something more drastic. There again he could have heard that the star of Opera North's new production was Olivia Fawley, and that she was the actress Caroline Fawley's daughter, and concluded that his father was likely to be at the first night."

"But not that he was likely to leave after half an hour and go to a crap-hotel like the Crescent," said Rani.

"Unlikely, I admit. But there is one possibility."

"What's that?"

"That Pete Bagshaw lied (if he did) because his mother was not home that night. He lied to give her an alibi, not *vice_versa*."

They pondered this for some time.

"Right," said Charlie. "Anybody else?"

"The sister," said Mike. "We really can rule out the father I'm sure, but not the sister. She fits into the pattern of the women in Fleetwood's life – a strong, independent personality. I have only her word for it that the contact between 'their Bert' and the Winterbottoms was practically nonexistent. It could have been much more frequent, and it could have left wounds."

"There's the same difficulty as with Pete Bagshaw and his mother," said Rani. "How could she guess his movements?"

"Yes, there is. Less so perhaps with another group – Olivia's lovers at the theatre. They would have had ways of finding out – in fact I wouldn't put it past that awful piece of self-obsession herself to tell them about the assignation, boast about it, taunt them with it."

"A nearly limitless pool of suspects opens up," sighed Charlie. "And there's a related one as well."

"Related?"

"Someone who may have been enraged by the Fleetwood-Olivia affair (if he knew about it) out of sheer chivalry."

"Jack Mortyn-Crosse?"

"Yes. He has this enormous protectiveness towards Caroline. I would have said he was the gentlest, most ineffectual of men, but then we're not into the quagmire of character, and any or all of us could be wrong about people we don't know beyond an interview or two."

"And he has a sister, doesn't he?"

"Yes. A nasty woman – a racist, probably a classist as well: she could well have thought of Marius as a common little tyke. Could have thought of Caroline as an actress in the old-fashioned sense of the word, tantamount to a prostitute. But those are not motives for murder. And I have to say she seems to me to be comic-nasty rather than dangerous-nasty."

"Character again," said Oddie. "The awful fact is, almost all these people could have had the opportunity, and unless we make a breakthrough over the weekend we'll have to get down to breaking alibis and charting opportunities."

"I still think," said Rani, "of those three kids wandering around Leeds at just the right time. What was the estimated time of death?"

"The Doc says any time between around half past seven and nine o'clock. With his betting being on the earlier part of the time-span."

"There you are, then: just when they were all three wandering around, not very sure what they were going to do with their freedom in the big city."

"But it's a part of Leeds nobody goes to," objected Charlie.

"The less you know of a city, the more likely you are to land up in dead ends and back alleyways," said Rani. They thought about that.

"Guy," said Oddie. "A first-time visitor. But I don't fancy him."

"They could have landed up in that area by following someone," said Charlie. "Most obviously they could have followed Marius."

"But unless they did it actually with the intention of murdering him, I can't see them doing that. They were out of bounds in Leeds, and Marius was the only real danger of their being caught, since they all knew he was likely to leave the theatre. To follow him would be to enormously increase the risk. It's much more

201

likely they'd have turned away and slunk in the opposite direction."

"That knowing girl Stella had some experience, saw something, that night," said Charlie. "I was sure of it when I interviewed her, and I'm sure of it now. But nothing likely has come up."

"I think you should have another go at her," said Oddie.

There was silence in the CID room.

"Then there's the weapon," said Oddie dispiritedly. "Where is the knife? Who had one, and why? Where has it gone?"

"I read the review of the opera in *The Times*," said Rani. "Wasn't there a lot of sword-fighting in it?"

"Yes, I think so, but that would have been in the second half," said Oddie. "I missed a lot of that. Bears looking into. But the description of the wound suggests a dagger rather than a sword. And carrying a sword around in the vicinity of a security-conscious new block of flats is likely to get you noticed. My wife tells me that the Olivia character gets stabbed off-stage at the end. I can't imagine she staggers on for the finale with a dagger protruding from her bos, but it's a mad world, and you never know. A word with the props man is called for."

A little voice in the back of Charlie's mind said that a visit to the Grand Theatre was called for, and not just to investigate the props. But before that he had to have another go at the pert young miss, Stella Fawley.

* * *

Caroline and Sheila found themselves in the odd position of wanting to ring each other up the whole time. Somehow, without any desire on their part, they seemed connected by some umbilical cord. Caroline had the best excuse, that of wanting to hear how things were going with Guy, then using that gambit to tell Sheila how things were going with the Doncaster Little Theatre chairman. For the truth was she suddenly cared very little about Guy, who had revealed his feet of clay quite as spectacularly as his father had. But Sheila herself she did care about, and felt with her a

202

kind of kinship which she thought could burgeon into a real friendship.

"No, I haven't changed my mind about coming to the funeral," she said when they talked on Saturday afternoon. "The wounds have *not* healed yet. There will be so much advance publicity for it that perhaps some of his other girlfriends will turn up – women whose wounds are less raw than mine. You should take their names and addresses and we could form a club."

"I have their names and addresses," said Sheila laconically. The two women laughed. "The idea of a club is not a bad one. 'The Women of Marius Fleetwood.' Just so long as we don't discuss sex."

"Why shouldn't we? It was the best thing about him."

"You'd find he used exactly the same techniques and ploys with all his women. It's humiliating. It makes one feel like one of several puppets, reacting the same way when he pulled the same strings. Otherwise we could talk about money, the legal status of mistresses, their financial rights ... Oh dear, the wife might feel out of things in all this. She has all the rights and standing. It would have to be you, Caroline, who went on all the chat shows and outlined the aims of the organisation."

The two women laughed again.

"How's Guy?"

"Pretty much the same," said Sheila with a sigh. "Going on about how he only wanted to go up to St Andrews with a bit of money to make a splash."

"Funny, my two are saying now that Guy never talked about anything except money. They never complained before."

"Because they wanted you to think that everything was fine and dandy between the young of the two families. Children *shield* their parents. Well, Helena does. I can't say I remember Guy doing any shielding."

"Don't give up on him, Sheila."

"Of course I'm not giving up on him. It's just that I'm realising that quite soon I shall be mothering two babies."

"Yes, I suppose he is a sort of moral baby ... Ooops, I must go."

"What's come up?"

"A car's driven up. DS Peace has just got out."

"Oh dear. I was hoping the police had finished with us for the moment. Watch Peace. He's sharp."

Caroline had been making the call from her bedroom. She slipped downstairs, but not fast enough to prevent the bell sounding through the house. She swallowed, then put on her most welcoming smile as she opened the door.

"Hello. I wasn't expecting you back so soon ... I don't think I've met your Constable."

"This is PC Rani. It was actually your daughter we've come to see, Mrs Fawley."

"My daughter? My daughter Stella?"

"That's right."

Caroline looked at him uncertainly for a moment, than backed into the hall.

"Stella!" A door opened upstairs almost immediately. The call had been waited for. In a moment Stella was coming down the stairs, a false brightness on her face.

"Do you think we could use the little study, as before?" Charlie asked. Caroline nodded. Charlie led the way, then closed the door and leaned his back against it, looking at Stella and saying nothing.

"You think I'm holding something back," said the girl.

"I *know* you are. But I want to hear what you saw in your own words."

It was a disgraceful imposture, old as the hills. It should never have worked. But Stella was only fourteen. She turned away to avoid his gaze and began to tell them.

Chapter Nineteen

Coup de Théâtre

Charlie and Rani stood at the back of the stalls in the Grand Theatre as the seats began to fill up. It was ten past seven, and as at all the performances of *Forza* the sense of expectation was palpable. Charlie found he was excited just at the experience of a packed theatre, and especially so at one that was clearly not just doing its cultural duty. Rani was cooler, more analytical: theatre was not in his blood, and he was not going to wallow in the experience, merely dissect and tabulate it.

The ladies on the door were rather satirical when the pair had used their ID to gain admittance to the performance. "Is the whole Leeds police force being given a musical education," asked the lady selling programmes, "and are you all getting free admission to our shows?" Privately though, when she had a moment, she took the two of them aside and said: "Joking apart, you get it sorted, and quickly. They say there's a really terrible atmosphere backstage, and even us front-of-house people are looking at each other and wondering – daft, isn't it? Mind you, every cloud has a silver lining: there's been full houses even for *Love for Three Oranges*, which they were papering half the house for last time it was on. Folk are strange, aren't they?"

"Papering," muttered Charlie as they walked away: "I think it means they beg people to come in for free."

And now the lights went down, and the heavy-framed conductor took his place and his applause, and the opera started. Charlie wished he could have been closer, to get a more authoritative view of what was going on on stage, but close views were reserved for luckier mortals who had paid money. At seven thirty-one Charlie, who had done a bit of homework on the opera in the Leeds Public Library, muttered: "Beginning the tenor-soprano duet – the only one in the opera." Rani wasn't sure whether this was just conversation or was meant to be noted down, so he entered the information in the little book Charlie had instructed him to carry. The pair were interrupted in mid-duet by the heroine's father, in a state of outrage. The gun was thrown down, went off with a crack and a flash that evoked little screams from parts of the stalls, and within a minute the stage had gone almost completely dark. Charlie glanced quickly down at his phosphorescent watch.

"Scene one ends seven forty-two," he announced, then resumed his intense scrutiny of the stage. A shadow flitted across it, barely glimpsed in the intense dark, and seemed to retrieve the gun, before darting off. "The hero is supposed to be of Indian blood," Charlie noted to Rani in the brief pause. "South American Indian, of course. They don't seem to have browned him up even a titsy-bitsy little bit. Like the retired colonels say in letters to the *Telegraph*: 'Political correctness gone mad.'"

The music began again, and in the darkness the set had acquired a couple of benches and tables. In the bright light of a daytime scene Charlie distinguished much more clearly the gun-like shape of the basic set. "Subtle," he thought sardonically. At the inn the solitary and lost Leonora, confronted by the sight of her vengeful brother, did the normal operatic gesture of concealment: she raised her arm so that the sleeve of her dress formed an impromptu yashmak. The music went on its full-blooded but boding way, until the scene was succeeded by the monastery – monks, the Prior, and the acceptance of Leonora as non-resident hermit. The music of the scene had Charlie's spine in a perpetual tingle, but when the curtain went down he looked at his watch in a business-like way.

"Eight thirty," he announced to Rani. "Interval."

They slipped out in advance of the thirsty mob, and went to the main entrance on Briggate.

"What put you up to it? Rani asked, as they walked round to the side of the theatre.

"Something Mike said. He'd seen it. He said 'They got separated.' Of course I didn't think at the time. You never do. But somehow it lodged there ... If Leonora was out of things for almost the whole of the second half –"

They had got to the stage door, and Charlie just raised his eyebrows at his companion. Rani nodded, and seemed to file it away, as if he were compiling some kind of handbook of detection techniques. Charlie pushed open the stage door and they tripped down the murky steps to the little guiche at the bottom. Syd's place.

"Ah, Syd. Me again."

"So I see," said Syd, trying to be genial. "No mistaking you, sir."

Charlie bared his teeth.

"I need to have a few words with the props man." Syd looked professionally dubious.

"Not the best time, sir."

"I realize that."

Charlie waited.

"I'll try him on his mobile." Syd dialled, and in a moment was talking. "I've got the police here, Bob. One of them's the one who talked to Simon on Tuesday. Yes, it would have been better if he'd talked to you then, but no doubt something has turned up ... OK, I'll tell him." He turned to the two policemen. "He says he can talk to you after the interval. It's the big scene between the tenor and the baritone. It needs some setting up, but once that's done it's a good long scene with nothing for him to do."

"Marvellous," said Charlie, moving away. "All right if we go backstage?"

"Er, no – if you wouldn't mind. Madam might cut up rough."

Charlie raised his eyebrows.

"I take it you mean Olivia Fawley?" Syd nodded. "She has got you well trained."

"And not just me," said Syd feelingly. "The whole theatre."

"I was backstage on Thursday and they told me she was around."

"That was *Oranges*. That's not her show. This is her show – and doesn't she let us know it! Just find a place to park yourselves and I'll give you a nod when the lights go down."

Charlie took Rani over to a bench in the far corner of the waiting space. He himself felt he'd had more than enough of Syd in the last few days, and he knew that Syd's sense of "humour" would be irrepressible, faced with not one but two non-white policemen. Rani tried to be blasé but tended to fume inwardly, and people who fumed almost always did the wrong thing. The interval seemed endless, but eventually Syd raised his finger and pointed in the direction of backstage.

Everyone there, of course, knew Charlie. It was like a remote village, where strangers were noted and watched. Even the baritone, waiting to go on, registered a police presence, and he was one that Charlie had not set eyes on before. The props man, Bob Holdsworth, came over to them, all no-nonsense and down-to-earthiness, and said: "I've got about fifteen minutes", and led them to a small, locked room so stuffed with this and that that it had more the feel of an overgrown cupboard.

"Now," said Bob. "What can I do for you?"

"Weapons," said Charlie, "used in the opera: are they real, and could they be used in earnest?"

Bob nodded.

"Borrowed from the Royal Armouries. All surplus to stock and of no particular value, but naturally we promise to take very good care of them. This room is locked, the cupboard where the swords are kept is locked, the case for the pistols is locked – we're pretty strict about it, because we might well want to borrow from them again for some other opera."

"Why not the standard stage props?"

Bob shrugged.

"Verisimilitude it's called. The actors look and feel right if they've got the right gear, the right props – that's the director's theory, and if you ask me why he has Alvaro in the first scene wearing jeans when he's wielding a flintlock pistol I couldn't tell you, though it's common enough in productions these days."

"The guns, of course, wouldn't be loaded, would they?" asked Rani.

"No, of course not. And quite possibly they wouldn't go off if they were. The swords are not particularly sharp, but they clang brilliantly, and – yes – they do add to the feel that these are two macho eighteenth-century men engaged in a life and death duel."

"I'm sure they do," said Charlie. "Can I see the swords?"

Bob unlocked the cupboard.

"These are not the actual ones. They're on stage at the moment.

But they're pretty much like these two, which are 'spares'." He handed a sword over to each of the policemen. They were long, thin, deadly-looking weapons, though when Charlie ran his finger down the edges he found they were far from sharp, as Bob had said. Charlie and Rani looked at each other and shook their heads.

"Even if they were sharper," said Charlie, "I don't think they could have been the weapon. They're so long, and flexible, that you couldn't get the force on that apparently was used. It really has to be a dagger. The programme says that Leonora is stabbed at the end. What with?"

Bob again shrugged, a favourite gesture obviously.

"It happens off-stage. Since the men have just been duelling, the logical conclusion is that her brother has run her through with his sword."

"No go, then," said Rani. Charlie pondered.

"At the end of the first scene, when all the stage lights suddenly go out, I thought I saw the tenor run over and pick up the gun he's just thrown down and killed her father with."

"That's right, he does. The audience is not supposed to see, but of course the darkness is never complete. You may have noticed the dead father sneaking off stage as well. He has to get off, and the pistol has to be got off too. The scene changes to an inn. As you'll have seen the set is basically a gun shape: at this point it fractures in the middle, benches and a table pop up, and the chorus and baritone come on. It's all done in less than a minute, and it's convenient for the tenor to remove the gun himself."

"It's a big gun?"

"Flintlock pistol, like I said. We wanted a big one. The producer wanted the shape of the gun in Alvaro's great-coat pocket to mirror the shape of the set." Seeing Charlie's sceptical expression, Bob shrugged again. "OK, I doubt whether anyone could really see that beyond the first few rows of the stalls, but that's producers for you."

He took another key from his pocket and opened a large box standing on one of the little room's tables. "See, here it is. When Colm gets off stage he then comes back here, with his own key, and puts it away." He pointed to three guns in the box. "These are the three the Armouries lent us – all pretty substantial weapons that had a chance of making a distinct shape in the pocket and being seen. That's the one we decided to use, but it doesn't much matter which."

Charlie bent down and looked more closely, first at the gun which had just been used on stage, then at the other two. Rani sneaked a look in from the side, and his body suddenly stiffened. Charlie straightened up and pointed.

"That's an odd one."

The props man nodded. He seemed to take it up with a certain reluctance.

"Quite common in the early nineteenth-century though. Combined percussion pistol and dagger. The blade slots in under the barrel of the gun, and can quite easily be flicked forward – like this, see." A short but substantial blade came clearly into view – menacing, dangerous. "It's a pretty basic, all-purpose weapon this."

"So we can see," commented Charlie. "Choose your weapon, bullet or blade."

"That's the idea. But that's not the weapon we decided to use on stage." There was tension in his voice, and had been since the box was opened. He looked down still, not wanting them to see his eyes. He knew what they were talking about. Charlie put his hand forward and ran his finger along the blade. His eyes were cold.

"On Saturday night," he said quietly, "did you check after the first scene that all these guns were back in this box?" Bob Holdsworth shuffled his feet.

"Not immediately. It was the first night, and we all had new, unaccustomed routines to follow. Checking the guns wasn't a top priority."

"When did you check?" Bob looked down still more obstinately.

"End of performance actually."

Charlie took from his pocket a plastic evidence bag, and gently took up the gun. Through the transparent plastic it gleamed, heavy and deadly.

"Do you have some kind of carrier, to make it less obvious?" he asked.

Bob Holdsworth nodded miserably, rummaged in a drawer and came up with a Morrison's bag. He then locked the gun box and the cupboard where the swords had been stored, and they left the room, Bob locking it behind him. Lured by the music Charlie strayed towards the stage, from which came the sound of two powerful male voices. The tenor one soared in angelic sweetness.

"Ah now I die contented ..."

"Oh dear," said Charlie, moved by the beauty of it, but not just that. He began to walk away. "Where's Madam?" he asked Bob.

"In her dressing room and not to be disturbed."

"Who is it tonight?"

"The man playing Fra Melitone. He must have come up to scratch. It was him on Thursday night too."

Charlie nodded, then he and Rani made for the stage door and out into the open air. Their walk to Millgarth Police Headquarters was done in total silence, and even when he handed in his prize for forensic tests Charlie felt a weight of depression on him that made him gruff and uncertain, with nothing of the triumph that often gripped him when the end of a case was in sight. He told the duty sergeant to ring Mike and tell him who they were about to interview. Then they went back into the night again, and for a long while tramped the streets, once again hardly exchanging a word. "I suppose coppers in the old days felt like this, only worse, when a man they'd convicted was about to be hanged," Charlie thought. Eventually they went back to the Grand and saw the last scene of the opera.

"She's singing like an angel," said Charlie.

"Lover-boy must have performed well too, at Interval," said Rani.

The cheers rang out at the final curtain, and when she took her solo curtsey Olivia seemed to be purring. Colm Fitzgerald was more sober, though he was generously cheered. Charlie and Rani let the happy, excited audience pour out, the triumph encouraging excited chatter among them. Then the pair of them slipped out and round to Harrison Street and the stage door.

"Mr Fitzgerald's dressing room number?" asked Charlie, looking Syd steadily in the eye.

"Number seventeen," he said. "Sir."

Backstage everything was a sixes and sevens, but even so Charlie had a distinct impression that people were determinedly not looking at them. There were moments when he hated his job, and hated himself, though they were few. He found the corridor of dressing rooms and knocked on the door of number seventeen.

"Come in."

The voice somehow sounded already defeated.

Colm Fitzgerald was sitting at his dressing table, and the mirror reflected a face with make-up smeared, the process of removal having been interrupted by their knock, or possibly by an access of remorse or despair, because from the sleeves of his shirt it looked as if his face had been in his hands. There was a horrible contrast between the strength of the body, the memory of the confident and clear voice he had heard on stage, and the dispirited, beaten air of the man caught in private.

"Have you come to arrest me?"

"We've come to have a talk with you."

"You've taken the pistol away, haven't you? The one with the built-in-blade?"

"Yes. It's with Forensics now."

"They said backstage you were there after the Interval. They said you went off with something in a bag, and I knew what it had to be. There doesn't seem much more to say, does there?"

Charlie left a silence, thinking it might be more useful than any words. Then Colm Fitzgerald started speaking again.

"The funny thing is, it didn't affect my performance tonight. Made it better if anything. I suppose poor old Alvaro is a defeated individual right from the start. Despair suits him ... I love her, you know."

"I guessed you must do."

"You won't understand unless you get that straight. She'll say things like that I wanted to be her standard tenor, getting engagements with her because managements would be willing to take the two of us as the price they paid for getting her. Or that I wanted to be her manager and get my share of the loot that way ... She can be a bitch when she wants to be."

"That certainly is my impression," said Charlie, sitting down in the one armchair and nodding to Rani to stand at the door.

"It made no difference – *makes* no difference. She's like no woman I've ever known. From the moment I saw her, at first rehearsal, I felt my blood boiling. I felt myself alive as I'd never been before. It was a wonderful time and a terrible time. You may not realize, but we have hardly any scenes together."

"We've seen the first half, and the ending," put in Rani.

"Then you've seen all there is of us together."

"We've only just realized that she has almost all the first half of the opera, and you almost all the second half. It meant you both of you had an hour or more when you weren't on stage."

"Yes. And it meant we had hardly any rehearsal periods together. They were so special, the ones we did have. Olivia realized we could make a really good looking pair of lovers. Like Georghiu and Alagna. She got very frustrated that Verdi had given us so little to do together ... I did too."

"But eventually the rehearsals got to your bits?"

"Yes. Some weeks into the rehearsal period. She'd been ... going with the Padre Guardiano mostly in the first weeks, and with one or two of the chorus. Then we started to do the opera as a whole. I realized she'd been tantalising me, saving me up. The coming-together of the two lovers in the opera had to be something special. Finally it happened, and I was on Cloud Nine. She was so vital, so crazy for me, so full of – passion you have to call it. For a week, ten days, she was my sun and I was her moon."

There was silence as he remembered.

"And then?"

"Then I'd served my purpose. Then I became her luggage-porter, her chauffeur, her dresser – whatever. Now and then she'd ... take me, if nothing else offered. Mostly she used me, and liked humiliating me. She'd have me drive her to Alderley, then dismiss me as if I was a hire-car driver. You can't imagine how painful that was. I'd been sure that what we were having was something special, something totally different from all her other beddings. And it wasn't. I was just another of her bedders."

Just like Caroline, thought Charlie. Just like Caroline and Marius.

"Did you ever meet Marius Fleetwood?" he asked.

"Oh yes, briefly. Caroline insisted that she bring me in for tea and cakes. I met the whole family. Liked them ... I got the idea then that something was in the wind between Olivia and Marius. I tried to tell myself I was imagining it, but the looks between the two told me different. And there was worse: I thought Olivia was *wanting* me to see it, wanting me to know that she and Marius were either lovers already, or were contemplating it."

"I think she probably did. It would be in character."

"Oh, I know her character. Better than you ever can ... After that I became insanely jealous for a time. I'd watch her, see who she went with, go to her dressing room when she wasn't there to see if there was any evidence of her and him, together."

"Hold it a minute. You knew Olivia was having other lovers now you and she were practically finished, didn't you?"

"Oh yes, I knew. Olivia was not the sort to be without lovers."

"But it was Fleetwood you were jealous of. Why did you feel that that was different?"

"Well, don't you?"

"Leave me out of it. Why did *you* feel like that?"

There was silence for a few moments, as he tried to sort out his emotional responses.

"I was jealous. But I was also nauseated. He was old enough to be her father, for a start. He was her mother's partner – not just lover, but in Caroline's eyes something tantamount to a husband. I could tell that from her ways of treating him: it was tremendous love, but also confidence that they were a stable couple. He was like a father to the two younger ones too. It made it so like ... so like *incest*."

He almost spat the word out. Charlie was horribly intrigued.

"Do you by any chance know about incest from close hand?"

Colm nodded miserably.

"Yes ... Do we have to talk about it? Oh, I suppose we do. My father abused my sister for years. He virtually destroyed her. It was the reason I left Ireland and went to study in America ... Nothing happened to him. When she finally accused him it was in the past and there was no way of getting evidence. There's a lot of covering-up in Ireland, especially where pillars of the community and the church are concerned ... So that's why I was nauseated by what was happening between those two."

"And did you find your evidence?" Charlie asked.

"Yes, I did. I found a pad on her dressing table, and a note had been written on the sheet above in biro. I tore the top sheet off, and took it back to my dressing room. When I sprinkled black powder on it it brought the words up."

"And what did it say?"

"I can tell you exactly. It read:
'OK. Crescent Hotel ca. 8.45. Looking forward to it. The eternal O.'"

"I see. But there was nothing to identify Marius Fleetwood."

"No, there wasn't. And when I'd looked up the Crescent in the telephone directory and gone along to take a peek at it, it seemed as unlike a place he would choose for an amorous assignation as you could imagine. So for a while I damped down my jealousy. But then I remembered that he always left concerts and musical events early – they'd told me that when I was down there. And eight forty-five was about when the first half of *Forza* would have finished and Olivia would be free for more than an hour. Thinking it over, the closeness of the place made it very suitable for a meeting and so – well, I changed my mind again, and I thought they just might be meeting there on the first night."

"So on the night you went straight out of the theatre after the first scene?"

"That's right, out the little door in the loading entrance, into the little side-alley – Harrison Street, it's called – and then down to Vicar Lane, which was likely to be more deserted that Briggate."

"Yes, it would be normally. But it was in Vicar Lane that you were spotted and followed."

Colm looked at Charlie dully. He didn't really care whether the police had evidence or not.

"Who was I seen by?"

"Someone who thought the big cinema that used to be at the top there was still going, and went to see what was on."

He shook his head. What did it matter?

"Anyway, I'm not denying anything or holding anything back."

"No, you're not. But how did you come to have that percussion pistol in your pocket?"

"I just dashed out as soon as the scene ended. It was still there."

"That *particular* pistol, sir. It wasn't the one that it had been agreed would be used in that scene."

"They were all three perfectly suitable. I just took the nearest one."

"Well, that was very much your bad luck, wasn't it? And his."

He glumly nodded.

"Anyway, I walked fast, and got to the part of North Street where the Crescent is, and when I stopped and looked back to see what traffic there was, there was Fleetwood coming towards me from the top of Briggate. He was walking along, very full of himself, practically dancing, dressed up like this was a first night at La Scala, Milan. He turned to look for the traffic too, and I came up behind him and said: 'Can I have a word, Mr Fleetwood?' He turned back, recognised me, and said: 'Oh God. I can't do with jealous lovers.'"

"What did you do?"

"I said 'Please, I just want a word.' I drew him up on to the grass, and he walked as if he was being dragged through a pig farm. We got a bit away from the road, and I said: 'Look, you're her mother's partner, practically a father to her other children.' And he just shrugged and said: 'Not much mileage left in *that* relationship.' I said 'You're practically a father to her,' and he said 'I'm nothing of the sort.' I was beginning to get hysterical I think. I said: 'I know all about incest. My father abused my sister for years.' That's when he made his mistake. He said: 'Look, get this into your head. I'm not her fucking father. I'm her fucking lover, or I will be in half an hour or so.'"

216

"That's when you took out the pistol?"

Colm Fitzgerald swallowed.

"Yes. He looked at it and sneered. He said: 'That's just your stage gun. I recognise it. You can't frighten me with that.' So I flicked the blade forward. Then he really went pale. He was a coward underneath."

"Most of us are cowards, faced with a man with a knife," said Charlie, who had been there, as had Rani.

"Maybe. Anyway he paled, like I said, then looked round as if for somewhere to run. That's when I plunged it in. And that's really all there is to tell."

"Where were you? Not where he was found."

"No. The bushes were a few yards away. I pulled the knife out. I knew he was dead, and I dragged him behind one of the bushes, so that he probably wouldn't be found at least until morning."

"If there'd still been life in him, would you have summoned help?"

"No."

"So you went back to the theatre. All this wouldn't have taken long, I suppose. The first part would still be on."

"It was. Olivia was singing like an angel. In *anticipation* I suppose. I went to see her at Interval. I wanted to tell her not to go to the Crescent. In the end I couldn't. Self-preservation, I suppose."

"And you went on stage and sang as normally, did you?"

"Yes, I did. Funny old game, isn't it? Funny old world. I'll come with you now. No need for handcuffs."

And he stood up, with a certain big, strange dignity, and let Charlie and Rani come on either side of him as he walked out of the theatre and towards the police car that Charlie had ordered Millgarth to have waiting for them outside. Both of the policemen felt for him something approaching admiration. They felt silenced by the terrible force of his passion.

Later, when Fitzgerald was in the cells for the night, they left the station for Rani to drive Charlie home and then go on to his own Bradford home. He was silent at first, then asked Charlie:

"What view will they take of it?"

217

"The Courts? Difficult to say," said Charlie, who had been thinking of the same thing. "I imagine Defence Council will have a stab at manslaughter – rush of blood to the head, happened to have the means to hand, no malice aforethought."

Rani looked at him, rather surprised by his tone.

"But that would be pretty much true, wouldn't it?"

Charlie shot him a glance.

"Were you convinced that he just took up the pistol with the built-in blade because it was nearest to hand? On the first night of a new production, when it had been decided a different one was the most suitable? I'm certainly not. He had it in mind. He might get away with it, of course – provided he didn't sharpen the blade beforehand."

"I liked him. I was sorry for him."

"So was I. But there's always a bit of 'There but for the grace of God' in these cases, you know. Maybe even if the man you've collared is a murderous pederast. You think: 'Thank God I wasn't given that sort of twist to my nature.' Here – this is me."

And he got out of the car, and went in to Felicity, a sleeping Carola, a late-night drink and a lot of talk, and all the round of love and routine domesticity.

Chapter Twenty

Afterword

The most immediate and frenetic reaction to Colm Fitzgerald's arrest was in the offices of Opera North. They were on the phone to agents and opera managements in Australia and South America the moment he left the theatre in the company (on either side of him – it had to mean trouble) of two policemen. "Just in case," they told the people at the other end, though they lied that he was going down with something nasty. Desperate to find a first-rate singer for the part of Alvaro they cursed the decision that had had them sing the opera in English, but thought that at a pinch they might be able to go bilingual. The work continued into the next day, Sunday, and by evening they had lined up a very promising Swedish tenor who would have a stab at learning the part in English by Wednesday, when the next performance was to take place.

"He's gay as they come," said his agent, "but it doesn't show on stage."

"Oh, that's quite irrelevant," said the woman at Opera North, but in her mind she noted that in the plus column.

Sheila Fleetwood was rung by the police on Monday morning and told that Colm Fitzgerald had been charged. She was in the middle of engaging a capable housekeeper to stay with her until the birth of Marius's last child, but her fleeting thought was that Marius's affairs were bound at last to take a shape that he could not duck out lightly from under. Guy was engulfed as usual in his concern for himself and he gave the matter little thought, but Helena had plans to be a writer (and she usually succeeded in getting what she wanted), and she thought that a biography of her father, with no secrets left in the closet, would be an interesting first project.

When the news made the papers, first in the *Yorkshire Post* on Monday morning, Peter Bagshaw confessed to his mother that on the night of the murder he had borrowed his girlfriend's car and driven down to Alderley, intending to ring on the doorbell, meet his father, and tell him publicly what he thought of him. When he found the house dark and deserted he had waited for an hour or so, then driven home feeling thwarted. His mother did not tell him that she had not been at home, having gone down to Les Formby, a widower further down the road, with whom she had a sort of arrangement.

Marius's sister, like his wife, thought that a career of such sexual irresponsibility as our Bert's had deserved to end in disaster. He had been, she concluded, deeply unlovable, whatever his surface attractiveness. Then she went along to the nursing home and heard her father talk on and on about what Bert had told him on his visit earlier in the day.

Olivia, who had had a very good idea who had killed her lover-to-be, hardly thought about him as a person at all. She regretted the loss of a capable tenor, felt glad they had not handed the part to the understudy, who had a bleat to his voice that combined badly with the purity of her own soprano, and wondered about the Scandinavian who was coming in his place.

And Caroline, momentarily sad for "such a nice boy", was full that Monday evening of her day in Doncaster. She had been round the Little Theatre with Philip Massery and talked to the small band of staff. Massery had contacted all the Board members, he told her, so that her appointment was now just a formality. He took her round a few possible houses in or just outside Doncaster, and took her to his home for a celebratory drink in the evening.

"He was the complete gentleman," said Caroline to her younger children later that evening. "He did at one stage put his hand on my knee, but I just gave him the *tiniest* shake of the head, and he took it away. No more of that for me! I feel so happy that finally I've seen the light about myself. I'm simply *not* a person for relationships – not *that* kind of relationship anyway. It's wonderful that at last I understand myself, even if it's taken an *age*! Now, you see, I can go on from there."

She did not see the look Alexander gave Stella, nor the look that Stella gave Alexander – both of them looks which said: "If only, if only."